D1247817

PRAISE FOR INTO THE MIST

"Cinematic and evocative, Into the Mist *is a tension-packed expedition into primordial terror.*
Murray's writing had me feeling the damp of the forest, seeing the mist curling through the fern fronds, and sensing the danger lurking there. Ancient myths, military men and scientists placed in remote, primordial locations – it had all the right ingredients for me, and it didn't disappoint for a moment.
Lee Murray is an author to watch."
– Greig Beck, best-selling author of the Arcadian series

"Creepy and addictive, Into the Mist *is an irresistible tapestry of military action, dark myths, and an ancient and terrifying horror.*
A must read for speculative fiction fans."
– Matthew Summers (Smashdragons)

Also From Cohesion Press

COMING SOON

INTO THE
MIST

INTO THE
MIST

LEE MURRAY

Cohesion Press
Mayday Hills Lunatic Asylum
Beechworth, Australia

Cohesion Press
Mayday Hills Lunatic Asylum,
Beechworth, Australia
www.cohesionpress.com

This book is a work of fiction.
All people, places, events, giant tuatara, and situations are the product of the author's imagination.
Any resemblance to persons, living or dead, is purely coincidental.

We are an Australian publisher, and even though we publish many overseas writers, we maintain a certain Australian house style of punctuation.

Glossary of Acronyms

CBD – Central Business District

CTR – Close Target Reconnaissance

DoC – Department of Conservation

DPM – Disruptive Pattern Material (combat camouflage material)

GNS – (Institute of) Geological and Nuclear Sciences

IRAD – Infrared Aiming Device, an inline night vision rifle attachment

SAS/NZSAS – New Zealand Special Air Service (elite combat regiment)

Glossary of Maori and Local Terms

Aotearoa – literally 'the land of the long white cloud', the Māori name for New Zealand

Haast Eagle – Giant eagle, which the Māori referred to as *Te Hokioi*, now extinct

Hine-pūkohu-rangi – the mist which occurs in the Urewera mountain ranges

Hongi – formal greeting that involves touching of noses, or sharing of breath

Iwi – tribe, people with common ancestry

Kāinga-tipu – ancestral home, place of birth

Karakia – a prayer

Kaumātua/mātua – elder, mentor, teacher

Kauri – conifer, New Zealand's largest and longest living native tree

Kiwi, kiwi – New Zealander, or small flightless ratite, symbol of New Zealand

Kōkako – endangered wattlebird, songbird

Korero – carvings

Koro, koro – grandfather, old man

Kuia, kuia – grandmother, old woman

Kupe – legendary discoverer of New Zealand

Matakite – fortune teller, seer

Moa – giant flightless ratite indigenous to New Zealand, now extinct

Morepork – New Zealand owl, Māori harbinger and messenger between the spiritual and real world

Pākehā – non-Māori, typically of British descent

Pīwakawaka – fantail bird

Pūrerehua – musical instrument, also called a bullroarer

Rūaumoko – God of earthquakes

Swanndri™ – popular New Zealand felted wool bush shirt label, typically in a check pattern

Tāne Māhuta – God of the forest

Tangata whenua – the People of the land

Taniwha – Māori legendary water monster

Tapu – sacred

Te Hoata – fire demon

Te Kooti – Māori religious leader, and guerrilla fighter (1832-1891)

Te Pupu – fire demon

Tōtara – endemic podocarp

Treaty of Waitangi – New Zealand's founding document signed on 6 February 1840 by representatives of the British Crown and about 540 Māori chieftains

Tuatara – only surviving member of the Family Sphenodontia

Tui – endemic passerine bird with dark iridescent plumage

Tūrehu – supernatural creatures of the spirit world

Tūhoe – Māori tribe from the eastern north island, famous for not acceding to European governance.

Wairua – spirit, soul

Wētā – nocturnal flightless insect resembling a katydid

Whakatane – an east coast town

Whio – endangered grey native duck

CHAPTER 1

Te Urewera National Park, late March.

What do you say we take a break?" Terry called hopefully, pushing up his hat and wiping his brow with the back of his hand. There was a hotspot on the ball of his foot that'd turn into a big-arsed blister if it didn't get looked at soon. In front, partially obscured by the undergrowth, Cam fended off an aggressive tree fern. He didn't turn.

"Cam!" Terry called, louder this time. "Give us a breather, will ya?"

Cam halted, one arm holding back the fanning branches. "What was that?"

"Break!"

"Nah. Reckon we should push on a bit. The hut can't be far off. We'll call it a day when we find it."

Cam released the bough as he passed underneath. Suddenly free, the branch whipped back in his wake, whacking Terry in the face.

"Ow!"

"Sorry."

Already, Cam was on the move again, the swish and whish of his movement trailing him like a reptile's tail. Groaning, Terry grabbed the straps of his pack, hoisting the weight up on his shoulders.

Maybe he should've thought twice before agreeing to another of Cam's crazy schemes. But he and Cam have been mates forever – since school – and one thing about Cam, Terry always felt alive when they were together. Probably because Cam was always trying to get them killed. Tramping was the latest in a long line of Cam's must-do challenges. At least this time they were on terra firma. Terry had nearly pissed himself the time they'd gone tandem skydiving. He *had* pissed himself black water rafting, but thankfully the water and the wetsuit had saved his dignity.

Their first hiking trip had been a one-day walk in Abel Tasman National Park, a rolling coastal track of sandy beaches, timber footbridges and leafy bush trails. Terry and Cam had set out early, covering the 34 kilometres in just under six hours. Their second trip was longer – a four-day hike out of Te Anau on the famous Kepler Track. A half a day in, Mount Luxmore had loomed 1490m overhead, prompting oohs and aahs from the overseas tourists on the trail. But Cam had bitched every time he saw a yellow trail marker. For him, even loaded up with gear, the traverse had been too fucking tame. He'd kept going on about how a girl scout could've done it, and in a double-decker bus.

That was their last holiday, six months back. Since then, Cam hadn't stopped telling Terry they ought to step it up a bit. Get out of their comfort zone. That's when Cam had come up with the plan to do this two-week hike in the Urewera forest ranges.

"It'll be great," Cam had said. "Something decent to get our teeth into. None of this namby-pamby touristy stuff."

Terry had agreed in a wink. A no-brainer really. At work, the company had been going through a restructure, and the atmosphere in the office was shitty. Terry figured if his job wasn't there when he got back, then fuck it, he'd go on the dole while he looked for something else. Terry's olds had bitched about it, but they could get fucked.

He was twenty-eight.

Ultra fucking responsible. This trip, he and Cam had checked the long-range forecasts, got themselves kitted up with borrowed gear, even given Cam's sister their proposed route. And everything had gone fine too, until today, when Cam decided they should venture off the trail – not too far, maybe just a kilometre or two – and do some bushwhacking. It had been great fun, a real adrenalin rush. Cam was like a dog pulling at the leash, keen to get to the next ridge, through the next valley, and 'round the next corner. He had the pair of them pushing through the foliage, clambering through thickets and stumbling across deep ferny valleys that looked as if they'd never seen a human footprint. Terry loved it. At first. Now, his patience, and his feet were wearing thin.

"Hey look at this!" Cam shouted. He pointed out some oddly spherical rocks protruding from a clay bank. "Reckon those could be fossilised moa eggs, probably uncovered when this bank came away. Looks recent, too. Probably came down in that big earthquake last August. Think about it, Terry, we could be the only people on Earth to see these eggs."

"If they're eggs," Terry said, dubious. He stepped up to the bank for a closer look.

"Course they are. What else could they be?"

"Rocks?"

Cam laughed, clapped him on the back. "No fucking imagination, Terry. That's your problem."

Terry shrugged. Buried in the bank, the rocks *did* look like a clutch of eggs. Cam's hypothesis was as good as any given that all this area had been swamp way-back-when. Maybe a moa had left her clutch here once upon a time. "Should we make a note of the location, let the park ranger know?" Terry asked, warming to the moa-egg theme.

Cam shook his head. "They've been hidden here all these years, what's another thousand going to matter? Let's just leave 'em."

They kept hiking, the hotspot on Terry's foot niggling as the afternoon wore on. But even more uncomfortable than his foot was Terry's growing suspicion that they'd managed to get lost. This little glade looked like one they'd passed through earlier. They should've reached the hut by now. More likely they'd shot by within metres of the shelter without realising it. Easy mistake. In places, this forest was as dense as mattress stuffing. The area was hardly swarming with people. Terry and Cam had only seen one pair of trampers – an old guy and what might've been his son – and that was two days ago.

The afternoon sun was weakening when Cam stopped and pulled the map from the side-pocket of his pack. Bracing his foot against a flat rock, he studied it.

"Where the hell are we?" Terry said, coming alongside to peer over Cam's shoulder.

"God only knows," said Cam. He indicated an area the size of a small coin with a grubby index finger. "Somewhere here. We must've missed the hut. Probably deviated off course when we went through that ravine."

When you charged off the track, you mean.

"Did you try your cell phone? We might still be in range." Terry was careful to keep his voice calm and matter-of-fact.

"What're we going to say? Boohoo, come get us? We've got enough food for a few more days, and plenty of warm gear. Let's just see if we can get ourselves out of this mess before we go crying for help, eh?"

"So what do you suggest?" Terry said.

"For today," Cam said, folding the map more or less into pleats, "I vote we find a place to set up camp, get some tucker in us, and rest. Tomorrow, we'll have a bit of a recce, and push on when we've got our bearings. My money's on finding the track before lunch."

They pitched the tent on an elevated site above a small creek, and soon a fiery pyramid crackled in the small clearing. While Cam got the tea brewed, Terry sat on a flat rock, took his boot off and examined the turgid bubble on the ball of his foot.

Bugger, that's going to hurt tomorrow.

The light softened to grey, and he fossicked around in his pack for his first aid kit to deal with the wound. He'd just finished repacking the kit, when Cam passed him a mug of hot tea.

"Get that down ya, mate."

Taking the mug, Terry wrapped his hands around its warmth and breathed in the steamy vapour. The fire popped, the cheerful sound of a soft-drink tab being pulled, its Fanta-coloured flames lighting the campsite. Mesmerised, Terry sipped the hot liquid and decided this wasn't so grim after all. They weren't really

4

lost, just temporarily misplaced. Cam was right. All they needed was some decent kip. Everything'd be sorted in the morning.

Terry woke, aware the space beside him was empty. Fumbling with his watch, he checked the time: 12:23am. Cam must've gone for a leak. Terry heard him stomping around outside the tent. *Geez, Cam, how hard is it to find a spot to piss?* Lifting himself up on one elbow, Terry gave his pillow – a bag of dirty clothes – a good whump, encouraging it into a more comfortable shape, then shifted his hips to avoid whatever'd been digging into him through the groundsheet. That done, he burrowed into his sleeping bag, pulling the fabric close to his chin. He was almost back in the land of Nod when Cam's yell filled the night.

"Jesus, Cam!" Terry scrambled free of his sleeping bag and charged out of the tent. He pulled up. Outside, the campsite was a patchwork of shadows, the fire long since extinguished.

"Cam?"

Nothing. Miles from civilisation, the silence was eerie, as if the forest itself was holding its breath.

"Cam," Terry said. "Quit fooling around, will ya? You're freaking me out."

The air was strangely heavy. At the base of his neck, Terry's skin prickled.

"Cam, you okay mate?" he said, reaching backwards under the flysheet for his boots. He strained his ears, just catching a faint rustle. Not bothering to do up the laces, he slipped his boots on, wincing when the blister touched home. Then, he crossed the campsite in the direction of the noise. He felt his way with caution, checking the stability of the ground before placing his feet. Cam had been making a bit of a racket earlier, stomping around out here. Could he have tripped on a hidden hollow and knocked himself out? Or maybe he'd wandered away from the campsite and couldn't find his way back? Except if that were the case, he would've called out. Terry figured Cam must've hurt himself. What possessed Cam to go off on a Tiki-tour in the dark? Not everything had to be a frickin' cross-country adventure. Why couldn't he just piss into the bushes behind the tent? Terry bashed his knee on a rock.

"Fuck!"

Hang on. Another sound. Possibly a whimper...

"Cam? Can you hear me?" Terry stopped still, listened for his mate and pushed back the panic that'd gripped his intestines. Dead silence. *Cam must be out cold.* Terry hoped it wasn't too serious. He increased his pace, trying to navigate his way in the murk, but his thoughts were way ahead. How were they going to get out of the bush if Cam was injured? Nothing else for it, they'd just have to pull their heads in and phone Search and Rescue. That was *if* they could get a signal. And even if they got through to someone, Terry didn't have a clue where they were. The forest park covered more than two thousand square kilometres. It could take days for anyone to get to them.

Terry shook his head, annoyed his imagination had run away with him. First thing he needed to do was find Cam. As far as getting him out of the bush, they'd deal with that later.

At the edge of the campsite, Terry stumbled on a fallen tree limb, bruising his shin and sprawling headfirst into some spongy bracken. Stunned and gormless, Terry picked himself up, casting around in the dark for the obstacle so as not to trip a second time. His fingers found a boot. Terry felt a rush of relief. Looked like Cam tripped over the same branch.

"Cam," he said jovially. "S'okay mate, I've found you. Everything's gonna be fine now."

Cam didn't answer, confirming Terry's suspicions. The duffer'd gone and knocked himself out on a rock or a stump or something. Concussed. Patting his way up Cam's legs to his trunk, Terry was pleased to note that at least there were no broken bones.

What the fuck?!

Terry shook violently, his body already grasping what his mind hadn't yet understood. Bringing his fingers to his face

Terry sniffed at the wetness there. Metallic. It wasn't dew. Terry jerked his hands away in horror. Cam's upper body was missing.

"Sweet Jesus!"

He'd been severed in half. Gulping air, Terry scrambled to his feet, backpedalling, using bloody hands to scrabble away, a low wail welling up from his stomach. *How did this happen?* He wasn't stopping to find out. He had to get the hell away from here. Turning his back on what was left of Cam, Terry charged toward the tent, plunging headlong through the dark, ignoring the branches that stabbed at his face and arms. He was half way across the clearing when the moon peeked through the forest canopy illuminating the campsite, and Terry knew getting out of the bush was the least of his worries.

CHAPTER 2

Maungapōhatu, Te Urewera Forest, late March

Rawiri Temera sat on a fold-out beach chair on the back porch of the farmhouse smoking a cigarette and listening to the familiar chatter of the morepork and weka. Some nights, from this spot, Temera could see the needle of Te Maunga thrusting its twisted silhouette against the darkened sky, the final spike of the Huia-rau mountain range in the Urewera forest. Tonight though, the mist maiden Hine-pūkohu-rangi had wrapped the mountain in her grey cloak, her earthy perfume overwhelmed by the scent of Temera's tobacco.

How many more nights would he spend on this porch? Not many – his great-nephew Wayne reckoned – if Temera insisted on smoking. He ignored his nephew's counsel; a man was entitled to one vice. At eighty-three, there was little enough pleasure in life. Even the journey in and out of the valley was misery these days, the ride in the truck jolting his bones and rattling his teeth. Perhaps, after all, this would be his last summer visit to *kāinga tipu*, his isolated ancestral home.

Flicking ash into the yard, Temera exhaled, lips pursed like a clarinet player as he stretched out his legs. From far away came what sounded like an engine, but he wasn't expecting anyone. Maungapōhatu was too far off the beaten track for visitors to pop in for tea and ginger-nuts. It was hardly a tourist destination, just a handful of hardy farmers, mostly rugged Tūhoe men, and fewer women. The lost and the lonesome. The year before last, the Search and Rescue helicopter had hovered around the settlement for close to an hour searching for some fool hunter who'd got himself separated from his party while chasing down an injured stag. It was the biggest fuss they'd seen in these parts since old war chief Murakareke rolled over in his sleep and singed his family jewels in a fire. Squashing his cigarette out in an old scallop shell, Temera leaned back in his beach chair and closed his eyes…

The morepork called; the owl's hoot far off and melancholy. Out of the darkened mass of the forest, a shape emerged, slowly growing, as if the mountain had broken off and plunged into the valley. The shifting form advanced until it was just metres from the house, its shadow stretching across the yard.

A taniwha, a monster of legend.

Temera knew that for the taniwha to appear he had to be dreaming. He'd never seen a taniwha before, but he'd heard enough to recognise one when he saw one, darkness or no. Here in Kupe's adopted home, every child knew of the taniwha – vengeful monsters that slaughtered warriors, kidnapped maidens and ate babies whole. Gruesome tales told and retold to children at the knees of their grandmothers. But taniwha could be protective as well as predatory, standing guard over rivers and mountains, and keeping the people of a tribe from harm. Warning them of coming danger.

And this taniwha? Was it friend or foe?

At last, Temera remembered what he should do. Quietly letting out his breath, he uttered soft, respectful words – a karakia-prayer in honour of his visitor.

CHAPTER 3

Landsafe Laboratories, Hamilton, early June

At the whump of the doors, Jules pushed back from her computer and looked down the length of the lab. It was Richard, her boss, the heavy double doors swinging closed behind him as he made his way towards her, a disposable coffee cup in each hand. Mousy-brown hair flopping over his face, he smiled. With his rubber-soled shoes squeaking on the polished linoleum, Richard hardly resembled the CEO of Crown Research Institute. He was more your salesman type, or a council contractor, or even a comedian, although the only stand-up he did was at scientific symposia – about four annually. He was a seriously good scientist with a PhD from Canterbury, post-doctoral stints at Texas and Cambridge universities, membership on some prestigious scientific committees, as well as ecological field-work experience on three continents.

And he was in love with her.

Not that Jules had done anything to encourage it – well, nothing more than your usual office banter. She just didn't feel that way about Richard. Although, if she was honest, she could do a lot worse. Richard was a good friend, but those Jake Gyllenhaal movies Hollywood kept churning out had her holding out for something more. Something special.

Richard passed her a coffee. "Milk, no sugar, right?"

Accepting the cup, Jules gave him what she hoped was a *professional* smile. She took a sip; the contents were still hot. Richard must have run all the way from the canteen.

"Okay, what's up?" she demanded, one hand on her hip.

Richard combed his fringe out of his face with his fingers. "Up? Why should something be up?"

Jules raised her coffee cup, and her eyebrows.

"It's not against the law to bring a staff member coffee, Dr Asher."

Jules drummed her fingers on the bench. "Did you get Mal one?"

"Hey, I've only got two hands," Richard protested.

Over the rim of her cup, Jules gave him a penetrating stare, and took another sip.

Rolling chair castors thrummed on the linoleum, and Richard sat down beside her, coffee in his hands and his elbows resting on the worn knees of his cords. "Okay, I'll come clean. I've just got off the phone with the Conservation Minister."

"The minister." Jules leaned back. "Should I be terrified or intrigued?"

"Don't panic. As far as I can tell there are no plans to sell off Landsafe." He threw her a wry smile. "At least, not this week. No, it's that gold uncovered in Te Urewera National Park. Did you see the news report?"

"The pair of Aussie geologists here on holiday?" Jules said.

Richard nodded.

"I read it online. Didn't that seem weird to you, them finding that nugget smack in the middle of the trail?"

Richard shifted his weight and rolled a little closer. "Actually, that's not so weird. The Aussies were crossing a riverbed when they found the nugget. Plenty of gold turns up in riverbeds. What's weird is that they handed it over to the authorities."

"It wasn't theirs to take," Jules said with a shrug. "Did you know that if you uncover a vein of silver in your vege patch, it belongs to the Crown? I expect the government can swoop in and confiscate your carrots, too."

"Yeah, but that nugget was the size of an iPhone: 1600 grams and close to pure. Fifty-four troy ounces, the minister said. At today's spot price, that's close to 100,000 US dollars. Imagine what you could do with that kind of money."

"For one nugget? Wow. I don't suppose the minister was calling to offer us a share."

Richard pulled a face. "I wish! He wants to know if there's more where this came from."

Biting at the edge of the paper cup, Jules waited for Richard to continue.

"So the ministers have overridden the Schedule 4 protection on the parkland. Granted a special prospecting licence. They're proposing sending in a Task Force to investigate the potential quantity of ore, and how it might be extracted. We've been charged with evaluating the impact to the environment."

Jules' pulse quickened. Of course Landsafe *would* be involved. Any eventual extraction would have to comply with the Conservation Act.

"I'm surprised at the Tūhoe though," Richard said, flicking away the hair that always fell forward over his face. "As co-guardians, I thought they'd have something to say about a bunch of strangers traipsing through their tribal lands, poking holes. But the tribe's elders have given it the go-ahead."

Jules wrapped her fingers around her cup. "I guess they're thinking of the economics of it." She managed to keep her tone even.

"Probably," Richard agreed. "There isn't much work up that way. But like you said, the government doesn't have to ask the landowner's permission."

Here it comes.

Jules held her breath.

"This Task Force. I want you to go, Jules."

Her heart sank. "Aw come on, Richard," she said, hating the whine in her voice. "I'm up to my eyeballs in this project." She waved at her computer screen. "What about Mal? Can't he go?"

"No, he can't, Jules. His wife is due next week and there's no way I'm getting on the wrong side of Gabby – she scares the hell out of me." He pulled an awkward grin.

"I can be scary," Jules whispered.

Richard laughed.

Jules dropped her chin, looking out at Richard from under her lashes. "What if I promise to wash all the laboratory glassware for a week? Every last Erlenmeyer flask."

Leaning in, Richard placed a hand on her shoulder. "Jules,

I've done my best to keep you out of the parks, but it's been two years."

"I can't go. Sarah needs me to look in on her."

"It's only for a few days. And Sarah has other people who can visit her."

"Yes, but I'm her best friend."

"She'll understand."

"What if she doesn't?"

"Jules…"

"Richard, I can't. It's too soon."

Richard's face was impassive. "Jules… there *is* no one else."

Dropping the crumpled coffee cup into the bin, Jules scrubbed her hands over her face, holding back her tears. It was bound to happen. She was going to have to face it sometime. Richard couldn't protect her forever.

She dropped her forearms onto the bench. "When is it?"

"You leave tomorrow. From Rotorua."

"Tomorrow! You said it was only a proposal."

"That's the official line."

"But it's the Ureweras. It'll be freezing."

Richard brushed his fringe out of his eyes again. "I agree, it could be bracing," he said, throwing his coffee cup in the bin.

Dinsdale, Hamilton City, same day

Jules stepped through the back door into the kitchen. At the laminate counter, a woman in her fifties stepped back from a pile of chopped vegetables, her voluminous bosom wobbling.

"Hello, Dr Asher."

Jules raised an eyebrow, tilting her head.

"I mean, Jules."

Jules gave her a warm smile. "Hello, Carol-Ann. How was she today?"

The caregiver wiped her hands on a chequered tea-towel. "Not bad, overall. We had a lovely lunch. Drove the van through to Rotorua to the Blue Lake, and had a picnic on the beach."

"Bit cold for that, wasn't it?" Jules slipped her handbag into the space between the chair back and the table.

"We wrapped up warm. Sarah likes it there, near the water and the bush." Carol-Ann lowered her voice to a whisper. "She's a bit melancholy tonight, though."

"Her parents?"

Carol-Ann nodded. "They left half an hour ago. Upset her, as usual. You go through, honey. She'll be pleased to see you. Give me a tick to get the dinner on and I'll bring you through a cuppa."

Jules headed to the lounge, the sound of the television greeting her.

'...Archie. Chris Tarrant on the line. I've got Phil here with me in the studio. He's doing very well, but he needs your help to win £16,000...'

On the battered leather sofa, a spot of spittle on her chin, Sarah's face was a picture of concentration. Jules' heart clenched, reminded of another evening her friend had sat on this same battered sofa. Back then Sarah had been wearing cut-off Levis, her long legs tucked under her, eating Indian takeout from a foil container, and nattering between mouthfuls about the pair of them partnering up for karaoke night.

"Hey, sweetie." Jules dropped a kiss on Sarah's forehead. Her friend looked up, blue eyes full of warmth. When rescue teams had pulled her out of the gully still alive, Jules had been overwhelmed with relief. Always a battler, Sarah had spent seven months in Burwood Hospital recovering from severe trauma to her frontal lobe.

"Do you mind if I turn this off?" Jules said, pointing to the television.

Sarah looked puzzled, so Jules picked up the remote and switched the television off. Poor Sarah. It wasn't just the partial paralysis of her legs. Where before she used to run marathons and play weekend touch rugby, these days Sarah struggled to process simple everyday things: socks before shoes; putting water in the jug first. Occasionally, she got aggressive, supposedly a result of the trauma, but anyone would be frustrated, humiliated and *pissed off as all hell*, if they couldn't manage to brush their own teeth.

Sometimes Jules woke in a cold sweat, reliving the accident. She could've been the one leading the team through the bush that day. It could just have easily been her at the bottom of that canyon; her struggling with the answers on a stupid game show.

"Carol-Ann said the two of you went up to the Blue Lake?" Jules said, cheerily.

"Hes." Jules tried not to wince at the monosyllabic answer, the result of Broca's Aphasia—the prison her friend was locked in.

"It's good to see you getting out and about. I'm going to be away a few days myself. Heading into the Ureweras."

Sarah didn't reply.

"I couldn't get out of it this time, Sarah," Jules said quietly. "I can't let Richard down – he's supported me often enough."

"Charrd."

"Hey, don't you start," Jules laughed. "You're worse than my parents. Richard's a friend, that's all!" Ignoring Sarah's frown, Jules went on. "Anyway, it's a mining exploration team and on conservation land, so it's all a bit cloak and dagger. I'll be working on the compliance issues. Looking out for the welfare of our native species."

Sarah's face twisted. She held up a hand and wiggled her fingers.

"How many are going?" Jules said, guessing the question from her friend's gesture. "I don't know. I'll be meeting the others tomorrow. What are the odds there'll be a gorgeous hunk amongst them?" she joked.

But, finding the remote, Sarah stabbed at the buttons and turned the television on, Chris Tarrant's voice booming, *'D-none of the above. Is that your final answer?'*

INTO THE MIST

Rotorua township

Temera woke and sat upright in bed.

That was one hell of a nightmare! Scared the bejeezus out of him. Again. Lately, he'd been dreaming every night. Haunting dreams. He lay down again and pulled the blankets up around his neck, but there wasn't much chance of getting back to sleep now. He checked his alarm clock: 4:18am. Sighed. *May as well get up, make a cuppa, watch some TV.* He had to go to the toilet anyway. Throwing off his covers, Temera swung his legs out of bed.

Offices of Geotech International, Sydney, Australia

Caren Murphy studied the report: graphs, tables, fault and shear zone information from the geophysical survey. The results didn't include any aerial data – dodgy atmospheric conditions in the area didn't allow for it, and anyway her two Aussie geologist 'tourists' had been on the ground. It didn't do to alert a country's government when you were prospecting for green field sites. Far better to gather the information quietly. She smoothed a mesh of blonde hair back into her bob. At least the results looked promising. Worth the initial investment. With the economic crisis and recent bad press affecting Geotech's share price, a big contract would be timely. Perhaps she could hurry things up even more?

Maybe a call…

CHAPTER 4

New Zealand Defence Force Army Base, Waiouru

James Arnold stared out the dusty window of the borrowed office, contemplating the army's training base – a vast tussocked wasteland. There it was again, a flash of reflected sunlight in the distance. A scope? More likely some fool in civvie sunglasses. James grunted. He'd have to follow up the incident with the training officer. Not so long ago, under the blazing mid-day sun of Afghanistan, a gaff like that could earn a soldier and his unit an all-expenses paid trip home in body bags.

A soldier and his unit. In body bags…

A rap at the door startled him briefly.

Private Karen Dawson and her perfect rump. James believed the modern term was 'bootylicious'. He turned away from the window as the private entered.

"Sergeant McKenna has arrived from One Battalion in Linton, Major," Dawson announced in a voice like melted chocolate. If James were inclined… Even then he'd be duty-bound to maintain a professional distance. In his sixties, James knew he wasn't without charm: the khaki uniform with its rainbow of service medals, the touch of silver at his temples, even the lines etched on his forehead gave him a Sean Connery look that certain women found appealing. He rarely indulged himself. Losing Brenda to breast cancer sixteen years ago hadn't meant he'd lost his appetite for female company, but one didn't rise up the ranks without learning to be circumspect.

He smiled. "Please show the sergeant in."

"Of course, sir," Dawson said. She headed for the door, allowing James a shufti at her magnificent rear.

"Go through, Sergeant McKenna," she said, turning sideways and offering the junior officer her prettiest smile as he stepped into the office.

James could hardly blame her. At thirty-four, Taine McKenna was closer to her age, and with steely blue eyes from his father's side and skin liked polished rimu – a legacy from his Māori mother – he was a handsome mongrel. What's more, the boy had all the power and dexterity of an All Black midfielder, and abdominals to match. James couldn't even *remember* the last time he saw his own abs. Today though, McKenna's musculature was hidden under regulation combat fatigues.

He came to attention before the burnished kauri desk. "Major Arnold."

James waved away the younger man's verbal salute as Dawson closed the door. "At ease, McKenna. Take a seat."

"Boss," McKenna said, using the SAS diminutive for his commanding officer. He folded his two-metre body into a chair with surprising grace.

James took his seat. "A job for you, McKenna. From Aitkens Street," he said, referring to the Defence Force head office. Not that there was anything much left to run these days, the force whittled away to the bare bones. The work of short-sighted suits in government – she'll-be-right types, who thought the country was perfectly safe, simply because it was stuck on the arse-end of the globe…

Clearing his throat, James continued, "A ministerial Task Force is heading into the Ureweras to undertake some mineral prospecting. You and your boys will accompany them."

"A Task Force, Boss?"

James snorted. "It's the ministers' term, not mine," he said, shaking his head. "Watched too many *Thunderbirds* shows when they were kids."

McKenna smiled.

"Made up of mainly government scientists and a couple of civilians, the Task Force will be led by a Dr Christian de Haas, from New Zealand Petroleum and Minerals… on the face of it, at least."

"A babysitting job."

"Of sorts."

McKenna's face darkened. "And the chain of command?"

"Dr de Haas will have full authority."

"A civilian." There was a ripple at the boy's jawline.

James ran his fingers over the manila file on the desk. The army had all the bells and whistles when it came to digital technology but, providing confidentiality could be maintained, James preferred a paper copy. Brenda used to joke that he could read between the lines. Maybe there was an element of truth in that.

"I know it's not ideal, but as it turns out, the civil expedition provides us with a plausible cover."

McKenna didn't say anything, waiting for James to elaborate.

Resting his elbows on the desk, James steepled his hands and took a slow breath before beginning. "Over the past three months, Urewera park authorities have received reports of people going missing in the forest. Lots of them. Fourteen," he said. "And they haven't turned up looking sheepish a few days later either."

Opening the file, he flicked forward a couple of pages.

"Campbell Edwards, 29, and Terry Hubner, 28, both of Johnsonville," he read aloud. "These two were the first to go missing. They set out on March 26th from Ruatahuna. Hut records show they stuck to the track for the first three days then disappeared. Edwards' sister rang the police when the pair didn't show up as planned. Seems she'd waited a week to call it in – in case they'd got it in their heads to finish up their holidays in Queenstown."

"Going AWOL isn't out of character for this pair?"

James shook his head. "No. But the sister maintains that staying away this long is unusual, even for these two."

"It doesn't necessarily point to foul play, sir. River crossings can be perilous if you don't know what you're doing."

"I agree, and I'd be tempted to discount those lads as unlucky adventurers and send out flowery condolence cards to the families. Except they're not the only holidaymakers to go missing." The timber armrest creaked as James shifted in his seat. "Only a week after Edwards' sister contacted authorities, a pair of German honeymooners went astray. Same general area. Conservation staff found their packs, intact and tidied to one side of the track, but no sign of the couple. Then there's a group of four from Otago, all experienced tramping club members. Their car was discovered parked at the campgrounds at Lake Waikaremoana. The last person to disappear was a farmer by the name of Samuel Waaka. Runs a small holding within the confines of the park. Wife reported him missing."

"Why haven't we heard about this on the news?"

"Things with the locals are still tense after police staged those terrorist raids in the Ureweras some years back. That's Tūhoe tribal land. Authorities have been keeping a lid on the media, especially the location of the disappearances, in case it's the Tūhoe separatist faction looking for attention."

McKenna nodded. "I make the count nine, sir. I believe you said fourteen."

"The rest are our own boys. Missing in action." James wiped his face in his hands. McKenna said nothing. "We sent them in ten days ago, after the army got the gig from the police. Our boys were following a lead from DoC – a bloodied glove belonging to one of the missing hikers. On their sixth day in, Corporal Gavin Masterton reported they'd discovered the remains of a woman aged around forty-five. From Masterton's description, we believe she was one of the Otago group. The communications operator taking the call said Masterton sounded shaken. She said... well, you can see for yourself." James thrust the folder across the desk at McKenna, and stabbed at the page. "The transcript's there."

McKenna picked up the file and read:

Masterton: 12 May 1700 hours. This is Corporal Gavin Masterton. Our current position – [redacted] – a half-day walk north of Mangatoatoa Hut, in an area of dense bush. [Up to this point, the officer sounds composed]. We've located a body... a woman. [Officer's voice wavers]. Fortyish, maybe 45. We suspect she's from the Otago party, although so far we've been unable to locate any sign of her companions. The body is emaciated and the extremities show various healed scratches and a number of broken nails, which is consistent with her having been lost in the forest for a period of time. [Exhales hard]. She's... the body... it's been... [Word muffled].

Operator: Could you repeat that last sentence please, Corporal?

Masterton: She's been mutilated. Murdered. Her stomach contents... [The officer breaks off].

Operator: Corporal Masterton?

Masterton: Whoever did this... it looks like they've tortured her. We think the victim was alive when they did it. Her eyes... [There's a pause of 5 seconds. The officer composing himself?]. We don't think she's been dead long. A day, maybe two, which means whoever did this could still be in the area. We'll store the body here for the moment – Pollock's bagging it now – and widen our search. Just days ago this woman was alive so there may be other survivors.

McKenna looked up from the transcript, his face grave. "This wasn't an accident."

James exhaled slowly. "I pulled Masterton's service file, checked his postings. He's been in a few skirmishes, is no stranger to atrocities, so for him to react this way..."

James stood and stepped across to resume his vigil at the window, taking a moment to gather his thoughts. His warm breath fogged on the cold glass, the shrinking vapour distorting like a globule in a lava lamp. Outside, Mount Ruapehu's snow-covered peak rose from the ocean of tundra. "Masterton's party were due to radio in again the following morning. We've had no further contact."

He turned back, put his hands on the desk, and fixed McKenna with a stare. "The problem is, we can't locate them either. The Urewera bush is so thick you could hide a small town in there and never see it – all that damnable mist, shifting and moving over the terrain, hampering satellite surveillance..."

"What's our brief, Boss?" said McKenna, matter-of-fact.

"I want you to go in and find out what the hell is going on in that backwater! The research team will provide you with your cover, and in return, your boys will keep the civilians safe."

"Sir." The sergeant's frown was almost imperceptible.

Suddenly feeling heavy, James sat. There was no fooling the boy. They both knew it wasn't army policy to send a second team in where a first had failed to return.

James wiped the bottom half of his face with his hand. "The first section's involvement was sanctioned. As far as the powers-that-be are concerned, those boys are still in there looking for the missing nine, whereas your team will be on the ground to escort the Task Force. But if you and your boys find anything untoward going on in that goddamned forest, *anything* that threatens the safety of New Zealanders we are mandated to protect, *then* it becomes army business. And should that happen, let's just say, how fortuitous it is that you happened to be there accompanying the Task Force."

"Understood, sir," McKenna said, closing the file and getting to his feet. "Since the platoon lieutenant isn't here."

James gave a grim smile; he'd picked the right man. A veteran of Timor-Leste, Afghanistan and Egypt, McKenna knew a thing or two about unrecorded missions.

"And one other thing, Sergeant," James said quietly.

"Boss?"

"My great-nephew Kevin was with the missing unit."

Outside the office block, Taine found his corporal, a New Zealand-born Chinese named Jack Liu, with the Pinzgauers they'd driven up from Linton, along with Private Matt Read, one of two 19-year-old FNGs in McKenna's section. Perched in the passenger seat, Liu's right boot was propped casually on the open door frame – his left leg hanging out of the vehicle, while he cleaned his fingernails with a small knife. Nicknamed Coolie, not, as one might expect, for his Chinese ancestry, but for his cool head in a crisis, the soldier was almost effeminate. In the army, his manner might've made him a ready target, but Coolie's light tread and quick reactions had gained him a reputation as a stealthy little bastard. No soldier in his right mind would creep up behind Coolie, even in jest. Not unless they were looking to get their head blown off.

Coolie dropped his foot when Taine approached.

"They give you our assignment?" asked Read. The newbie had been slouched against the vehicle, sunning himself. He stepped forward, pulling the buds from his ears. "We heading out, then?"

"I'm going to need you to round up the others, Read. We're leaving at 0800 hours. Going up country to the Urewera ranges."

The boy crammed the leads into his pocket. "Whoa! We gonna be dropping into the forest, Boss?" Taine smiled at the boy's enthusiasm. For Read, every day was like an episode from a Marvel comic.

"No choppers today, Private."

"But this isn't a training exercise, right? It's a proper assignment. Searching out separatist cells or something?" Read looked hopeful.

"We'll drive in as far as we can then head into the forest on foot. It's a proper operation, yes. We'll be accompanying a research team. And we need to keep it under the radar, so try not to make a song and dance when you round up the others."

Read's eyes widened. "Awesome!" He scampered off across the quadrangle to round up the rest of the section.

"Were we ever like that?" Coolie said. "All bright-eyed and bushy tailed?" He shook his head. "The way I heard it, we just got ourselves another babysitting assignment, and Read there is all Indiana Jones – tally-ho we're off in search of the lost ark."

Taine gave Coolie a grim smile. "The lost ark might be a fair assessment. Seems we've got fourteen people unaccounted for in there." Coolie raised his eyebrows as Taine continued. "And five of them our own boys."

Coolie whistled under his breath. "Fourteen! I don't suppose they're just lost, then?"

Taine shook his head. "Unlikely. There's more. One of the missing diggers was a Private Kevin James Arnold, twenty years old."

"A relative of the major's?"

Taine nodded. "And the platoon lieutenant wasn't present when I received the orders."

Coolie's brow creased. "No chain of command. So, it's an unofficial mission."

"Oh, it's official, Coolie," Taine said. "We're going to protect a scientific team in an area where the locals could be hostile."

Coolie scuffed his boot in the dirt. "And the fourteen people gone AWOL is just an aside?"

"Something like that."

"That'd explain why we're not getting a chopper." Coolie said. "Let me guess. We don't come back with the kid, we can forget about being written up for any medals."

Taine grinned. Won over long ago by the glitzy 'go places' army recruitment advertisements, Coolie couldn't give a rat's arse about medals. Read wasn't the only one here for the adrenalin fix.

Squinting against the sunlight, McKenna glanced across the quadrangle; the new boy disappeared into the mess.

"So, will we be taking all the normal kit?" Coolie asked.

"Yes, but I hope we won't need it. Whoever's causing the disappearances, whoever we encounter out there in the bush, greenies, Tūhoe separatists or just pissed off locals, they're all going to be Kiwis, aren't they? Personally, I don't like the idea of pointing a machine gun at anyone, least of all one of our own. If we're forced to shoot, let's go for casualties, not corpses."

"Hide the rocket launcher under our lunchboxes then?"

"That's the plan."

Coolie glanced in the direction of the mess then cocked his head. "You know Trigger isn't going to like this. He fucking hates babysitting."

Taine nodded; Coolie wasn't wrong. A few years older and built like a small refrigerator, Trevor Grierson had done a couple of tours with McKenna. Their last babysitting assignment had been on tour, on a morning not unlike this one, the low-angled sunlight glancing off dusty buildings…

They were in Afghanistan, part of the International Security Assistance Force, teaching the Afghans how to protect their own when the Taliban announced their intent to target central Kabul and then went about doing just that, launching simultaneous assaults on the Wazir Akbar Khan district, as well as in the eastern townships of Jalalabad, Pul-e-Abam and Gardez.

Taine's section was assigned to extract some administrators from the British Embassy, but at the eleventh hour the orders changed: the embassy was in lock-down, so they were to secure the adjacent French-run school instead. Taine and his boys had arrived at the school just as insurgents stormed a nearby construction site. From this vantage point, the cool-headed fanatics assaulted the district. For hours, machine-gun fire and striking shells of rocket-propelled launchers performed a deathly opera, the wail of sirens and pop of machine-gun fire providing top notes to the periodic bass explosions of NATO's air support. Inside the school compound, the screams of the kids put everyone's teeth on edge.

The noise didn't bother Taine particularly, but a little girl of six wearing a pale blue smock did, one of the three girls lucky enough to attend school. She was terrified. Wisps of shiny black hair escaping from under her hijab, she curled up under a table, whimpering as she sucked her thumb, rocking back and forth to squeeze out the din.

An hour passed. Then another. The insurgents' rockets hit the school building more than once. Taine doubted the Afghans had the situation under control. Their track record was dismal. Less than a year before, the US embassy had been the centre of a 19-hour siege by the Taliban. Finally, suicide bombers had put an end to the waiting, attacking the compound and killing nine civilians. No way was Taine going to have a repeat of *that* snafu on his conscience. Besides, this group wouldn't handle a prolonged stand-off. Already one of the teachers was showing signs of flipping out. It wouldn't be the first time. Last thing they needed was him running out into the street in a panic. For a Taliban sniper, a hysterical teacher could be brought down like a housefly with a single squirt of fly-spray.

Better to get the kids out. They'd take the back route out of the compound while the allied air support had the fanatics boxed in.

Taine had already given the order when Trigger pulled him away from the civilians. "What the fuck, McKenna?" he'd hissed. "We can't go out there! We gotta just sit tight and let the local boys handle this."

"Like they did last year?"

"I don't like it either, but we have to take our chances. There are little kids here. How are we supposed to get them out under fire, man?"

"But this is a *school*, Trigger," Taine had retorted, wrenching his arm free. "If the Taliban can't make a dent in the diplomatic compound across the road, how long do you think it'll take them to turn their fire on the next best target, one that'll make the western world sit up and take notice? What if they've got someone out there strapping on explosives as we speak? Some jihadist nutter prepared to run in here and blow himself and everyone in here to Hawijah? Tell me what chance these kids will have, then?"

They'd hardly made it two blocks before Taine knew it was a mistake. The street was choked with smoke and fumes. Full of debris. Empty car carcasses stood in the middle of the road, the doors flung open. Overhead NATO Black Hawks bombarded the construction site, kicking up rubble to contain the militants. Taine's group made themselves small, moved swiftly. It might've worked, but friendly fire kills just the same.

The girl took a hit to her femoral artery. Trigger had picked her up and carried her to cover, but by that time she was as good as empty. With a tiny gasp, she expired in Trigger's arms, her blood seeping into his uniform, the white of her skin and serenity in her face a contrast to his horror. The girl's hijab had slipped off in the scuffle. McKenna recalled a tiny ribbon clinging tenaciously to a braid.

Afterwards, the official story had been positive: twenty-three civilians safely extracted with only one fatality. For once, western media played it down, supposedly out of respect for the girl's family, but mostly because no-one wanted the Taliban to clock up the point. There was a debrief. Reports were written and filed. Life went on. But Taine hadn't forgotten and neither had Trigger – although to be fair, the big man had said little about that day. Not that it mattered. Taine carried guilt enough for both of them...

"McKenna," Coolie said, interrupting Taine's nightmare. "Before Read gets back with the others there's something else you should know."

Taine kept his face deadpan. "I'm listening."

"Lefty and Eriksen have an issue."

Folding his arms across his chest, Taine sighed. Skilled combatants both of them, mostly the pair are mates, but lately they'd been as compatible as a small boy and soap.

"So what are they squabbling over this time?"

Coolie shrugged. "They're not saying, but it's getting pretty tense."

McKenna nodded, imagining the pair stalking about glowering at each other. "Let's just keep an eye on them. Anyone else got a problem? Miller? Winters?"

"Not that I know of."

"Excellent."

Wrapping on his ballistic sunglasses, Taine strode into the sunlight to meet his section.

CHAPTER 5

Rotorua township, Monday evening

Nathan Kerei popped the last piece of crumbed schnitzel in his mouth. Still chewing, he placed his knife and fork neatly on the plate, and swallowed his mouthful. "Got a call today. I'm off in the morning, love."

From her armchair in front of the telly, her eyes on her *Downton Abbey* rerun, Paula said, "Another group? It's late in the year for tourists."

"It's not tourists. The army called me up."

"Why? There a war on?" said Nathan's grandson. The teen sat alongside Nathan, geography homework laid out on the kitchen table: a textbook, a couple of coloured pencils and a tatty refill pad.

Brandon had been with them for a few months now, since Nathan's daughter Mary had hooked up with her new man and they'd had baby Kimbra. Mary was happy enough, but poor Brandon had never really hit it off with his step-dad. When the atmosphere between them had become too tough for Mary, Nathan and the wife had stepped in, offering Brandon a home until things settled down.

"They've asked me to be a guide."

"Why don't they use a map?"

"Because they want someone familiar with the area up near Maungapōhatu."

Brandon flicked through his textbook then pointed out a page to Nathan. "They need a topography map, like this."

"It's not the same as knowing a place, son."

"But why do they need to know?" Brandon demanded.

Nathan pushed back a speck of annoyance at Brandon's constant questioning. These days, teenagers asked a lot of questions. They taught them that in school. It was how they learned, apparently. "Not sure," Nathan replied. "Some scientists are going."

"I bet it's a cover for something."

"And I bet it's just a regular science trip."

"So, why send in the army?"

Nathan shrugged. "Just helping out. The army helped out when the Rena was wrecked off the coast in Tauranga, remember? They cleared the beach of oil and those decomposing meat patties. It's part of their job."

"But aren't they like trespassing?" Brandon insisted. "The beach belongs to everyone, but Te Urewera belongs to us Tūhoe."

Nathan carried his plate across to the sink and scraped a piece of fat into the rubbish bin with the back of his knife. "I assume they've asked permission, otherwise we wouldn't be going." He rinsed his plate and put it on the draining board.

"But who would they ask, Koro? There's more than one group thinks they're in charge of the whole tribe."

The boy had a point. Maybe asking questions wasn't so bad for the kid's learning.

"Will you be gone long?" Paula said, interrupting the discussion. She stretched one arm out wide, unravelling more of the cupcake-pink wool.

"Few days. A week. That's all."

"I'd better get some warm clothes ready for you then," she said, getting up. She wound the wool around the bonnet, bending to pop her knitting back in her workbag before switching off the telly then disappearing down the hall. A few minutes later, Nathan ducked out to the garage to get his tramping boots.

Brandon reckoned he had about fifteen minutes to make the call while his koro had a smoke out back. When he heard his grandmother opening and closing the drawers in the bedroom, he grabbed the phone.

"There's an army group going into the park," he told the boy at the other end. He kept his voice low. "My koro's going in with them."

"The army? That's effing bold."

"I reckon."

"What do they want?"

"Koro didn't say."

"Looking for our separatist training groups again?"

"Like I said, Koro didn't say. Just that they needed a guide."

"My dad'll know. Or if he doesn't, he'll find out."

"What'll he do?"

"I dunno. Something. The army's got no business coming here. The park belongs to the Tūhoe Nation."

Brandon cut him off; he'd heard the power-to-the-people speech before. "Just remember to tell your dad that Nathan's going to be with them."

"Yeah, okay, I'll tell him. Don't worry, nothing'll happen to your granddad. I better go. Thanks for the tip."

"No worries."

CBD, Sydney, Australia

The hostess of the Collar and Thai ushered Caren into a booth where richly-woven wall tapestries glinted in the low lighting. It was early for lunch, just after 11:00am, yet already several groups were scattered amongst the tables, their shopping bags stacked against the black lacquered table legs.

Caren slipped into the bench seat, annoyed with herself for not stopping in at a boutique downstairs so she, too, could tuck a shopping bag at her feet, making her anonymous amongst the ladies-who-lunch crowd. Caren almost laughed – a lady who lunched.

Not *this* lady.

Minutes later, a tall florid man in his late fifties, his lips too thick and too wet, wove his way through the labyrinth of chairs and tables. Caren checked her watch and smiled; right on time.

The Texan extended his hand as she stood. Caren clasped it in her own, turning the handshake into something more. His hands were damp.

"Vernon. Kind of you to take time out from your vacation," she said, making a conscious effort not to wipe her palms dry on the front of her skirt.

Inclining his head, Vernon motioned to the booth and the pair sat.

"It can be crazy here at lunchtime so I took the liberty of ordering," Caren said. She scooped her hands under her buttocks, tucking her skirt tidily beneath her. "Barbeque Duck Curry and Spicy Beef Salad."

A scowl flitted across her companion's face.

Stupid, stupid, stupid.

Caren could have kicked herself; she shouldn't have presumed to order for him. Men like Vernon Bonnar needed to feel they were in control, that they were making the decisions. Calling the shots. That tiny mistake could cost her the deal. Uneasy, Caren twirled the opal on her finger, hardly daring to hold her breath. But Bonnar must have been feeling sweet, because he ignored the blunder, summoning the waitress with a click of his fingers. He pointed to the wine-list then shooed the girl away.

"These trials – the info – it's legit?" he demanded finally, his Texan drawl booming about the restaurant.

Caren wanted to hiss at him to keep his damn voice down. Instead, she delayed answering, pouring herself a glass of water – the fact Bonnar hadn't offered her a drink not lost on her. This was a game, after all.

Caren chose her words carefully. "How we got the data is irrelevant. The results speak for themselves. We're looking at extensive reserves – perhaps better even than gold output from the Martha mine at Waihi – and with minimal extraction costs."

"Anyone else seen this?"

"Only you, Vernon." Caren fingered the stem of her water glass. "For the moment."

"Now, just a minute. If you're thinking—"

Deliberately, Caren took the serviette from her lap, placed it on the table, then stood, pulling her handbag over her shoulder. She kept her action slow, knowing this was a bluff she could only play once. "If you'll excuse me. I believe we're done here."

But Vernon didn't move. "Hey, there's no need to get all huffy," he protested, his hands palm up. "I just need to be sure what you're offering is exclusive to OreGen. You're asking us to commit a fuckload of money to this."

Caren smiled inwardly. Backtracking *and* swearing. She set her handbag down and settled herself back in the booth before continuing. "We've *already* invested a lot of money in this project, Vernon, and I'm letting you in on it. I don't have to do that."

"As a matter of interest, why *are* you doing that? Why not exploit the information yourselves?"

"Let's just say that right now the Geotech name might throw up a few hurdles."

Vernon's piggy eyes bored into her. "Because?"

Twirling the opal again, Caren shrugged. "There've been some site safety allegations."

Vernon's eyes narrowed. "OreGen won't buy an unsafe plant, Caren."

"Nor will it be. Our equipment meets the highest compliance standards, Vernon. So our mines have had a couple of accidents. You know as well as I do that more often than not, accidents are caused by human error."

"So you need us."

"We need a front. I'd *like* it to be OreGen, but it could just as easily be someone else. China Mining Corp, for example." Caren kept her voice offhand. "In fact, I had lunch with the Chairman Xu only two weeks ago in this very restaurant. He was particularly fond of the chili tamarind snapper—"

Bonnar's lip curled. "You're forgetting that OreGen could go ahead without you. I have the data," he snarled, cutting her off. A spray of his spittle hit the glossy table top.

"It won't help you, Vernon. You'd be starting from behind."

"At least we'd be looking in the right place."

"Yes, but it could take you years to get permission to prospect on that parkland. I have a strategy in place which should see us underway within six months."

"Providing OreGen agrees to purchase a new plant from you."

Caren stared at him, raising her water glass to her lips.

"Okay, so tell me more," Bonnar drawled.

She didn't, of course. Why would she tell Vernon Bonnar *anything* that would allow OreGen to go ahead without her? By the time the waitress arrived with the duck, she'd told him enough to hook him.

Army Leave Centre, Rotorua township, Tuesday morning
"Sergeant McKenna?"

Straightening, Taine turned away from the truck to face the man behind him. Wide-faced with cheery features, he was more like a student than a 31-year-old consultant.

"Mr Fogarty."

"Ah, so you know who I am."

"Process of elimination, you're not female, which rules out Dr Asher or Ms Hemphill, and I've already met Dr de Haas. And the Australian accent helped."

"Incredible. I didn't even mention the words *pool* or *six*," Fogarty said, giving Taine an easy grin. "Call me Ben, please."

"Pleased to meet you, Ben."

They shook hands. Ben Fogarty's grasp was firm. Solid.

"So," Ben rocked lazily on his heels. "I don't suppose there're any coffee kiosks where we're heading?"

"Not a lot of call for them. The milk tends to go off."

"I figured as much. Will I have time to grab a last brew before we pull out? I'm told this little jaunt could take a week – a long time to go without a double shot of Columbian Arabica."

Laughing, Taine checked his watch. "We'll be leaving in twenty minutes. Briefing here in fifteen."

"I'd better be quick, then." Ben's hand was already diving into his pocket for his wallet.

When the consultant had left, Taine spared a moment to observe the other civilians. No obvious couch potatoes at least. Not far away, Louise Hemphill, de Haas' research assistant – a striking woman in her late twenties – set her pack down on the asphalt next to a second canvas bag. Louise opened the second bag and checked through its contents, lifting out notebooks, fabric sample bags, a geologist's pick, a few chisels. Not a single strand of hair escaped her ponytail. Taine's dossier said she'd once won a junior national single sculls title. She'd kept up her training from the looks of it, with decent shoulders and a leanness to her.

Taine smiled as the section new guy, Miller, ambled towards her, obviously believing the NZDF recruitment slogan that he's *Got What it Takes*. Still, it was clear to Taine, if not yet to Miller, that even without the ten-year age gap, Louise was way out of his league. Luckily the private was spared from finding out, his approach cut off by a woman crossing the parking lot in fluid efficient strides.

Jules Asher.

Taine recognised the biologist from her file photo. Petite and dark, she looked fit enough despite her lack of recent field experience.

"Louise?" the biologist asked. Taine detected a hint of tension in her voice. Just nerves at meeting someone new? Pushing the pack deeper into the truck, he strained his ears.

"Yes?"

"Jules Asher. Your tent-mate. Thought I'd pop across and reassure you that any snoring you might hear won't be coming from me." Taine glanced over to see Asher push a wisp of hair off her forehead with one hand while extending the other.

Smiling, Louise shook Jules' hand, the movement sharp and efficient. "Good to know. Where do you stand on teeth grinding?"

"Only in daylight hours."

"Sharing a toothbrush?"

"'Ew." Jules screwed up her face, but her dark eyes sparkled.

"I think we're good, then."

A pause.

"Good to see someone else still getting their gear sorted," Jules said, gesturing at the equipment bag.

"Yes, we didn't get much notice and Dr de Haas likes to be prepared." Louise nodded in the direction of her boss. Near the rear of the second truck, the stocky geologist had intercepted Miller, bellowing at the private to stop what he was doing immediately and help him load his pack into the vehicle.

"Have you worked with him long?" Jules asked.

"About a year."

"And is he always so... so..."

De Haas' barking carried across the lot, prompting Coolie to stride over to see what the fuss was about.

"Exacting?" Louise said. "Yes, he is."

Jules didn't look surprised by her companion's choice of adjective.

"Can I ask you a question?" said Louise, her eyes on Miller and Coolie.

"Sure."

"What's with all the rippling muscle? Why are we getting an army escort when we already have a guide?"

Jules threw a backwards glance in Taine's direction, and he leaned into the truck, hiding his face.

"I don't know," Jules said. "Maybe the army hasn't got enough for them to do? You know how it can be with boys. Too much testosterone left to idle and they get themselves into trouble. And we've got plenty to keep them busy here."

Taine straightened, to see her waving at the packs lined up on the asphalt.

"You're right," Louise agreed. "Let me rephrase. What I meant was, isn't it wonderful to have all this rippling muscle and rampant testosterone to help us carry our gear?"

"There you go," Jules said with a laugh, Louise joining her.

Christian de Haas washed his hands at the basin, allowing the cold water to run over his wrists, a trick he'd seen his mother use to calm her nerves. Little wonder he was rattled. That stupid soldier wasn't capable of following even the simplest instruction. *"I'll just squash it in here,"* the idiot had said. There was a microscope in that pack! De Haas shook his head. No finesse whatsoever. Although, it was what he'd come to expect from Kiwis, always worshiping brawn over brains. For God's sake, New Zealand's annual competition to find the best farmer – hoary blokes riding around in tractors – got more press than any academic achievement.

Sighing, he dried his hands under the blower, and smoothed the hair over his ears. Then, about to check his watch, he stopped himself. There was no hurry. In fact, it wouldn't hurt to make a point and turn up to the briefing fashionably late. They could hardly leave without the Task Force Leader, could they? De Haas smiled at the man in the mirror. It had been a thrill when the minister's aide had called him about the appointment. De Haas stepped back and straightened his collar. An entire expedition, civilians *and* soldiers, and all under his leadership.

Task Force Leader.

Such a satisfying ring to it. Not that the title would impress his old man. Nothing less than Springbok rugby captaincy would have been good enough for *him*. But Christian had his moments. Being headhunted by New Zealand's Petroleum and Minerals, and handing in his notice at his father's company, for example. The satisfaction of departing his home country within the week, finally free of the bastard. He'd hoped to shoot up the ladder, but as always, he'd been disappointed, instead spending a decade pushing paper. There'd be no pushing paper after this. Not after he'd distinguished himself with a momentous discovery in the Ureweras. Let's see his father ignore that.

A momentous discovery...

De Haas had every intention of making that happen. With a last look in the mirror and a final tug to the bottom of his jacket, de Haas exited the bathroom.

Her gear stowed in one of the trucks, Jules joined the others for the briefing at the edge of the car park. In green combat fatigues, the army sergeant waited for the group to settle.

"Good morning, everyone. My name is Sergeant Taine McKenna," he said, his voice reminding Jules of a well-known newsreader, its timbre solid and trustworthy. "I'm heading up the army escort accompanying this party into the Urewera forest. It seems our Task Force Leader has stepped away for a moment, so in the interests of expediency, I'll get started on the logistical briefing. We'll be leaving at 0800 hours, travelling by army vehicle to the head of the trail. It should take us…" He paused as the man who went off earlier re-joined the group. Panting slightly, the man raised his takeout coffee cup at the sergeant.

A last coffee.

Damn, Jules could've done with one of those. Might have calmed her nerves. Still, it was worth taking the time to make a friend of Louise. And the technician was good value. Just the right kind of tent-mate to help her survive a week in the wop-wops.

"It should take us around two hours to drive in," McKenna said, "and a half day to reach the Conservation Department hut where we'll spend our first night. It'll take a further day to get to the approximate site where the nugget was found, and where Dr de Haas and Dr Asher will conduct their studies." He gave Jules a short nod, fixing her with his steely blue eyes as he pointed her out to the rest of the group. Embarrassed, Jules dropped her eyes and examined her boots.

The sergeant went on. "Introducing my section, we have Corporal Jackson Liu, who answers to Coolie, Privates Trevor

'Trigger' Grierson, Adrian Eriksen, Eddie 'Lefty' Wright, Jugraj Singh, our medical officer, Anaru Winters, communications..." When McKenna called their names, the men stood to attention, and then at ease when the next soldier in line was announced. The last of the team were barely out of school uniform – Matt Read and Hamish Miller. Possibly their first assignment, if Read's face was anything to go by. Flushed, the soldier looked as if he could scarcely contain his excitement.

"And our local guide is Nathan Kerei."

Sitting on a bollard, Kerei was puffing on a cigarette, blowing blue smoke into the air above his head. He acknowledged the group with a nod.

McKenna was about to go on when de Haas bustled forward. Jules noticed the geologist made a point of placing himself directly in front of McKenna, his action only serving to highlight the difference in their heights, the sergeant looming head and shoulders over the geologist.

"I'll take over from here, Corporal," de Haas interrupted. He flapped his hands at McKenna, as if he was a preschool teacher sending his charges off to recess.

The sergeant made no comment, but Jules detected the slightest twitch of his jaw. He took a step back, closer to his men.

"Dr Christian de Haas. I'm your Task Force Leader for this expedition. Up until now, the Ureweras have been of only low to medium interest when it comes to mineral exploration, but new information has changed that. The Government has appointed this group to determine the mining potential. We're here to find the golden goose."

The latecomer raised his coffee cup. "Dr de Haas."

"Yes, um...?"

"Ben Fogarty, engineer, Australian Minerals. No offence, but why are the army coming?"

Jules shot a quick look at Louise, who raised her eyebrows.

So we're not the only ones to wonder.

"Ah, well, ordinarily we wouldn't mount an expedition of this sort in the winter – there's the added risk of flash floods and landslips – but the government are keen to move quickly on this, which is why we've been offered the extra help," de Haas replied. "The army will be carrying the bulk of the camp gear, our equipment, and any samples we collect. Think of them as our pack horses." He laughed at his own joke. From the looks on their faces, the soldiers weren't amused.

Ben Fogarty raised his arm again. "That doesn't explain why McKenna's men are *armed*. I've heard rumours about separatists hiding out in this forest. I'm not keen on going in if there's a chance I might get shot at by a bunch of crazy radicals."

De Haas clucked. "Rumours!" He waved a hand airily. "I'm a scientist, Mr Fogarty. I prefer to act on hard facts, not speculation and conjecture. The army's role is to transport the apparatuses necessary to carry out the geophysical objectives of this mission, and to carry the rocks home. As for the guns..." He shrugged. "We all know how the army like their toys. If they choose to cart their weapons around for no good reason, that's up to them. Right, if we're all done, let's get underway."

Chapter 6

Winter conditions had pitted the track, making it uneven and treacherous, although not as treacherous as driving in the border desert between Sinai and Israel. Taine manoeuvred the vehicle to avoid another giant pothole, causing Jules to grab for a handhold. The pothole avoided, Taine noted the set of tyre tracks. Someone'd been down this road ahead of them, and given the rain earlier, only an hour or two back. But why? Unless you were a hiker or a local, there wasn't much call to come out this far. Not in the winter.

A kilometre on, they came across a 4-wheel drive parked hard to the left. Taine slowed the Pinzgauer, squeezing through the narrow space between the parked vehicle and a clay bank to the right. Red-brown clay spackled the 4-wheel drive like blood splatter from a cop show. He shot a look inside when they passed. A crocheted bedspread was laid out on the back seat, a box of tinned food on top. No obvious weapons – not unless someone planned to bombard them with baked beans...

Taine took the bend. About thirty metres ahead, in the middle of the track and blocking the way, were two men: an old man in his seventies or eighties, and a younger one, possibly a son. Clad in heavy Swanndri shirts, they were seated on canvas fold-out chairs arranged about a steel thermos. A couple of white plastic cups stood upright like lighthouses in the sea of gravel.

Taine pulled to a stop.

"Wait here," he said. Stepping down from the vehicle, he trotted over to meet with the locals.

Jules climbed out of the vehicle, glad for the excuse to stretch her legs. The truck's other passengers get out too. Behind her, Trigger slipped discreetly into the bushes.

Tipping her head to one side, Jules rubbed at a kink in her neck. The past half hour on this road had thrown them about more than an unbalanced centrifuge. Army vehicles weren't built for comfort. It hadn't helped that going back into the forest had her wound as tight as a clock spring.

At the blockade, McKenna greeted the old man, the pair touching their noses together in a hongi, sharing their breath. Jules detected a measure of respect in the way the soldier softened the line of his shoulders and dropped his gaze.

Interesting.

"What's going on?" Eriksen said, coming up on Jules' shoulder.

"Not sure," Jules answered, her hand still working at her neck.

Christian de Haas got out of the second truck and marched over to join the party in the middle of the road. The geologist hadn't exactly endeared himself to the group when they'd met this morning. Something about the ironed-in crease of his trousers, or the slightly too-pinched bridge of his nose.

Or his officious posturing.

Up ahead, voices were rising. Clearly upset, the old man waved his arms, stretching them out as wide as he could reach, as if describing his latest fishing catch. De Haas shook his head, responding sharply. Jules didn't catch the words, but his tone was clear enough.

"Oops. Looks like our Mr Christian has a mutiny on his hands, doesn't it?" Eriksen said softly from behind Jules.

They watched the younger man – Jules suspected he was a relative – place a calming hand on the old guy's shoulder. McKenna took advantage of the movement to position his own body in front of de Haas. Jules doubted the change in stance was for the Task Force Leader's protection.

"Now what?" she asked Eriksen.

The soldier shrugged. "I don't know. They're like elephants, the people who live in these parts. Never get over a grudge. I wouldn't be surprised to find out someone ran off with the old fella's great-granny half a century ago and he's still pissed."

The old man made a lunge for de Haas.

"Aha!" said Eriksen. "I was right. Seems great-granny got about."

Jules stifled a snort at Eriksen's irreverence. But the altercation surprised her. De Haas was prickly, but to have upset the old man enough to provoke a punch? And in that short a time?

The old man's lunge fell short of its mark, encumbered by the wall of McKenna's body. The relative pulled the old guy back.

"Get over yourselves, guys," Eriksen murmured.

McKenna turned to de Haas, clearly trying to stop the geologist from inciting any further conflict while the younger man held the old man in check. A stalemate.

Nathan Kerei had been travelling in the other truck. Stepping out of the bushes, he made his way to the front. It looked like he recognised the blockaders. The guide spoke a few moments with the younger man, who in turn spoke to his older companion. A few tense minutes passed, after which the group broke up and the beach-chair cordon was removed.

McKenna was the last to slide back into the vehicle. He put the truck into gear and pulled out.

In the passenger seat, Jules couldn't stand the suspense. "What was that all about? Who were those people?"

McKenna fixed his eyes on a deep rut in the road. "The old fellow's name was Rawiri Temera and the other was his great-nephew, Wayne. They're from the local iwi. Tūhoe people."

He swung hard to the right. Jules grabbed the dashboard as the truck jolted. A little further on, when the travel was less hairy, Jules asked again, "So what did they want?"

"Temera wanted us to turn back."

"That's just bloody typical, isn't it?" Eriksen moaned in the rear. "One day you appoint a top secret Task Force, and the next, every man and his fucking dog know about it."

"I don't think they knew about the Task Force. We only knew ourselves, yesterday," McKenna said.

"But it wasn't hard to guess the government would do something when that gold nugget was found, was it?" said Trigger.

McKenna swerved around a rut. "Except the nephew said the pair have been parking up here on and off since the summer. Apparently, Temera had some kind of premonition. Claims he saw a taniwha roaming the forest, and he wants to warn people not to go in."

"A taniwha?" Jules said, her hand still on the dash. A mythological monster? Did McKenna really believe that? She looked across at him; his face was impassive.

"Sounds to me like the old codger's lost his marbles," said Eriksen from behind.

"The nephew says not."

"He's lost his marbles, and all."

Coolie placed a hand on the front headrest, pulling himself forward. "Here be dragons," he murmured, his voice sending a shiver up Jules' spine.

"What's that about dragons?" Read said eagerly from further back in the truck. It was a wonder he could hear anything over the rumble of the engine.

"Here be dragons," Coolie said, louder this time. "Cartographers wrote it on maps when they didn't know anything about an area. They'd draw a sea serpent marking the unexplored territory. Warned travellers to be on their guard. Some people reckon Māori legends about taniwha had the same intent. You know, as an indication of danger."

"I thought taniwha hung out in rivers or swamps," Read said.

McKenna lifted his chin, glancing at the private in the rear view mirror. "Usually, but not always."

"Anyway, there are plenty of rivers in the Ureweras," Trigger said.

Eriksen snorted. "Load of mumbo-jumbo!"

"It's all in the interpretation, isn't it?" said Coolie thoughtfully. "You could say the Māori are superstitious, but others would argue they're intuitive."

"Yeah right," Eriksen scoffed. "Interpretation. The way I see it, the old guy watches the same news as everyone else. He figures the Tūhoe should be the ones to get the golden egg, so he goes and conjures up an imaginary bloody dragon."

"I'm with Eriksen on this one," Trigger said. "It's just a way for Māori to get their hands on some free money."

Jules looked across sharply. "Did he ask for money?" she asked McKenna.

"No," McKenna replied. "He didn't mention compensation, or the Treaty. He was just warning us off, telling us it's too dangerous to go in."

"These forests *are* dangerous if you don't know what you're doing," Coolie said. "There's freezing fog, rock falls, flooded rivers, landslips..."

Trigger grunted. "And we're army. So there's a few rock falls. We don't scare that easy."

Jules heard the seat exhale as Trigger sat back, his point made. A glance over her shoulder showed him sulking good-naturedly in the back. Read had popped his ear buds back in. Jules looked at McKenna; the soldier's lips clamped tight, he navigated the vehicle over the pitted terrain.

Subject closed then.

Leaning back, Jules hugged her arms across her chest. The forest was closing in around them. Tree trunks stood on parade, row upon row of them like platoons of soldiers guarding the dark and dense interior. The tribe who lived here were called the Children of the Mist, after the clouds of mist that drifted in and out of the valleys like dragon's breath. Perhaps there was something in the old man's warning. Jules wasn't superstitious, but she knew the forest was deceptive. Darkened byways promised adventure, and yet a single false step could change an outing into something sinister, even deadly.

The engine strained as the vehicle climbed over a ridge,

allowing Jules a glimpse of the wispy brume that hovered over the mountain tops and descended into the valley. She pushed down a tremor of fear.

McKenna parked the vehicle and ratcheted the handbrake. "End of the line, people. Dragons or no, from here we go on foot."

The next fifteen minutes were a nightmare, anticipation and fear making Jules queasy. Her bootlaces tightened and her pack already on, Jules waited for McKenna's soldiers to distribute the rest of the equipment and supplies, praying they'd hurry up. She scuffed her feet in the grit.

Let's just get this over with.

But the roar of a vehicle – Temera and his nephew again? – made them all turn.

A white Nissan Pathfinder streaked with clay-coloured mud. Like a newly-licensed teenager, the driver skidded to a halt, kicking up the shingle in a wet crunch.

Jules strode across and pulled open the driver door. "Richard! What are you doing here?"

"You said it'd be cold. I brought you my spare beanie," he teased, swinging his legs out of the truck.

"Richard. Be serious," Jules scolded.

One hand on the top of the door, Richard stepped out of the vehicle. "I had some leave owing, and after you left it got very quiet at work, so I thought, why not be spontaneous?" He glanced around. "Which one of these chaps is de Haas?"

Stupefied, Jules pointed out the geologist, who was sliding his geologist's pick through a band on the side of his pack. Richard covered the distance in seconds and thrust out a hand.

"De Haas? Richard Foster, CEO, Landsafe. Thrilled to meet you. I've read some of your work, of course. Pre-requisite background reading for our soil and rock research."

Obviously as bemused as Jules, de Haas shook Richard's hand, and waited for him to come to the point.

"Look, I'm sorry to barge in unannounced, but I'd like to join you if I may?"

Richard is going to go in her stead? Fantastic!

Already, Jules felt the tension drain from her shoulders.

"I'm not asking in any official capacity you understand, but as a volunteer," Richard told de Haas. "As Jules' boss, I've already been briefed…"

Jules clamped her teeth shut, afraid of what she might say. If Richard had wanted to come, why all the song and dance yesterday about not being able to spare anyone, and how her colleagues were all too busy? Richard knew what she went through; knew how she felt about fieldwork. She hadn't slept at all last night thinking about this week in the forest. And here he was, saying he'd got leave?

"Jules is rusty where field work is concerned," Richard said. He stepped back and clapped an arm around her shoulders. "I'm sure she'd appreciate some help."

Help? Now he was undermining her ability as a scientist, too?

Moving out of Richard's hug, Jules fiddled with the straps on her pack, tightening it although it fit her perfectly. These feelings… she was being unreasonable. Richard had always supported her career. If he thought she was lacking confidence, it was because she *had* been hiding behind her lab work. Most likely, he wanted to allay her fears about being back in the forest, his presence meant to ease her back into field study. Jules frowned. But if that was the case, his actions were a step beyond the conduct of a concerned boss. She should probably think about the implications of *that*, but right now there was no time. De Haas had obviously agreed to Richard's request because the man was yanking his gear from the back of the Pathfinder.

"No point taking that, Foster," de Haas said, pointing at the rectangular bulge in Richard's shirt pocket. "Where we're going I very much doubt there's any cell coverage."

Richard pulled a goofy face. "If you don't mind, I think I'll take it anyway. I've got a bit of a fetish for Angry Birds."

"Suit yourself," de Haas said as he turned and motioned to Kerei to lead on.

CHAPTER 7

Te Urewera National Park, Day One

Half an hour in and already Jules' palms were clammy. A trickle of sweat rolled between her breasts. Concentrating on the trail and the regular movement of Private Wright – Lefty's – boots in front of her, she was in that moment in a horror flick when you'd held your breath for too long, waiting for the fright. She forced herself to exhale slowly and hoped no-one suspected she was near panic. Maybe they'd think she was a bit unfit.

Instead of terrified.

Every step took them deeper into the mist. So far the going hadn't been too bad, the track properly formed and reasonably flat, but soon they'd hit the deep valleys and soaring crests the park was famous for. Treacherous, unforgiving ridges dropping into steep ravines – the kind that reminded her of that long night clinging to a cliff – and the broken twisted body of her friend lying silently at the bottom of the chasm...

She needed a distraction. But there was no chance of a cheerful chat with Richard, Louise, or even Lefty for that matter. The track was too narrow, forcing them all to travel single file, like Peter Pan's Lost Boys. Jules focussed her eyes and feet on the trail, and tuned in to the sounds of the forest. The Ureweras were bursting with birds. *That's it!* She'd occupy her mind by identifying the songs of native birds. A brain teaser. It was exactly what she needed.

She strained to isolate birdsong over the jingling of packs and trudge of boots. Easy enough to detect the boisterous warbles of tui and bellbird carrying over the top-note chirps of a flighty fantail. A kākā chirruped somewhere nearby. The occasional turkey-like gobbles of native woodpigeon filtered through the trees, and then at last, she was not entirely sure... although it might've been… there it was again… the heart-shattering lament of a silver kōkako, some way off, but unmistakably beautiful. Jules strained for another chance to catch the sound… in that moment remembering why she loved the forest. It was so glorious. So vibrant.

So alive!

She looked skywards, marvelling at the branches of a silver beech draped in grey-green lichen, and breathed in the rich damp smell of detritus.

So stupid! How could she have given this up? Being outdoors like this? The purity, the *serenity* of it. All this time Jules had been blaming *the forest* for what had happened to Sarah. For her own terrifying night on the ledge. The accident had been a one-off. A fluke. An unforeseeable act-of-God. It had never been the forest's fault. If she hadn't been so stubborn, she could've been enjoying all this rather than denying herself. It might've been therapeutic.

Yes, of course she was frightened. Who wouldn't be after what she'd gone through? The forest could be a dangerous place. But perhaps she'd held the grudge long enough.

Jules caught the iridescent plumage of a tui as it hopped in the leathery branches of a five finger tree and, in spite of the weight of her pack, her step felt lighter.

Jugraj Singh grappled for a handhold. It wasn't the first time today his feet had disappeared from beneath him. Leaning heavily on a tree trunk, Jug struggled to regain his balance. The steep banks were so slippery, and the descent was rutted with water channels. Already the tread in his boots was caked with red clay. It didn't help that he was near the back of the group. Parts of the track had been eroded by their passage, the scuffs and skid marks making the going difficult.

Jug envied the way Miller made easy work of the slope. The soldier was as wily as a mountain goat, descending in short, carefully-placed steps. Jug tried to emulate the man's speedy technique, but a misstep sent him sliding on his bum again, his pack scraping the ground behind him.

Shit!

He skidded a few metres, but remembered to turn into the slope as he'd been trained, bringing his body close to the ground to slow his momentum.

Still slipping…

He dug his fingers into the clay, slid a bit further.

Make a grab for something.

A root.

Bugger! Too smooth…

A rock.

Grab it!

At last, his fall arrested, Jug paused, breathing heavily. That had been bloody close. Any further and he might've made it to the bottom before everyone else.

He looked down the incline. Miller had opened up a bit of gap, leaving Jug behind. Jug tried not to beat himself up about it. *Let's face it, I'm at least twice Miller's age.* In fact, apart from the local guide, Jug was probably the eldest in the group and right now he was feeling every one of his 42 years, as slow as an old cart and just as rickety. He'd have thought going downhill would be easier, but his legs were quivering with fatigue. Stabilising muscles didn't get much use when you stood all day working in a hospital. Well, they were getting a serious work-out now. On the plus side, there wouldn't be much further to go today, but Jug was already dreading tomorrow's hike. The second day always hurt more than the first.

Jug made a mental note to hit the gym more often when he got back, and maybe cut down on the custard squares too. Priya'd be pleased. Since the scare with her brother, she'd been after him to take better care of himself. 'Doctor, heal thyself,' she was fond of quoting. Jug wouldn't want to be in his brother-in-law's shoes. With two kids in high school and one at intermediate, heart disease was the last thing he needed.

Jug glanced forward. Miller was moving too far ahead. Soon

Jug wouldn't be able to follow the soldier's footsteps. Better get a wriggle on or he'd have to find his own route to the bottom. With aching limbs, Jug grabbed hold of a supplejack vine and scrambled his way down the slope.

Te Urewera Forest, First Campsite, Day One
McKenna kept them to the schedule they'd set at his morning briefing. By mid-afternoon they'd arrived at a grassy camp area near a small creek – the Department of Conservation hut to the rear of the site. Jules saw the sergeant have a quick word with de Haas, who waved him off. Then, a few minutes later, the geologist announced, "We'll set up camp here. I'll take the hut." Everyone dropped their packs, making off to select their tent sites.

"What say we pitch our tent here?" Louise suggested.

Jules considered the spot. They were on the leeward side of a small knoll at the edge of the campsite, and a stone's throw from the hut. "Looks as good as any."

Crouching, she began to brush stray sticks and stones from underfoot. It may have been years since she'd been in the field, but not so long that she'd forgotten to search for sharp objects that could damage the tent fabric.

"So what's your story, Louise?" she asked.

"There's nothing much to tell," Louise answered. She dropped a few strands of grass in the air to check the wind direction.

Still bent, Jules flicked a broken twig into the trees. She'd sleep better without *that* poking into her. "No-one at home?"

"There was, but we broke up a while back."

"I'm sorry."

"Don't be. It's no great loss," said Louise, taking the tent out of its bag and shaking the fabric free. "I joined a film festival club instead. A group of us meet up once a week at someone's place to watch and critique films. A highly satisfying alternative: the dialogue is better, and conflict gets resolved by the end of the movie."

"Good for you."

"Although it was a bit of a blow when he ran off with my best friend," she confided.

Piecing together sections of fibreglass tent pole, Jules grimaced. "Ouch!"

"Uhuh. Not very original, is it? What about you? Are you married?"

Jules snorted. "No. The only person waiting at home for me is a cat named Mr Cato, and to be fair, ours is more a master and slave relationship."

"At least you know where you're at with him." Louise held the door of the dome away from the wind, while Jules pushed the tent poles through the fabric sleeves.

"Oh no, he's cheating on me, too," Jules said over the top of the dome. "He's been seen leaving my neighbour's place right after breakfast." Stopping what she was doing for a second, she put her hand to her mouth and feigned a conspiratorial whisper. "I caught him rubbing himself up against her."

"No!" Louise exclaimed. "The cad!"

They were still laughing as they pegged out the dome and put up the flysheet.

Jules zipped her jacket against the early evening chill. The group sat dotted around a campfire, getting to know each other. Inevitably, the conversation returned to this morning's roadblock.

"Most people around these parts know Rawiri Temera by reputation," said Nathan Kerei from his perch on a fallen log. "Some are even a bit scared of him. He's well-known for being a matakite—"

"A what?" interrupted Ben.

"A matakite. It's a fortune-teller or soothsayer," Coolie told the Australian quietly.

"Okay," Ben replied.

"He seemed very agitated," said Louise, sitting cross-legged on the groundsheet beside Jules. Opposite them, on the other side of the fire, McKenna whittled a piece of wood, while the communications officer, Anaru Winters, propped up against a backpack, was trying to read a battered version of *To Kill a Mockingbird* in the waning light.

"A lot of people put stock in what the old man says. They reckon the next time Taupō is about to blow, Temera will be the one to tell us," said Kerei.

Ben laughed. "The last time Taupō erupted, the whole world knew about it. 186 AD if I remember rightly. There were reports of ash as far away as Greece."

"Well, there'll be no need for crack-pot fortune tellers then," de Haas snapped. "GNS has teams of scientists dedicated to monitoring volcanic activity. That old man is nothing but a trouble maker. I told him as much. He was trying to stop us – a legitimate Government Task Force – from entering the park."

Coolie butted in. "With all due respect, Doctor, these *are* their lands. The Ngāi Tūhoe held out, refused to sign the Treaty of Waitangi."

"What's that supposed to mean?" Trigger said. "That they're not subject to the same rules as the rest of us?"

Kerei nodded. "For some, yes."

"They may not have signed the Treaty, but it didn't stop them taking an enormous settlement from the government, did it?" said Singh. "What was it? 170 million?"

"It's always about money," said Trigger. "Remember when that tribe in the Waikato manipulated Transit New Zealand into re-routing State Highway One—"

"That was the Ngāti Naho," said Nathan Kerei quickly.

"Whoever," Trigger said, continuing. "All of a sudden the tribe's oldies, the kaumātua, get all riled up, demanding their taniwha be placated, and next thing, the tribe gets a fat little pay-out. No offence to you, Nathan and Taine, I know these are your people we're talking about, but the way I see it, anytime anyone wants to put in a road, build a bridge, whatever, along come the local Māori digging up some old taniwha and demanding their cut."

"Small price to pay for two centuries of disruption to our way of life," Kerei said, his cheeks twitching.

Jules glanced at McKenna. The sergeant had stopped his whittling, slipping his carving, and the knife, into his pocket.

"Well, the land is never really owned by anyone, is it? Only borrowed until the next generation comes along to take over its guardianship," Richard said.

Jules grinned at him. They both knew Richard's sentence was lifted straight from a Landsafe policy document.

"170 million," whistled Miller. "That's better than winning Lotto."

"It's a lot of money," agreed Singh, stretching out the band of his watch. "That kind of coin would fund the army for a few years." He laughed. "We might've avoided last year's IMPing programme."

"IMPing?" Richard asked.

"Army short-hand. Means making an endangered species out of certain personnel. Warrant Officers mostly: First and Second Class. The army's been retiring them as a cost cutting measure."

"Tell me about it. You want to see the budget cuts in science. Isn't that right, Jules?" Richard said. "These days we're so busy jumping through funding hoops, there's no time left to do any science."

Nearby, several birds broke cover, their silhouettes flapping away over the canopy.

A shout reverberated around the campsite.

CHAPTER 8

Taine and Coolie were the first to get there. Behind a copse of scrawny mānukā, Eriksen and Lefty were locked together and rolling about on the ground. Eriksen, heavier by about ten kilos, had Lefty in a rear chin lock straight out of the World Wrestling Federation handbook – his knee forced into the middle of Lefty's back with his forearm wrapped around his neck, Eriksen pulled back with all his weight.

Lefty swung blindly for his opponent, but the hold had him immobilised.

"Eriksen, let him go!" Taine roared, but Eriksen maintained the hold. Lefty's face was turning purple. "That's an order, soldier!"

Glaring, Eriksen released the green skin. Kicked him away.

Lefty collapsed on the ground, holding his throat and panting noisily.

"What the hell is going on?"

Neither man answered.

"Eriksen!"

"Nothing, Boss. It's personal."

"Lefty?" Lolling in the grass, Lefty gave Taine a small nod. Whatever it was, both men had decided to keep it to themselves.

"Well, if it's personal," Taine said, "it can wait until the assignment is over. You can kill each other then. In the meantime, I'll expect you to behave in a manner appropriate to soldiers of the NZDF. Am I *clear!*" He looked first at Eriksen then at Lefty. Not waiting for their confirmation, he turned on his heel and strode back towards the campfire.

"Nothing more to see people…" he heard Coolie say to the onlookers behind him.

Now Taine noticed de Haas was dogging him, skip-walking to keep pace.

"McKenna."

"Yes." Taine didn't break his stride.

"Well, aren't you going to do something about them?" de Haas demanded.

"Like what?"

"Like punish them? Set an example for the others."

"They said it was a personal matter." Taine said.

"But they were *fighting*."

Taine whirled to face the geologist, and found himself looking down on the man's bald patch. "They're soldiers. They're trained to fight, Dr de Haas."

"It's not good enough. I want those men punished."

Taine felt his nostrils flare. "That won't be necessary."

"Sergeant McKenna, I hope I don't have to remind you that *I* am the leader of this Task Force?" De Haas drew himself up to his full height and jutted his chin out.

So this is the way it's going to go, is it?

"I'm fully aware of the chain of command here, Doctor. However, Privates Wright and Eriksen are New Zealand Defence Force personnel," Taine said, keeping his voice even, "which makes their conduct my responsibility."

De Haas snorted. "Yes, exactly, and we've just seen how well *that* worked out."

"Nothing more than a friendly altercation," Taine said. A pulse throbbed at his temple. "Think of it as a bit of high-jinks on the first night of school camp. I've told them to put a lid on it."

Like a school marm, the geologist put his hands on his hips. "I won't have your men jeopardising the success of my expedition. If you can't keep them under control—"

"As I said, I've told them to put a lid on it," Taine said coolly. "Now if you'll excuse me."

De Haas bailed up Jules and Louise on their way back to their tent.

"You and Dr Asher will share the hut with Dr Foster and myself, Louise. Given the altercation earlier, I've decided it would be best," he said, hooking his index fingers in the air to punctuate the word altercation.

He's decided?

The pained expression that flitted across Louise's face told Jules her tent-mate wasn't keen either. If they let him bully them now, he'd likely keep it up for the rest of the trip. Best to tell him politely they were nobody's dishrag.

"If you don't mind, I'd prefer to sleep in my tent, Dr de Haas," Jules said. She threw him an apologetic look. "I'm afraid I'm a bit self-conscious about… um… men sleeping in the same room as me."

"Nonsense. This is a field expedition."

"I'd really feel a lot happier."

"Dr Asher, I can't be responsible for your safety if you insist on sleeping in the tent. I'm concerned about McKenna's ability to keep his men under control."

"I think Sergeant McKenna will vouch—"

His face reddening, the geologist cut Jules off. "You'll both sleep in the hut."

"I'm sure the two of us will be quite safe if we're together," Louise said in a rush. "We've pitched our tent within calling distance of the hut. See? If there's any trouble, we'll shout."

"That's settled then," said Jules. Taking Louise's arm, she threw her sweetest smile at de Haas. "Have a good night, Doctor."

De Haas' eyes narrowed. "Very well," he said, his lips thin, and stalked off towards the hut.

Taine pulled Coolie aside. "Any idea what's going on with those two?" he said, inclining his head in the direction of Eriksen and Lefty. Across the campsite, the soldiers – both on sentry duty – were glaring at each other like a couple of stags about to lock horns.

Coolie nodded. "I had a talk with Anaru, who had the lowdown from Lefty."

"And?"

"It's Sheryl."

Taine should've seen it coming. Sheryl Howell. A pretty girl with a thing for men in uniform. Sheryl was rumoured to have 'dated' more than one or two of the guys at the Linton base over recent months, including Adrian Eriksen.

The problem was, she was Lefty's sister.

"She's pregnant," Coolie added.

Taine figured as much. "Let me guess. She's naming Eriksen."

"Uhuh. Only he's denying it. Doesn't believe the kid's his. He told Anaru he's not about to raise some other guy's brat just because the battalion bike fingered him."

McKenna groaned inwardly. "And Eriksen's reaction has Lefty outraged about the slight to his sister," he said, summing up the situation.

"You have to admit, Sheryl likes her fun."

"Even so, no man wants to see his sister's name dragged through the dirt. Well, let's hope they suck it up until we get back. De Haas has us pegged as undisciplined rabble as it is."

It was mid-morning on the second day when Jules got her first fright – a hunter startling her by stepping out of the bush to her right.

Māori, he was fat with a broad nose, his skin the same gnarled texture of the adjacent beech trunks. A grimy yellow charity bandana tied loosely around his thick neck, he was carrying a small pig slung across his shoulders. A muscled pig dog, its jowls wobbling, ran silently at his heels. The hunter acknowledged the group with a sharp tilt of his head. The mongrel wagged its tail.

"Hey." His voice rasped from disuse. Bushmen like this existed in the forest. Some were loners who preferred the quiet company of the tōtara and rata trees, others were hiding from people or situations they couldn't bear to face. They lived in the forest for months, even years at a time, but this was the first time Jules had ever come across one.

"You fellas better go back, eh," the hunter said.

De Haas muscled his way through the group to face the hunter. "What did you say? Go back? Why?"

"This way's no good."

"No good? What do you mean no good?"

"Tūrehu. Patu-paiarehe."

"What the devil is he on about?" de Haas snapped.

Jules frowned; the geologist had the manners of a gorilla. She extended a hand to the hunter. "Hi," she said, smiling. "I'm Jules."

"Ira Bidois." Still grasping the pig, Ira was about to offer Jules his free hand, but seeing the blood and crud on it from his tussle with the pig, Ira obviously thought the better of it. Instead, he brought his hand down and wiped it on the back of his trousers, his fingers spread wide. It didn't help, his trousers were just as grubby.

"Sorry."

Jules grinned. "No worries. I can see you've got your hands full. You were saying something about us not being able to go this way?"

"It's not safe."

Jules felt an irrational leap of panic, her mind jumping to Sarah at the bottom of the landslip, but she stifled it quickly. That was a *freak* accident, she reminded herself sternly.

McKenna stepped forward. "Ira. Sergeant Taine McKenna. I heard you mention the patu-paiarehe?"

Ira nodded.

"The what?" said de Haas.

"Patu-paiarehe. They're light-skinned people who live in the forest and hide themselves in the mist," Kerei said. "They're said to come out at dusk to make trouble."

"Trouble," Ira echoed.

"What do you mean they're *said* to come out?" de Haas demanded.

"The patu-paiarehe are legendary. Like fairies. Or ghosts," Kerei explained.

"*Legendary?*" de Haas spluttered. "We're expected to turn around because this nutter says there are some *legendary fairy* people about?"

The hunter gave de Haas a derisive look. "Plenty of smart people believe in the patu-paiarehe, reckon they've seen them even."

"Oh for goodness sake!" de Haas threw his hands in the air theatrically. "First you people try to scare us off with your taniwha, and now it's bloody fairies. Any moment I expect we'll see Tarzan swinging out of the trees on a supplejack vine. You deal with this, McKenna. I've got a job to do here and it doesn't involve dealing with nutters." He stomped off to the edge of the clearing.

Insulted by de Haas' outburst, or just deciding he'd outstayed his welcome, the hunter turned to go, his dog tucked close to his heels.

"Wait," McKenna said. "I apologise for Dr de Haas."

Ira made no comment. Jules couldn't blame him for being offended.

"I'm really sorry," McKenna said, dropping his voice. "The man's a scientist. A genius, or so they tell me. There's a bit of a fine line, you know?"

Ira's wide features relaxed into a grin. "Sure. I get it. Don't worry about it. I got thick skin."

"So, you know this area well, Ira?"

Ira widened his stance to support the weight of the pig before tilting his chin upwards in assent. "Lived round here most my life."

"In the bush?"

"Some of it."

"What about lately?"

"Yeah, I've been here..." The hunter appeared to calculate the time in his head. "Maybe five months."

"And there's been some trouble?"

"In the bush, you see plenty."

"What about recently? In the past month?"

The hunter rolled his shoulders, shifting the weight of the pig across his back again. "Yeah, that's what I was trying to tell you." McKenna waited for him to elaborate. "There's been some weird stuff."

"Weird?"

"Mischief, you know."

"What kind of mischief?"

The man's eyes shifted to the edge of the forest. "Fairies..."

"You know, I think we'll stop here for a bit," McKenna announced. He looked across the clearing at de Haas as if daring him to say otherwise. "I reckon it's been a while since Ira here has enjoyed a hot cuppa with company." He gestured to one to the young privates. "Read," he called.

Read jogged over. "Yes, sir?"

"You and Miller brew up, will you? Let's show our guest a little hospitality."

Read and Miller set to organising a tea party, while the rest of the Task Force fanned out about the clearing, dropping their packs, rolling their shoulders and stretching their backs. Jules watched Jugraj Singh lie flat on the grass, his head on his pack and his arms outstretched.

Ira leaned his gun against the trunk of a tree then dropped the pig on the ground where it landed with a heavy thud. The smell of blood and the proximity of the dead animal whipped the dog into a frenzy. It rushed over to worry at the dead animal. The bushman gave the mutt a swift kick and sent it yelping into the undergrowth. Jules winced.

"Shuddup, Tip!" The dog cowered under a fern where it watched warily. "Stupid dog. He's been out of his head lately."

McKenna took a seat on a stump alongside Ira, wisely downwind from both the pig and the man. Jules followed suit, settling on her pack alongside the two men. Close by, Coolie and Kerei remained standing, leaning against tree trunks.

"I'm grateful for your warning, Ira," McKenna said.

Ira nodded.

"But the thing is, it would really save us a lot of time to

continue this direction. Of course, I don't want to do that if it means endangering the group. I'm responsible for their safety."

"Yeah? What is this group?"

"It's a civilian scientific team."

"And you army guys?"

"Security detail."

"Security? What kind of science are you doing? Radioactive testing?"

Kerei laughed, giving his leg a slap. "Radioactive testing! That's a good one."

"Nothing as exciting as that, I'm afraid," McKenna replied. "Just some routine government monitoring."

Jules caught the warning in the sergeant's glance. "Sergeant McKenna is right, Ira. It's very routine stuff, I'm afraid. I'm with Landsafe. I'll be monitoring native species – frogs and birds mainly – to see how they're faring." Jules talked from behind her hand, pretending to share a secret with him. "These army guys are just here to put up the tents and make the tea. Very hard to get good help these days."

Ira grunted.

Read interrupted, handing Ira a steaming mug of tea. "I stuck in three sugars. That okay?"

Ira wrapped his hands around the mug. "Yeah. Thanks, bro."

Job done, the soldier moved off.

McKenna waited for Ira to take a sip of his tea, then said, "Do you think you could tell me exactly what we're up against? That way, I can make an informed decision."

Elbows on his knees and the cup cradled in his hands, Ira glanced nervously at Kerei. The guide nodded his encouragement, and Ira took a deep breath. "They're always up to something," he said. "You know, fairies, aye? It's their personality." He talked in staccato phrases.

"It's well known the patu-paiarehe like to meddle," Kerei agreed.

"But this is more serious, right?" McKenna said. He turned to the pig hunter. "You don't strike me as the sort to tell us to turn around just because your billy went missing, or something got into your beef jerky."

Ira took another swig of the steaming tea. "I seen some stuff, you know. Weird scratches on trees. Funny prints like little hooves in the ground. Bends in the trees."

"Those are normal signs of the patu-paiarehe," Kerei said. "The fairy folk live in the forks of trees. Usually on the tops of high misty ridges."

"Plenty of high misty ridges in here," Jules said, in an attempt at light-heartedness.

"But, but..." Ira hesitated.

They waited while Ira found the words. "Their night music, the music of their flutes, has changed. It used to be soft, beautiful, eh. Now it's deeper. And there's this strange hissing. I don't like it," the bushman said finally. "And after that, I found a dead pig. A good one. Just left on the track. Gutted and left. Why would anyone leave a good pig like that and take off? Doesn't make sense." He shuddered.

"Could it have been an offering?" Kerei suggested.

Ira shrugged.

Kerei warmed to his idea. "You know, it *could* have been an offering. The patu-paiarehe have been known to talk, whispering in people's ears, telling them the next crop or the next kill should be theirs."

"But a whole pig?" Coolie said.

"It's a sign of respect," Kerei told him. "Before the People came, the land belonged to them."

Coolie shook his head, and let out a low whistle. "That's a whole heap of respect. In my family, offering someone a pig gets you a bride and all her extended family."

Jules had to admit, the corporal had a point.

Ira lifted the cup to his lips, throwing his head back to get the last drops. "The forest is a big place," he said when done. "I've been here five months. Youse are the first people I've seen for ages. That's strange too, you know. Normally, there are other people." Ira handed his cup off to Jules, the only woman in the vicinity.

"You haven't seen any other army guys in here, then?" asked Coolie.

Jules' ears pricked. *What other army guys?*

"Nup." The hunter stood.

Sensing his master was on the move, the dog scuttled from its spot under the fern. McKenna leaned over and gave the dog a quick scratch behind its ears, making the mongrel's tail wag. "Thanks for your help," he said.

"Yeah, no worries."

"But what about you, Ira?" said Jules, clutching the empty cup. "Aren't you afraid for your own safety?"

"Think I'm gonna head on home," he replied, on one knee now. He hoisted the pig onto his back with a grunt. After a few seconds, he stood up like a clean-and-jerk competitor. McKenna helped him shunt the animal's weight evenly across his shoulders. "Been bugger-all pigs in here lately, anyway. Other than this one here, that dead one was the last one I'd seen in ages. Going to head off tomorrow, soon as I can get this fella packed up." Bending slightly at the knees, he picked up his gun. "Thanks for the tea. C'mon Tip," he called.

Then, giving Jules a gentlemanly farewell nod, he crossed the clearing, pig on his back, and disappeared into the forest.

"Interesting," said Coolie.

Jules agreed. What was that comment Coolie made about there being other soldiers in the forest? She was about to ask when McKenna cut in, "Would you mind returning the cup to Read please, Dr Asher?"

When Jules was out of earshot, Taine pulled a topographical map from the inside pocket of his DPM smock. Safely waterproofed inside its plastic zip-lock bag, the map was already folded open at their approximate location.

"What do you advise, Nathan?" he said, holding the map out in front of him where the guide could see it.

Nathan examined the map a moment. "If we want to get to the site quickly for de Haas, then I like this route..." he replied, tracing a line on the plastic with his finger. "...particularly since this is a fairly able group. If we follow the park markers – the white slats nailed to the trees – it saves us a couple of kilometres over some dirty great hills. I expect we should get to your investigation site by mid-to-late afternoon."

"And Ira's warning?" Taine asked.

Nathan looked awkward. "Look, I'm not doubting what Ira says – our people have always co-existed with the patu-paiarehe – but in all the stories I've heard they tend to come out at night. And in twenty-odd years of guiding, I've never seen one. Anyway, we've been warned, haven't we? We know to keep a look-out."

"Coolie?" Taine said, turning the map for his corporal's input.

"There are other explanations for the things Ira told us. Could be there's another group operating in here," Coolie said. "One that doesn't want to be noticed. Our infamous separatists, for example. Or someone else. Unusual night sounds could be their night-time activities carrying on the wind. The scratchings, sure it could be fairies like Ira said, but it could be someone using gouges to mark the trail for their own purposes."

"We shouldn't forget the forest either," Nathan observed. "You spend a lot of time in here, you start to dream stuff up. Go a bit crazy."

"Then how do you explain the pig?" Taine said. "For a hunter to leave a valuable animal like that doesn't make sense."

"Could be there was no pig," Nathan said. "Like I said, you're in here too long, you can go a bit crazy."

"Maybe Ira came across the pig's hunters – our separatist group – as they were about to take it back to camp," Coolie speculated. "They couldn't take the pig without him being able to follow their trail, so they dumped it."

"Well, if they wanted to stay hidden from Ira, a lone hunter, then they'll want to stay hidden from us too. I don't reckon we'll have any bother," Nathan said finally.

"Okay, we continue on this route," said Taine, folding the plastic bag and putting the topo map back in his pocket. He approached de Haas. "We might need to carry on, sir. If we want to make the campsite in the daylight."

De Haas got to his feet. "Yes, yes, I was just about to get everyone up." Picking up his pack, he called, "Right, break's over, everyone."

As the group moved off, Taine pulled Coolie to him. "Tell the guys to keep their eyes peeled," he said, under his breath. "Half a section has already gone missing in here. I'm not so sure a show of force will scare these guys off, even if they do turn out to be a bunch of fairies."

CHAPTER 9

Wellington

Ken Chesterman, Director of Regulatory Policy for the Department of Conservation, received the call in his lunch hour. This time, he wasn't in the office, but out power-walking the capital's waterfront pavement despite the biting southerly. Trying to avoid turning into a spineless overweight hypocrite, unlike some colleagues he could name.

Keeping his head down out of the wind, he answered, "Chesterman."

"Kenneth, dear." He recognised the voice – oilier than a Swedish massage – and his heart sank. He should've changed his cell number.

"So pleased the Task Force has gone ahead," the voice said. Ken suspected its owner was middle-aged. He imagined her looking like Glenn Close, which was probably not far from the truth, since the bitch was a real bunny boiler. "Have you heard from them yet?" He decided her accent was Australian, narrowing her identity down to just a few million possibilities.

"Why should I hear from them? They don't report to me."

"That's true. Though I suppose you'll hear soon enough. It's going to be quite a find."

"Like the nugget you planted?" he guessed.

"You sound so sceptical, Kenneth," the caller said, not giving anything away. "There is gold in there, you know."

"Of course. Why else would you plant a nugget the size of a teacup?"

"You really are too cynical, Kenneth. But that's not why I called. I need you to do something for me."

He gritted his teeth. "I've already done something for you. As I recall we had a deal. I was to alert the minister to the find and recommend he establish the Task Force, including your man Fogarty, and you would send me certain incriminating photos. I did that. You returned the photos. That's it. I have no intention of doing anything further."

"Oh no, did you think that would be all? How deliciously naïve. Of course, I haven't sent you *all* the photos. That would've been terribly short-sighted."

"Who are you?"

"You know who I am. I am the person who is about to blow the lid on your liaison with a certain male student."

"So? I'll just go public myself. People won't give a shit."

"You're right. *People* don't care, although I expect your wife and daughter might, and your father-in-law, since you've been using his beach house for your trysts."

Ken said nothing. Where *was* she getting this? Not for the first time, he wondered if his lover was feeding her information. Andrew had denied it, but then he had nothing to lose, did he?

"And another thing. It seems your lover might have lied about his age."

His blood froze. "He's twenty-two."

"That's funny, his passport says nineteen. Remind me how long you've been seeing one another?" the bitch said. "Nearly four years? Now that might not look so good with you being an elder in the church. By the way, have you always had that birthmark?"

Ken stopped. The cold southerly did not. "What do you want?"

"Really, there's no need to be so hostile. It's nothing illegal, Kenneth. When the Task Force evidence comes in, it will be significant. The data will be conveniently leaked and as a result, representatives of a multinational company will approach you to broker a deal with the government for extraction of the ore."

"You want me to leak the data?" Ken said, his voice sounding as brittle as the wind in his face.

"Thank you, but no. I have someone else to do that. I want you to use your influence with the minister to push the resource consent through by Christmas."

"Christmas!" Ken spluttered. "You give me too much credit."

"Not at all."

"No really. You don't understand how these things work. It's a complicated process. There's the local tribe to consider, for example, and the public consultation process. All that can take years. I have no control over how long it takes."

"I see. Well, I guess you can only do your best. But let's just say that if I don't get what I want for Christmas, then the press can expect a rather juicy present."

"You bitch."

"Super talking with you, Kenneth."

"You're with the multinational, aren't you?" Ken said quickly.

A peel of laughter. "Wrong again."

Ken slipped his phone into his jacket. He was going to have to hoof it back to the office if he was to make his afternoon meeting. He snorted derisively. Well, if he was going to be a spineless hypocrite, at least he wouldn't be overweight.

As it turned out, there were no bushmen, pigs, or fairies en route and Taine was pleased with their timing, reaching the site where the stream intersected with the track by mid-afternoon. Taine was about to set up his own tent when he passed de Haas deep in conversation with the two women.

"Dr Asher is quite capable of setting up the tent on her own. She has a PhD," the geologist said.

Taine slowed.

"Oh, I agree she's quite capable, but I should really be—" Louise said.

"Leave that tent pole there," de Haas said, snatching the pole from Louise. He handed it off to Jules, who glanced at Taine over the billowing tent fabric, and rolled her eyes.

"I've already checked out the site," de Haas said impatiently. "It's over this way. I think we should start straight in on some baseline sampling, and not waste time while the light's still good…" His hand at the small of Louise's back, de Haas guided his assistant away, leaving Jules looking bemused. Shrugging, she smiled at Taine, then got back to the task of erecting the tent on her own.

Taine detected a quiet movement to his left.

"McKenna, would you mind stepping over here a moment, mate?" Coolie said. "Eriksen's found something interesting." The corporal used standard patrol hand signals to indicate the location of the 'something interesting', essentially, north-east, referencing a young kauri protruding from the canopy.

Taine hoped he wasn't about to be shown Lefty's head on a stick, although, to be fair, since his warning, the two men had been giving each other a wide berth. With a final glance at the campsite – more out of reflex than anything else – Taine followed Coolie towards the base of the kauri tree.

Eriksen and Read were there waiting, the bush about them, dense and oppressive.

"What have you got?"

"There." With a flattened hand, Coolie indicated the subject of interest. Draped over the fronds of a scraggly flax was a crumpled yellow CanTeen bandana. The grimy fabric was soaked with blood.

"It might be just a coincidence," Eriksen said. "But I thought the hunter we met on the trail earlier today – the guy with the pig – was wearing a bandana just like it."

"That's definitely his!" Read said excitedly. "I saw it. He was wearing it around his neck when I handed him the tea."

Taine nodded. Eriksen and Read weren't the only ones who'd observed the splash of yellow at Ira's collar. The children's cancer awareness bandanas weren't uncommon. For a while, there was quite a craze for them. But yellow wasn't everyone's favourite colour. And two in the same day? Unlikely.

"Did you find anything else? Tracks?"

"Read and I had a pretty thorough look-see. Went approximately twenty metres in every direction. Didn't see anything. We were gonna extend the search, but we thought we better report it in first."

"Good call," Coolie assured Eriksen.

"I still reckon it's that hunter's," Read said. "He left a few minutes before we did. He could have come this way. Maybe he just dropped it?"

"An eighty kilogram pig on his back and he gets here before us?" Eriksen said, shaking his head. "Sure, a tramper can make better time travelling on his own, he can keep to his own rhythm and only stop when it suits him. But even so, that pig hunter would have to be The Flash to get here that fucking fast."

"Maybe he dropped the pig off somewhere first," said Read. The other men considered this.

"Ira said he was going to head home tomorrow," Taine said. "I guess it depends where his vehicle is, but if his campsite was a distance from the road, it's possible he stowed the pig, intending to come back after packing up his gear. Why lug the animal all over the forest if you don't have to?"

"Well, how do we explain the blood?" Coolie said quietly.

"It was already on there?"

"This much blood?"

"Maybe he stopped to butcher the pig," Read suggested.

Eriksen snorted. "He stopped off somewhere to slaughter the pig and *still* made better time than us? Yeah right."

Taine rubbed his chin. "There's every chance we're overreacting. Ira might've made better time than us if he'd dumped the pig. It's possible he simply dropped his bandana. But this amount of blood could also mean he's hurt himself—"

"I reckon something's happened to him," interrupted Read.

"—so we can't rule out foul play," Taine continued. "Coolie, round up Miller and Lefty, will you? Tell them, they're to join Read and Eriksen and look for signs of the pig hunter. Cover as much area as you can while the light holds. And check down low under the bushes. He could be injured. I'll give Singh the heads up to expect a possible casualty, and post Winters and Trigger to monitor the campsite."

Read turned to go.

"Wait," Taine said. He picked up the bandana and stuffed it in his pocket. "Until we know more, let's keep this to ourselves. There's no point upsetting the civilians."

De Haas laid his geologist's pick on the ground. "Sample bag," he said. Louise held out a white calico bag. "Wider, for heaven's sake. How am I supposed to get it in there?"

She opened the bag wider and he dropped the rock into it. Then she labelled it, and slipped it into the bag with the others. "I should probably run over and check that Ben has enough sample bags," she said.

De Haas snorted. "He's got legs, hasn't he? If he needs more, he can come and get them." The engineer was working higher up and further along the streambed, not far from where Jules Asher had set up a transect line for her ecological study.

De Haas took up his pick. Ben Fogarty was like every mining engineer de Haas had ever met: over confident, overpaid, and with an over-inflated sense of entitlement. The kid had brought a hand-held mineral identifier with him, for goodness sake. Typical. Relying on gadgets rather than knowledge and hard work. Still, it'd be important to have an independent consultant to support, if not corroborate his findings. Ben's credentials with Australian Minerals wouldn't hurt that.

"De Haas!"

The idiot was running across the dry streambed, waving one hand in the air and his silly machine in the other. De Haas stood; it was a wonder the engineer didn't break his ankle.

"What is it?"

"Look!"

Fogarty thrust out his palm revealing a rock the size of a small walnut. "Gold."

Another nugget? The potential of this area! De Haas felt a rush of excitement. Perhaps he wouldn't need to salt the samples after all – a good thing too, given the industry's caginess since the Bre-X scandal.

"Let me see." He handed his pick off to Louise and took the nugget from Fogarty, leaning over to examine it under his magnifying glass. He scratched at the surface with his fingernail. "It certainly has the look of gold," he said.

"The whole area's volcanic. There's plenty of porphyritic rock about," Ben said. He lifted his gadget. "I'm picking up all the right indicators."

De Haas screwed up his mouth. "Either way, the lab assays will confirm it."

Jules Asher came over. "What's up?" she said, slipping a blue-grey feather into a plastic specimen bag.

"Ben thinks he's found some gold," Louise gushed.

Jules ran her fingers along the top of the bag to seal it. "Wow, that was quick," she said.

"I know, right?" said Ben, beaming. "Just a couple of hours work and already we've uncovered what could be a gold deposit. Streets paved with gold – the potential of this area could be incredible!"

De Haas frowned; did Fogarty plant the nugget? He shrugged. So what if he did? De Haas had it now, as well as control of the entire exploration programme.

"That's great news, Ben," Jules said, patting Ben's forearm. "Just try not to get too carried away yet. There are the ecological impacts to consider," she said, before going back to her transect. Watching her slip the bag in with her other samples, de Haas snorted.

As if a few insects could hold back a gold rush.

"Nice work," he told Ben. He could afford to be magnanimous. "Sample bag."

Louise passed him a bag and de Haas dropped the nugget inside then put the bag in his coat pocket. Ben's eyes widened.

"Um, Dr de Haas…" Louise started.

"I think it's best if I keep this one on me, don't you?" he said, patting his pocket. "Given its size. We can't be too careful. Now, I think we should call it a day."

Retrieving his pick from the ground, de Haas grinned. Hand-held identifier aside, on this mission there was no guessing whose pick was largest.

Chapter 10

Rotorua Township

"Come on, Pania," Wayne groaned, dragging his eyes from his tablet. "You're making out like it's worse than it is."

"Really?" Wayne's girlfriend stood up from behind the kitchen island, snapped the dishwasher shut, and set the wash cycle to run. "That's three weekends in a row the two of you have been up there in the bush."

"He's an *old man*. It's important to him."

"Yeah, well having you here on the weekends is important to me. I've been asking you to fix the lock on the back window for a month. It'll be too late when some kid jimmies it and we come home to find the house cleared out." She picked up a sponge and ran it under the tap.

Wayne shook his head. "This is about me not fixing the window?"

Pania squeezed out the cloth. "No, it's about us spending some time together." Leaning over the oven, she wiped bacon grease off the splash-back.

Wayne craned his neck to steal a look at her arse, her jeans stretched tight over smooth hips. It was true, he'd been neglecting her lately. But she didn't understand how important this was. Uncle Rawiri was a *matakite,* and if he said something unusual was going on near his ancestral home, then it wasn't to be sneezed at. It wasn't her fault. Pania hadn't grown up with Uncle the way Wayne had.

Once, when Wayne was a small boy, maybe four or five, Uncle Rawiri had come to his parents' house. Over a cup of tea and a gingernut biscuit, Uncle warned Wayne's parents that the fire demons Te Hoata and Te Pūpū were about, and that for his safety it was imperative Wayne be kept indoors. Wayne hated it – being stuck inside – but a couple of days later a fumarole appeared, spitting and snorting right under Wayne's sandpit. Since the geyser came with a ready-made sandpit box surround, it got a mention in the paper. Fire demons with a sense of humour, the headline said. Except, it wasn't funny. If Wayne had been out there making tracks in the sand with his dump truck, he'd be dead now.

Wayne flicked his eyes back to his tablet before Pania caught him staring at her butt. Probably not the best strategy when they were in the middle of an argument.

"I'll pick up a new lock on my way home from work," he mumbled.

What if Uncle's on to something this time, too?

For a remote place, Maungapōhatu was attracting a lot of activity. That band of scientists they'd met on the road, for example. Wayne hadn't liked the head guy much – an arrogant SOB in his opinion – but the army guy was good value. And another thing that was odd; since when did a scientific team need a bunch of army guys with them? Something strange was definitely going on up there. If the weather stayed good, he and Uncle Rawiri planned to go out again.

If he can get Pania onside.

Maybe if he took her to the movies tonight? He pulled up the cinema listings. Smiled. There was a girly flick on. Ryan Gosling. Pania liked Gosling. Said he was a good actor—

"Wayne, are you even listening to me?"

"Yes."

"Then what did I just say?"

"I was listening." Wayne looked up.

Frowning, Pania had her arms folded across her chest, the pink sponge protruding from behind her elbow.

"Okay, I wasn't listening. But look, there's a Ryan Gosling movie on tonight…" he said, lifting his tablet for her to see. Her arms still folded over her chest, Pania clamped her lips tight and closed her eyes.

It was no use. She wasn't buying it.

"I'm sorry, babe. What did you say?"

"I said, it's not just this idea your uncle's got in his head about something bad going on in the bush. I'm worried about these nightmares he's been having. Calling out in the night. Waking himself up and then having trouble getting back to sleep. The night before last, I woke at 2:00am thinking someone must've gotten in the window, but it was him, tinkering in the kitchen, making himself a cup of tea. Then, when I got up for my shift at the hospital, he was already up and dressed."

"So he got up instead of going back to sleep."

"It's not good, Wayne, this big change in his sleeping patterns. I really think we need to get him checked out by the doctor." Tossing the sponge in the sink, she joined him at the table.

"You know Uncle doesn't hold much store by modern doctors," Wayne said, swiping idly at his screen.

"He would if you encouraged him."

"It's just a few nightmares." He scrolled down a couple of pages.

"They're affecting his sleep."

"Well, it's not like he has to get up for work. He can nap during the day."

Pania put her tiny hand on Wayne's larger one, stopping his fiddling. "It's affecting our sleep, too."

For the first time, Wayne noticed the grey smudges under her eyes. She was right – neither of them had been getting their full night's kip.

"Wayne," Pania said, her voice deliberate. "The fact you cared enough to have your uncle come and live with us is one of the reasons I love you. Don't get me wrong. I love having Uncle here, too. But we need to face up to this. It's not healthy for anyone to be this obsessed. I think there might be a medical reason for it, maybe a chemical imbalance or something." She gave his hand a squeeze. "We have to remember he's an old man."

Wayne nodded.

Outside, Temera ran a wrinkled hand through thinning hair. His niece was right. He was an old man. Too old. Perhaps his mind was going, like Pania said. Some wires shaken loose in his old brain. It happened. One of his mates from the sawmill had Alzheimer's. Couldn't even remember how to do up his own zipper.

Temera pulled his smokes out of his pocket. Lit up. Smiled in spite of himself as he brought the cigarette to his lips. Unlike Wayne, Pania said it was probably too late for him to give up smoking. She said, at his age, forcing Temera to give up the habit was likely to cause more stress than carrying on. But she didn't like him smoking inside the house and he didn't like to upset her. She was a good kid, Pania. Pretty. Head screwed on. And a good cook, too. His great-nephew had done well to get her. Perhaps he and Wayne shouldn't go up the bush again for a bit. Maybe they could go to Hammer Hardware instead – get the bits they needed to fix that window and keep the girl happy.

Temera took a long drag on the cigarette, savouring it. He closed his eyes and listened to the still of the morning. Imagined himself back at Maungapōhatu, on the porch at the old homestead. It seemed so far away now, but thinking about it, Temera's heart beat a little faster.

What if Pania was right? What if Temera's old body had some sort of disease that made him see things in his sleep?

It wouldn't hurt to see the doctor. Get checked out. Sucking in the last of his cigarette, he leaned over and dropped the butt in a bucket of browning water he'd been saving to spray the aphids.

If they suggested it, he'd go along to see their doctor. Maybe there was something wrong with him after all.

INTO THE MIST

Te Urewera Forest, Second Campsite

"I'll walk you down to the water, Ms Hemphill," Anaru said, shifting the Steyr across his body. "Until we know what's going on, the sergeant wants us to stick together."

When the pig hunter's dog had limped into the campsite just before sunset, the game was up as far as keeping the situation from the civilians. McKenna had been forced to tell them about the bloodied bandana – not that it had bothered de Haas. That git couldn't care less about anything other than sampling for his precious gold. The guys had gone out again after that, searching the area until well after dark, ferreting around under bushes, turning up nothing. Dr Asher had fed the dog – seemed she'd known its name was Tip – and found a warm spot for it under the flysheet of her tent, tying it to a tree so it couldn't run off again. There wasn't much more they could do until morning. Perhaps tomorrow the dog would lead them to the big Māori.

They walked to the water's edge, Anaru behind Louise, the torch on the picatinny rail of his rifle lighting the way. On alert, Anaru scanned the ground for signs of the hunter, distracted by Louise's long fingers as they brushed the tops of the ferns.

At the creek, the surface of the water glittered like a silver Christmas garland in the smoky moonlight. Louise took her time to fill her water bottle. Seemingly oblivious to the cold, she let the silvery liquid run over her fingers. When the bottle was full, she made no move to return to the campsite, although it had started to drizzle. Instead, she crouched on a flat rock in the middle of the stream in a gauze of mist.

On the bank, Anaru watched as she savoured the quiet. No doubt she was grateful for the respite from de Haas. They'd hardly arrived before he'd started bossing her about. He would've had her work through dinner too, if Dr Asher hadn't gone over and pulled her away.

Louise sighed. "It's a lovely spot, isn't it?"

"Yes."

"The way the torchlight picks up the droplets..."

A wisp of poetry surfaced in his mind. "A note as from a

single place, A slender tinkling fall that made, Now drops that floated on the pool, Like pearls, and now a silver blade," he quoted, feeling awkward the second he finished. Citing poetry to a woman he hardly knew. What was he thinking? He was *working*.

But Louise Hemphill didn't laugh. She said, "Then the moon, in all her pride, Like a spirit glorified, Filled and overflowed the night, With revelations of her light... And the Poet's song again, Passed like music through my brain, Night interpreted to me, All its grace and mystery..."

Anaru raised his eyebrows. "Yeats?"

"Longfellow. And yours?"

"Robert Frost."

"Pretty." There was nothing to say to that. They watched the water rush by, Anaru on the bank and Louise on her rock. "So you like poetry," she said. A statement.

"A thug like me shouldn't like poetry?"

"I didn't say that. It was more of a refreshing revelation. My ex-boyfriend was in finance. He didn't like poetry. Thought it was girly."

Anaru noted the prefix, *ex*-boyfriend. "It's like you said: the poet's song. Poets put the world into words for us."

"They do."

They stayed there a while longer, watching the play of the light on the water. Anaru heard Singh and Lefty chatting amiably further along the bank.

After a while the drizzle started to set in. "I should probably get you back or you're going to get soaked," Anaru said. Louise stood and jumped the gap to the bank. They picked their way through the brush and up the narrow path to the campsite. A few paces in, Anaru caught a rustle a little way off the path.

He stopped. Louise slowed too.

"Did you hear that?" Anaru asked.

She half turned in the direction of the sound. "That rustling? Probably nothing. The wind."

"Hmmm." Anaru was unconvinced.

"It could be an animal. A possum maybe, or a bird? We might've frightened something."

"Or it could be our hunter."

"You think so? I thought your sergeant said he had this area searched."

"McKenna also said the man might be injured. People in shock often react strangely. They'll crawl into a small space and hide, even when it seems odd. It happens all the time in house fires. I suspect it'll be nothing – most likely a possum or a bird – but I should probably take a quick look. Just to be sure." He hesitated. "Are you okay if I leave you here a second on the track?"

"Of course."

"I'll have to take the torch."

"It's not that dark, and Singh and Lefty are just behind us at the creek. You go ahead. I'd feel awful if the poor man was lying there and we walked right past."

"I won't be a minute."

Anaru didn't like leaving her, but this drizzle looked like it'd turn to rain soon. If the hunter was in here, without warm clothing and shelter, even with no injury, he could die of hypothermia by morning. Anaru didn't want that on his conscience. It would only take a moment to check.

Wishing he hadn't left his Mini N/SEAS night vision goggles back at the campsite, Anaru stepped into the bush, the undergrowth brushing softly against his legs. He'd only advanced a few metres, when the rustling came again. Definitely *something* close by.

He stopped. Listened hard.

Nothing.

But now he could smell something. The sour odour of an unwashed body? He took a step forward.

"Private Winters? Can you see anything?"

His blood thundering, Anaru nearly leaped into the treetops. *Jeepers, she gave me a fright!*

He took a second to inhale deeply before replying. "Ms

Hemphill, shush please, I'm trying to locate the origin of the sound—"

Pain exploded in his chest. Heart attack? He gasped as the agony tore through his ribs and legs. His chest was constricted, crushed. He couldn't get any air, couldn't breathe – his breath stalled. Suddenly, he was yanked upwards as if tethered by a cord. Battling the burn in his torso, Anaru tried to twist. He couldn't move. He was pinned. Dangling. Was he in some sort of animal trap? A metallic stink hit him. Another animal. Or the pig hunter?

His arms were free...

...and he still had hold of his rifle! If he could just point the gun's torch forward. Get a sight on what had him caught. Turning the Steyr was the hardest thing he'd ever done. Lacking control, the beam of light spiralled widely, glancing off the trees in violent angles. Anaru fought white hot pain. His vision blurred, his body was wracked with nausea. He inched the rifle sideways. Not much time before he passed out; the stabbing in his chest excruciating as he manoeuvred the gun light, holding it still just long enough to see... the horizontal blink of a scaly-rimmed eye.

Lord help me. I'm being eaten like a fly.

A wail pierced the air. Jug leaped to his feet. Beside him, Lefty did the same.

Immediately, the forest around them was alive with birds screeching and flapping.

"What the fuck was that?" Lefty said, raising his Steyr and pointing it into the blackness at the edge of the water.

"Don't know," Jug said, scanning the brush.

"Sounded like a chick shrieking."

"Louise Hemphill? She was just upstream with Winters. I heard them talking."

Lefty sighed, and lowered his gun. "That'll be it then. She'll have a huhu beetle crawling on her, or a wētā in her hair."

"Yes, probably," Jug said. Women and creepy crawlies. Priya could wake the dead with her squealing if there was a daddy long-legs in the bathtub. Although Jug wasn't convinced what he'd just heard was an 'eek-get-it-off-me' kind of scream.

"Anaru was with her, so she'll be safe enough," Lefty said. Perhaps he wasn't convinced either.

"The pig hunter is missing," Jug said. "So maybe we should check it out anyway?"

"Yeah, I reckon. Just to be on the safe side."

They left the river, heading up the path at a jog.

Louise ran for her life, heart pounding so hard it hurt. Frantic, she scrambled through the undergrowth. In the darkness, the branches jabbed at her, grabbing at her hair, and scratching her face. She whacked her shoulder against the trunk of a tree, reeling as the air was forced out of her lungs. She got up, turned her bruised shoulder sideways to push past the obstacle, and ran on, staggering.

She hadn't heard anything behind her for a while. Perhaps she'd outrun the danger? Escaped? *Oh please, let me escape.* But the sound came again. That rustling. Closer. It was coming closer! Louise let out a tiny squeak of terror and jumped away, tearing off in the opposite direction, running hard, her arms spread out in front of her like a blind man without a cane.

Even so, she hit another tree and stumbled. Half-stunned, she got to her knees, and closed her hand, feeling the stickiness in her palm. A deep cut. A new thought filled her with dread. Could it smell blood? Panicked, she hauled herself up, snatching in the dark for branches to hold on to, her raw hands stinging. She ran again, sobbing silently, not daring to look behind her. The sounds of pursuit followed her anyway, and in her head was the image of Anaru Winters, flopping.

God help me…

Why had she followed him in? She should have stayed on the track and waited like he'd asked. Lefty and Eriksen were just there. *They were there.* She should have waited. But minutes had passed and she'd got nervous. Before that, she'd heard him brushing through the ferns and cracking twigs, but then, after he'd told her to shush, everything had gone quiet. Uncannily quiet. So, she'd taken a step off the path into the bush…

There was scraping, like a log being dragged. Over there. She turned away from the sound and ran on.

I can't keep this up. I can't…

She had to. Because if she didn't, the alternative… She pushed herself to run faster, ignoring the scrapes, the branches cruelly whipping backwards to smack her face, her eyes. She wiped the back of her hand across her forehead. It came away wet.

Suddenly, she was seized by an awareness of space in front of her, whether it was the movement of the mist, or the lilt of moonlight through the canopy, she didn't know, but she pulled up, her feet kicking stones forward. The pebbles tumbled away below her, clattering as they fell. She was at the top of a gully. She'd nearly gone over the edge! Reaching out her injured hand, she grasped at the air until she found a support. Bracing herself against a tree trunk, the spike of adrenaline drained away. She'd come *that* close to falling.

A hiss.

No…

It was there. Behind her. Louise turned slowly, too scared to breathe. The feckless mist chose that moment to clear, allowing Louise a glimpse of her pursuer. Its body slung low to the ground, the predator lowered its head. Feathers? Are those feathers? And the smell of it! Like a rotting carcass.

They were eye-level now, just metres apart, staring at each other, predator and prey, Louise's body wracked with tremors.

Go away… please God, make it go away…

But in her terror, she had allowed it to corral her here, turning and turning again from the sound of its passage. It had played with her the way a cat plays with a mouse. Now she was cornered on a precipice. Almost as if the creature was waiting, testing her mettle. Would she jump, or wouldn't she?

INTO THE MIST

It opened its jaws; pink ooze dripped from the side of its mouth.

Fuck that.

Louise jumped.

CHAPTER 11

Jug stayed with Anaru while Lefty raised the alarm. Within minutes McKenna dispatched Coolie and Read to watch over the civilians, leaving Jug and Lefty to look after Winters' body while the rest of the section searched for Louise Hemphill.

Those first few minutes on his own in the forest had been the longest of Jug's life, standing over Anaru, waiting for Lefty to return. Even with him back, the last hour hadn't been much fun either. Jug didn't think McKenna and the others would be long; the conditions were too poor, the rain really setting in now, and none of them knew the terrain. Plus, the sergeant would want to avoid a second surprise attack by Winters' killers.

Except there was only one killer.

"So," Jug said carefully. "What exactly did you tell McKenna?"

"Just that Winters had been attacked and killed, and Louise Hemphill's missing."

"You know he's going to come back and ask us what happened."

"Yeah," Lefty said, his eyes skittering over Winters' corpse.

"What are we going to say?"

Lefty shook his head. "Fucked if I know."

"But you saw it, right?" Jug whispered, his voice cracking.

Jaw tight, Lefty nodded.

Jug slumped. "Crap. I was hoping my eyes were playing tricks on me," he said.

A creak sounded behind them. Panicked, Jug turned, swinging his rifle upwards. Lefty pushed the barrel down and away with his hand. 'Singh, not at me, you arse!"

Jug had come close to shooting him, spooked by the trees, scraping together in the storm. Just as well he hadn't. Jug didn't fancy standing out here on his own. "Sorry. I'm a bit jumpy."

"Yeah," Lefty said. "Me too."

"They'll be back soon."

They said nothing, listening to the rain hit the tarpaulin they'd slung across the trees to keep the attack site dry. After a time, Lefty said, "What if we say we didn't see anything, that it was too dark?"

"We're equipped with infrared gear," Jug countered. "They'll think we're incompetent."

"Yeah. But what's the alternative?"

The question hung in the air between them.

"Did you cop a look at its teeth?" Lefty said, shuddering.

Jug nodded. "They're never going to believe us."

Taine cast his eyes over the site, Trigger at his side. There wasn't much to see. Some trampled undergrowth, and Winters' body, washed clean of blood in the ensuing rain. The soldier has been dead three hours now, but Singh and Lefty were still shaken. Pale and sluggish, they were like a couple of zombies. Even Singh looked white – no mean feat given his ethnicity.

"I'm going to need a fuller account of what happened here," Taine said. "You say you were both at the creek when you heard a shout?"

"We heard *something*," Singh said, plucking nervously at the cuff of his tunic. "We thought it was a woman…"

"Or it might have been Anaru…" Lefty said softly.

"At the time, we thought it was Ms Hemphill, you know, scared by a bug or something. We went straight to where we thought the sound was coming from. It was just a little way up the path, but it took us a few minutes…"

"And that's when you saw Winters' killers?" Taine noted that both men paused, each throwing a glance at the other.

"Not killers, killer. It was an… animal," Lefty said, hesitant.

Taine frowned. "You're sure? Not a bunch of men?"

"No."

"I was a couple of paces behind Lefty," Singh said. "It was definitely an animal of some sort."

"A wild pig?" Taine asked. "It's the only animal in these forests capable of killing a man."

"Bigger," Lefty said.

Bigger than a wild pig?

"You're positive it wasn't a group of men? The visibility is pretty poor with all this mist."

"It was an *animal*," Lefty insisted. "And it was as big as a fucking bus. Big enough to have Anaru clamped between its jaws."

"There was nothing we could do," said Singh. His eyes blurring, the medic stared over the tarp-covered corpse into the forest. Lefty too, was close to tears. Taine needed to tread softly. He'd seen enough PTSD to know these two could be close to flipping out.

"Lefty?"

The private exhaled slowly. "For a second, it didn't move," he said. "It just stood there bold as brass looking at me with Anaru in its mouth. I... I was paralysed. I didn't react. I should've taken a shot. I know I should've. Maybe if I'd... I don't know why not... in shock, I guess, and I didn't want to hit Anaru..." He trailed off.

"What happened next, son?" Taine prompted.

"It just dropped the poor bastard on the ground," Lefty said, "spat him out as if he didn't taste good and went after the girl."

"There was nothing we could do..." Singh said again.

Taine leaned forward, looking hard at Lefty. "You *saw* it chase Ms Hemphill?"

Lefty shook his head. "No."

"We could hear her," Singh said. "That's how we could tell she was running away. She must have seen the animal and panicked."

"This animal, what did you say it looked like again?"

The men fell silent. Lefty looked pointedly at Singh. Inviting the medic to speak?

"Jug?"

But the medic's eyes slid away. "Like you said, Sergeant, the visibility is poor."

"Okay, so when Ms Hemphill ran, the animal followed the sound. What direction did she go?"

"We told you before," Lefty said.

"Tell me again."

Now it was Lefty's turn to look sidelong into the bush. "She went that way," he said eventually, pointing into the trees, and Singh nodded.

"What happened then?"

"I came to get you, Boss."

"And I went to see to Winters," Singh said quickly, "in case he was alive, only by that time…" He broke off.

"I'm finding it hard to imagine an animal big enough to attack a man, let alone an armed soldier."

Lefty blurted, "Look, it was straight out of Jurassic-fucking-Park, okay? It was a bloody T Rex."

Trigger snorted. "A T Rex? Yeah right!" he chortled.

Taine shot him a glare. Whatever Lefty saw, it had him rattled. Ridiculing him wasn't going to help.

"A tyrannosaurus," Taine said gently. "You mean, as big as a tyrannosaurus?"

Lefty looked at the ground. "I know you think I'm nuts, but Jug saw it too. It was a T Rex. We both saw it."

Taine turned to Singh. The medic fiddled with his tunic.

"Singh?"

Singh lifted his chin. "I don't know about a T Rex, but it looked like a lizard. A huge one. And before you ask, no I haven't been prescribing myself anything from my medical kit. I'm sure of what I saw, just not what it was."

"Oh come on, a fucking dinosaur?" Shaking his head, Trigger folded his arms across his chest.

"Trigger!" Taine snapped. Taine nodded at Singh to go on.

"I know it sounds crazy. It's true the light was bad, and we only got a glimpse of it, but that's what it *looked* like."

After another ten minutes, Taine dismissed them. Their shoulders slumped, Lefty and Singh trudged their way back up to the tent site.

"We're going to have to keep an eye on those two," Taine told Trigger as he watched them go.

"Yeah. They're both off their fucking heads," Trigger said. "You'd think a medic would be used to blood and guts. Not fall apart. Did you see him? He was shaking like a girl!"

Taine watched the twin torches of Singh and Lefty advance up the slope like two beams of a car. "You never get used to seeing someone die," he said, crouching to lift the tarpaulin off Anaru's mutilated body.

Confronted with the cadaver, Trigger wiped the humidity off his face with his hand. "Yes, well, that's true enough."

"Where's his gun?" Taine demanded.

"What? It isn't with the body?"

"No."

They searched the area for the Steyr, finding it buried in the ferns a few paces away.

Taine picked it up. Examined it. "It isn't jammed," he observed, puzzled. "Why didn't he fire?"

"From what those two are saying, he might not've had a chance. But what they're saying is—" Trigger stopped himself, taking a deep breath before going on. "Come on, Boss, surely you don't believe that cock and bull story? A dinosaur? That's just fucked!"

Taine frowned, the rain dripping off his eyebrows. It *was* bizarre. But both soldiers were singing from the same song sheet, and unless they were on drugs, which Singh denied, Taine had no reason *not* to believe them. Besides, they'd both been carrying infrared gear: Wright with the IRAD inline night device attached to his rifle, and Singh wearing a pair of Mini N/SEAS goggles. That kind of technology, they could hardly have failed to see Winters' attacker, even given the drizzle.

"Taine?" Trigger prompted.

"Sometimes stress plays tricks on a man's memory."

"Yeah, but a T Rex?"

"Why would they lie and risk becoming a laughing stock, Trigger?" Taine said. Someone carrying a torch was making their way down the creek towards them. "The thing is, the evidence fits: the injuries here on Winters' body, the pig hunter's disappearance, and before that, more than a dozen other missing people. Arnold was right. Something weird is going on in this forest."

Trigger looked up sharply. "Major Arnold knew?"

Taine filled him in.

"Something weird's going on, I'll give you that," Trigger said when Taine had explained. "But a *dinosaur*...?" He shook his head; Taine's account of the missing section wasn't enough to convince him.

"I know," Taine said, grimly. "Even Ira's fairies were more plausible."

The torch turned out to be Coolie, who joined them under the tarpaulin out of the rain. "I've left Read, Miller and Eriksen on sentry duty in case whoever did this comes back," he said. "Singh is going to try and write up the post-mortem report. He's shaky, so Dr Foster is helping him. Lefty has asked to bag up Winters' body to take back. I've told him he can, but later, when we've finished the incident investigation." Coolie shifted slightly, droplets of rain rolling off his wet weather gear. "Anaru isn't going to be able to call this in, so one of us will have to do it."

"And say what?" Trigger snorted. "They're going to think we're crackers."

Taine told Coolie what they'd learned so far. His corporal gave a low whistle. "Interesting."

"Don't tell me you believe them?" Trigger said, incredulous.

Coolie shrugged. "Hey, I'm Chinese," he said. "In my family, they believe cutting your toenails can conjure up a ghost. A dinosaur isn't such a big jump."

"You do believe them, then?"

Coolie scraped a clump of mud from his boot. "Singh doesn't

strike me as the kind to make this up. He's a doctor. In his job he has to look at the evidence and, based on that, make a best guess about what a patient might be suffering. Sounds to me that's what he did here. Examined all the evidence and came up with dinosaur."

"So you *don't* believe him?"

"No, that's not it either. I believe he saw what he thinks he saw."

Trigger did a one-handed face-palm. "Say that again in English."

"He's saying we need more information," Taine interjected. "It could have been a bunch of separatists armed with a saw and dressed to look like a taniwha. Based on that evidence, Singh's best guess would still have been dinosaur."

"That's his *best* guess?" Trigger puffed the air out of his cheeks. "Geez, remind me not to get a pimple. He's just as likely to decide it's cancer and slice my bleeding nose off."

"Boss, we have to report," Coolie said, interrupting Trigger's bluster. He inclined his head at the mound. "We have a dead soldier."

He was right. They needed to report in. "For the moment let's tell them the attack on Winters was witnessed, but the attacker has yet to be identified."

"Can't argue with that," Trigger said.

"Except the witness in question is MIA."

"We'll resume our search at first light tomorrow, report in again as soon as we've found her," Taine said, hoping when they did, Louise Hemphill would be able to tell them exactly who or what they were dealing with.

CHAPTER 12

Taine had Coolie and Trigger assemble the civilians.

Released from his tent, de Haas emerged like an enraged ferret from its hole. "What the hell is going on, McKenna?" he demanded. "Your goons have practically had us under house arrest all evening! If this if some kind of stupid power game—"

Taine cut across his tirade. "One of my soldiers has been killed."

Eyes wide, Jules brought her hands to her face.

"Jesus," said Ben.

"Well, I'm hardly surprised," de Haas said, turning on Taine, and poking an index finger into his chest. "I warned you, didn't I? First night of camp high-jinks you called it! Which one was it? Wright or Eriksen? I sincerely hope you've put the other hothead under guard. We can't have a crazed murderer sleeping amongst—"

Taine looked down at the geologist's finger, then to his face. "Neither Wright or Eriksen were involved, Dr de Haas. The camp was attacked by an... an outside threat. Anaru Winters was ambushed and killed."

"Oh no," Jules said softly.

"An outside threat?" de Haas ranted. "What outside threat? What sort of army-speak is that? And don't tell me any more of your fairy stories."

Fairy stories! Taine rubbed his hand across his chin. What should he say? He could hardly believe it himself. "It's too early to say more about the attacker or the attack," he said carefully. "But we suspect Ms Hemphill witnessed the incident and was sufficiently traumatised to run into the bush in a panic. She has yet to be found."

Jules looked around the group. It was clear to Taine she

hadn't been aware her friend wasn't with them. "Louise? Out in the bush? But she's been with Dr de Haas, in his tent, discussing their results."

"What?" De Haas screwed up his face. "She hasn't been with me."

Jules' face drained of colour. "But she *must* have been with you."

"It's true, Jules," Richard Foster said. "There was just the two of us. Louise wasn't with us when Corporal Liu asked us to stay in our tents."

She turned to Ben, her eyes imploring him for an alternative explanation.

"Ms Hemphill isn't in the camp, Dr Asher," Taine cut in. "Singh and Wright are certain she ran into the forest after witnessing Private Winters' death."

She looked at him, stricken. "Then go and find her! Please, Sergeant."

"We *have* been searching for her. My men have been out there scouring the bush for the past three hours."

Jules turned to push him, her palms flat against his chest. "Then go back and look again. Find her."

Taking her wrists gently in his hands, Taine shook his head. "We'll resume our search in the morning when conditions improve."

Jules wrenched free, and turned to Richard Foster. "Richard, please, *please* help. Make them do something. Louise is out there in the dark. She could be injured. Cold..." She swivelled back to Taine, her face twisted in anguish. "We have to find her. We *have* to."

Richard put an arm around her shoulders. "Jules, it's okay. I'm sure Louise will be fine. She was dressed warmly, and she's sensible. She'll have found herself somewhere sheltered..."

Jules buried her face in Foster's shoulder.

Taine suppressed a wave of irritation. Foster just couldn't keep his hands off her, could he? Had to be the hero. His fists clenched, Taine looked away. It was none of his business. *She* was none of his business. He was a soldier. He needed to concentrate on getting on with his job.

Taine sucked in a breath. "The safety of the rest of the party is our first priority," he said. "Until we can be sure what we're dealing with, we're asking you to please go back to your tents. My soldiers will mount a guard overnight, and we'll resume the search for Ms Hemphill at first light. Corporal Liu will see you to your tent, Dr Asher."

"Winters is dead," Taine heard Foster say to Ben when the civilians moved off.

"It'll be separatists," Ben muttered.

"Anti-mining protesters more likely," Foster replied. "It wouldn't be the first time an environmentalist has done something reckless. But sneaking into camp and killing a man – a soldier – that's pretty serious."

"I just hope it wasn't one of my people who did this," Nathan said quietly.

Wiping her eyes with the back of her hand, Jules looked like she was about to follow Coolie, but instead she paused, turning to Taine. "Sergeant?"

"Yes, Dr Asher?"

"I'm very sorry about Anaru Winters. I didn't know him, but he seemed like a nice man."

Taine nodded. "Yes, he was a good man."

And he was also a soldier. Winters knew when he'd signed up that he'd be putting his life on the line. But like this? Taine had had to inform families before that their loved one had perished in the course of duty. It wasn't common, but it happened: a shell hit the vehicle your son was driving; your brother was the victim of an unseen sniper; the building collapsed while his section was helping to evacuate civilians. This time though, the wording would be deliberately vague. Anaru Winters was killed tragically while carrying out his duties. Because how was he supposed to tell the man's family, 'Sorry, we're not entirely sure, but reports suggest *your loved one may have been ripped in half by an oversized reptile?*'

Jules turned to go, shoulders hunched.

Taine reached out; his fingertips grazed her forearm. He snatched them back, then cleared his throat. "Dr Asher, I know you're concerned about Ms Hemphill. I promise we'll do everything we can to find her."

She looked at him a moment, and gave him the smallest nod before Coolie led her away.

When the civilians had dispersed, Taine and Trigger hurried to catch de Haas. "Doctor, can we have a word?"

The geologist put his hands on his hips. "What?"

"As soon as my men have located Louise Hemphill, I'll be taking this team out of the forest."

"Sergeant McKenna," de Haas said in a tone one might use with a small child. "It's out of the question. This afternoon, after less than half a day of study, Ben Fogarty and I discovered a significant nugget where the trail crosses the stream bed. We'll need time to verify the quality of the ore. This site might be New Zealand's most important prospecting find ever. I don't plan to leave without further investigation."

"I'm sorry, Doctor, but one of our party is dead – two if we include the pig hunter – and now Ms Hemphill, *your assistant*, has gone missing in the bush. We have grave fears for her safety."

"If they're dead, then there's no hurry, is there? They can wait another day, at least. And I'm sure Miss Hemphill will be fine. The silly woman will be holed up under a fern somewhere. You and your men can look for her tomorrow while I carry on with my work, which is the reason we're all here in the first place." He dropped his hands, a signal the interview was over.

"Dr de Haas."

De Haas rolled his eyes. "What now, McKenna? It's been rather a long day and I'd like to get some sleep."

"I'm afraid I'll have to assume leadership of the Task Force."

"Really?" de Haas smiled.

Taine wanted to throttle the man. People were dying.

More might still die and yet de Haas insisted on playing these ridiculous little power games.

"Well, we'll see what the minister has to say about that, shall we? I'll radio him first thing in the morning. I have my doubts about this outside threat. More likely it's one of your men. We've already seen—"

"What about a T Rex?" Trigger blurted, echoing Lefty's account from earlier in the night.

Dammit, Trigger, keep your mouth shut.

"What?"

"The *outside threat* that killed Winters," Trigger said. "What if it was a lizard the size of a fucking shipping container? Would *that* change your mind?"

"What's he on about, McKenna?"

"It's what Singh and Wright are saying," Taine said, aware of how it must sound.

"A giant lizard? There's no such thing."

"I realise it's hard to believe – I'm finding it difficult to believe myself – but both men were equipped with night vision gear. They claim it's what attacked Winters."

De Haas moved his face closer to Taine's. "You must think I came down in the last shower. I expect your jarheads were fooling about with their toys – no doubt half of them are out of their skulls on drugs – and they've had some sort of mishap. It'd be just like the army to cover up their blunders—"

At the geologist's slur, Trigger stepped forward. Okay with passing comment on another soldier himself, Trigger wouldn't tolerate it from an outsider.

Taine stopped him with the smallest tilt of this head. "My men aren't equipped with serrated kitchen knives, Dr de Haas," he said quietly, his anger simmering just below the surface. "They could not have caused the kinds of injury sustained by Private Winters."

De Haas shrugged at that, his indifference infuriating. "Can I suggest you start searching the forest for someone with a kitchen knife then?"

Taine bit back a retort. He inhaled, flaring his nostrils. "As it happens, Winters isn't the first casualty. There have been other reports—"

De Haas puts up his hands. "Not my problem. I will not be disbanding this Task Force."

Trigger spun away to face the bush.

Taine cleared his throat; time for de Haas to understand his place in the pecking order. "Since you don't believe there's a creature killing people in the forest, I'll assume you won't require a security detail?"

"I didn't say that, McKenna. We can't be too careful. Winters is dead, so there's obviously some nutter running around out there. I'll need you to leave some of your beefcakes here while you go off looking for the girl." He turned to go. "Now if you don't mind, I'd like to get out of this rain."

"It's a wonder he trusts any of us *jarheads*," Trigger said, his eyes following the geologist across the campsite to his tent.

Jules trembled, cocooned in her sleeping bag, rain thwacking on the tent fabric. Poor Louise, out there somewhere in the bush, alone, soaking wet and possibly injured. It was like Sarah all over again. Only this time, it definitely wasn't the forest's fault. Louise hadn't been the unlucky victim of a landslip or a rapidly rising river. McKenna said she'd been a witness to Anaru Winters' murder and panicked, running into the forest to escape. It occurred to Jules that, unlike Sarah, who was assaulted by the forest itself, the shrouded mists and dense undergrowth might be Louise's best allies, since Anaru Winters' attacker was still out there. Whoever it was could be tracking Louise, hunting her down. She'd been a witness to murder after all. What if she could identify the killer? What if, because of that, the killer decided to eliminate her...

Stop it! Too much late-night television. Anaru Winters was a soldier. Whoever had ambushed him – separatist, environmental fanatic, *whoever* – would have seen a soldier with a gun and felt it was a fair fight. In a war, there were always casualties. People with causes often thought like that.

But Louise was a *civilian*.

Jules turned sideways and curled herself into a ball, pulling the hood of her sleeping bag tighter around her head and neck. Even so, the chill crept down her back, making her shiver. She didn't want to think about what might happen to Louise if this weather kept up.

Or if Winters' killer found her.

Stop it. Just stop it!

She was going to make herself sick if she carried on like this. There was no point worrying. There was nothing anyone could do until morning. All she could do now was hope Louise was safe and that she'd found somewhere warm to hide.

But Jules' mind strayed to Sarah's crumpled body, and Louise huddled in the undergrowth. Perhaps she should've taken up Richard's offer to share her tent so she wouldn't have to be alone.

"Jules, we're all shocked," Richard had said, after Coolie had seen her to her tent. "A man died tonight. Times like these it's normal to want company." Jules had been tempted, but there was something oddly cheerful in his manner. Did his comfort come at a cost? Jules had pushed that ugly thought aside. It was *Richard*, who knew her better than anyone. Not just her boss, but a man who'd been her friend for almost a decade. It was uncharitable of her to think Richard would want to take advantage of tonight's situation. Jules had said 'no' politely anyway, telling him she'd prefer to be alone. Richard had sulked a bit, his shoulders sloped and his hair flopping forward as it always did, and urged her to think again, but after a few minutes and another promise to send for him if she started to freak out, he'd headed off to get out of the rain.

Maybe it had been a mistake. It might have been nice to have someone to talk to. Anything to take her mind off tonight's events. She wriggled, finding little comfort in the ground beneath her.

She wondered how Winters had died. McKenna had been

tight-lipped with the details. She hadn't heard a gunshot, so it couldn't have been a shooting. Unless separatists had silencers. Jules didn't know. In any case, she hoped it was quick. Hoped he hadn't suffered.

Just hours ago Anaru Winters had been alive. Yesterday he'd sat across the campfire from her reading *To Kill a Mockingbird*. His second time, he'd said. His family would be devastated. Burying herself even deeper in her sleeping bag, Jules turned to the other side where Louise Hemphill's bedroll lay empty.

Oh God.

Jules turned again, and willed sleep to come. Outside the soldiers murmured, moving about the campsite.

CHAPTER 13

Rotorua township

"**P**ania, have you seen my training thermal?"

Sitting cross-legged on the sofa, a magazine on her lap, Pania flicked through the pages while holding a cup of tea. "Isn't it in your drawer?"

"I can't find it."

"Did you have a proper look or a man-look?"

Wayne popped his head around the door. "Baby, I looked hard. Believe me, it's not there." He tilted his head to one side and showed her his helpless puppy-dog eyes.

Pania snorted. "Try the laundry cupboard. I might have put it in there."

Wayne's head disappeared. "Got it, thanks."

A few minutes later he emerged in his rugby kit and socks, his big toe separated from the others by the thong of his jandals, and his boots slung over his shoulder in a drawstring bag.

"You planning to stay on for a drink afterwards?"

"I thought I might. I said I'd drop Greg home. His car needs a warrant."

He leaned in to give her a peck goodbye. She held her cup out wide to avoid a spillage and returned his kiss.

"Have you seen Uncle Rawiri? I'm just about to set the table."

"I think he's pottering around in the back shed. Want me to go look?"

"No, you're late. I'll go. Have a good practice. Try not to wake me up when you come in."

Wayne thwacked down the front steps. The four-wheel drive gave a throaty roar and he sped off.

Closing her magazine, Pania went through to the kitchen, tipped the dregs of her tea into the sink, and checked on the potatoes. Then she picked her way along the cracked concrete path to the back shed.

She knocked on the door before she entered. "Uncle Rawiri?"

Like his room, the shed had become Wayne's uncle's private space. Ignoring the daddy long-legs spiders hanging cheerfully in the corners, she ventured in. An earthy odour of potting mix and seedlings pervaded the lean-to – and the sharp tang emanating from the half bag of left-over sheep pellets stored alongside the motor mower. On the scarred worktop, a battered radio played an AM station, the tune barely recognisable through the hiss of static. Most of the seed pots had been stacked away now for the winter, but a small jumble of odd pots and some used window cleaner bottles filled with Uncle's home-made bug spray remained.

"Uncle Rawiri? It's almost tea time."

Looking up, the old man leaned over and flicked off the fan heater with the tip of his chisel, the soft whirr dwindling away. "Ah, Pania."

"What's that you're up to?" Pania said, perching on the wide arm of the chair.

Putting the chisel down, Uncle Rawiri held up his handiwork for her inspection. "I've been making a pūrerehua."

"A what?"

Pania was ashamed she didn't speak more Māori. She knew the words to the national anthem, well most of them, and a spattering of other words like library and family, but beyond that, her Māori was pretty shabby. She wasn't the only one. They said there was a chance the language could die out.

"It's a pūrerehua," Uncle Rawiri said patiently. "A musical instrument."

Pania examined the object in his hand. Elongated and oval – a bit like a TV remote control – it was strikingly beautiful, made of a deep golden wood naturally swirled with darker lines and knots, and the blade overlaid with surface carvings. Pania admired the strong sweeping whirls and delicate spirals of the design. It wasn't quite complete yet; pencil marks outlined spirals Uncle Rawiri still had to etch and whittle, but Pania had never seen anything quite like it.

She put out her hand. "Let's have a look."

To her surprise, Uncle Rawiri snatched it away. "Please, you mustn't handle it. Pūrerehua are very tapu, too sacred for womenfolk to touch."

Pania was disappointed. She'd like to touch the little instrument, and imagined those swooping ridges under her fingertips, the aromatic tang from the heart of the matai tree.

"I'm sorry," he said.

Pania shrugged. Tapu was tapu. Nothing you could do about that. "That's okay. How does it work?"

"See this little hole here at this end?"

Pania nodded.

"You thread a string through it and then swing the instrument, whirling it at differing speeds around your head. You know, the way a cowboy uses a lasso. The wind carries across the blades over the little dog's-tooth notches I've carved on either side of this end – see? – and that's what creates the sound."

"What does it sound like?"

"Like a piece of corrugated iron thrown about in a tornado apparently, although they're *supposed* to sound like the wings of a moth. I guess it's an acquired taste. Like that DJ music Wayne likes."

"You mean David Guetta?"

"Is that his name? Guetta. More like Get-a-Headache." He laughed at his own joke. "Tell you what, when I've finished making it, I'll play it for you and you can hear for yourself."

"Well, it's very pretty. Is it a gift for someone?"

"Not, not a gift." He frowned. "I'm not sure why I made it." He closed his eyes...

Temera was eleven. It was the summer holidays. He and his Mātua Rata had climbed the narrow track to the top of a nearby hill and sat in a clearing in the trees looking over the valley. It had taken them a long time to get there because the day was hot and Mātua was old, so old years of learning were fixed in the wrinkles of his skin, like the words in a book or the rings of a tree. At the summit, Temera sat on his haunches while he waited for his mentor to catch his breath and consider the topic for the day's lesson. To pass the time he took a stick and drew a picture in the dust – a WWII Spitfire. But when it was time for the lesson, Mātua wiped a bony finger through the wings and tail of Temera's aircraft, leaving just the fuselage shape, which he then embellished with swirly patterns – the kind you saw on meeting houses.

"Looks like a torpedo," Temera said.

"Hmph," Mātua grunted. "It's much stronger than a torpedo."

"No way."

"Much, much stronger."

"Can it blow up a submarine?"

"Hush. Sometimes you talk a lot of rubbish. This is a pūrerehua, a musical instrument."

"A musical instrument. How can a musical instrument be stronger than a torpedo, Mātua?"

"Because the pūrerehua is infused with powerful magic," Mātua said.

"What sort of magic?"

"Old magic."

This time it was Temera's turn to grunt. Picking up a little stone he threw it over the ridge. The pebble rattled through the foliage on its way down the hill until eventually it fell quiet. Mātua lit a cigarette, passing it to Temera before lighting another for himself. For a time they puffed contentedly together, the boy and his teacher. The cigarette half smoked, Mātua stubbed it out on the ground and put the other half of the butt in his pocket.

He said, "Pūrerehua are powerful enough to connect a person's wairua, his spirit, with others in the physical world."

Temera had reflected on that. "You mean like seeing ghosts? But when I follow the morepork in my sleep, that's my wairua travelling, right? My spirit travelling, not my body. My wairua hears the messages in that dream-place and I have to come back to my physical body to warn people about what's going to happen. That's how it works."

"Not always. A pūrerehua like this one can serve as a conduit through which a spirit and an earthly body can talk directly."

"A conduit?"

"A passage."

"Like a telephone?"

"Maybe."

"So, this musical instrument lets my wairua talk to people."

"It's not exactly words."

Temera had frowned. This lesson was so confusing.

"That doesn't make sense. How can they talk if they don't talk? Some kind of telepathy?"

"I don't know. I'm only telling you what my own mātua told me. It isn't the same for all seers. I've never experienced it myself."

"Then how do you know?"

"Not everything requires proof, Temera."

Annoyed, Temera flicked his cigarette butt into the bushes. Mātua had frowned at that. He didn't approve of littering. Said desecrating the bush was the same as shitting in your own bed.

"So how's it supposed to work?"

"I believe it's in the particular music of the blade: a combination of the instrument's shape, its surface korero – the carvings – and the material itself. These days pūrerehua are made of different woods but in the days of our ancestors, they were made of stone. Even the string attachment is significant. All these things influence the sound of the music when the musician swings and whirls the instrument."

"The magic is in the music itself then," Temera had concluded, pleased with himself. "The way it makes you feel." It wasn't so hard, now he'd figured it out.

Mātua smiled. "Ah, but Temera, you forget about the musician. If you give two guitarists the same guitar, do they make the same music?"

"No," Temera said thoughtfully.

"What if they play the same tune?"

"Still no."

"How are they different?"

"That's easy. It depends on the musician's skill, or the amount of practice they've had, or their preference for a particular style of music," Temera said proudly. But Mātua said nothing so Temera understood there must be something else. Perhaps the answer had something to do with playing the pūrerehua, which were swung in the air, and not guitars, which were plucked and strummed.

"Is it to do with the speed the musician whirls it?"

Mātua shrugged, opened his cigarettes and lit another, shaking the match to extinguish the flame.

"The size of the circles?"

Mātua looked out over the ridge. He exhaled a cloud of smoke. Made it long and slow so Temera knew he was waiting on an answer.

"Well, am I even close?" Temera said crossly.

"You're close."

Temera huffed, impatient. He lay back on the ground and chewed on his lip. The clouds passed overhead. He was just about to drift off when the answer came to him. He sat up abruptly. "It's about the wairua, isn't it?"

"Uhuh."

"Is that why they call it soul music?"

"What do you think?"

"I think yes. If you want a song to be meaningful, you have to put your heart into it. I think when a man plays a pūrerehua, one he's fashioned himself, he puts his *soul*, his wairua, into the performance. He plays it in a way that allows the voice of his spirit to travel through the string, through the blade, through the music. The song becomes like a prayer, or a chant. A song of the soul."

At that, Mātua had cuffed Temera's hair affectionately with the flat of his hand. "You know what? I reckon you're not as dumb as you look."

Excited, Temera stood and faced his tutor. "People have done this right? Other seers? They have to have, or what would be the point of this lesson?" Not waiting for an answer, Temera spun on his heel, striding away from the old man, only to turn and retrace his steps when he reached the start of the trail.

"Holy shit!"

The old man grinned.

"The pūrerehua *is* like a telephone. It's a link between the living and the dead. Between the spirit world and the earthly realm. When you told me before, I didn't really get it, but this... this... it's amazing."

The old man nodded. "It is, Temera. Can you see now, how, when used correctly, a pūrerehua can be more powerful than a torpedo?"

"Yeah." He flapped his arms in the air, letting them slap against his thighs. "Cool."

After that, Temera had lain on the ground, his hands cradling his head, once again watching the inexorable drift of the clouds. In his ear, Mātua continued the lesson, his old voice mellow.

"As well as being a beautiful object, the pūrerehua's uses are many. The right man can use it to call forth a soul-mate, farewell a loved one, even summon the rain..."

Pania's heart softened. Uncle Rawiri had drifted off. She patted him gently on the shoulder. "Uncle? Are you awake?"

"Just thinking, that's all. Did you know these little objects are supposed to be able to summon a person's soul-mate? I should call up Jessica Alba, see if she wants a date." His eyes twinkled, the crow's feet around his eyes forming merry creases.

"Forget Jessica, how about getting Wayne to come home early from the pub?"

Uncle Rawiri laughed. "Nothing's *that* powerful." Chuckling, he hauled himself out of the armchair, put the instrument in the vice, and turned the handle to lodge it there. "Shall we go in then? The spuds aren't going to eat themselves."

Chapter 14

Te Urewera Forest, Day Three

Still wearing his rain gear, Taine's breath formed swirls of condensation, adding to the early morning brume that drifted softly in and out of the campsite like a sad melody.

He skirted the camp's northern edge. Unable to sleep, he'd taken over Coolie's sentry duty at 0300. He walked wide of the camp perimeter heading south, his eyes scanning the surrounding bush. Had Louise Hemphill survived the night? And if she had, would they be able to find her in this pea-soup? They'd mount a full search in an hour or two, after he'd dealt with de Haas.

Taine gritted his teeth. The geologist was a liability he didn't need – a bad-tempered terrier yapping at passers-by from behind the safety of the fence. Well, let him bark all he wanted. Taine's soldiers were trained to follow *his* command.

Taine caught a glimpse of Trigger's form up ahead, visible through the gap in the tents. Nathan Kerei emerged from his tent wearing a heavy red and black check Swanndri. He stopped briefly to talk with Trigger before ducking into the trees. Lefty was up too, stoking the fire with dry wood stored last night under a fly sheet. Ben chatted to him over a mug of something brewed on his camp stove.

Good man, Ben. The best way to find some normality is to pretend…

The early-morning mist had finally lifted, the drifting clouds separated…

Taine's breath caught.

A monster.

Surveying the scene, the creature stood motionless and silent at the southern edge of the rag-tag bunch of tents.

Taine's body swung into flight or fight mode, but he resisted the call to action. Lefty and Singh had warned him. A giant lizard, they'd said. And neither of them liars. In his heart though, Taine had been sure they were mistaken. It had been a trick of the light. Or a deliberate plan by an unknown opponent to confound them. He hadn't truly *believed*.

But now he saw it with his own eyes. A giant lizard, as big as a fucking bus, just as Lefty described it.

It was magnificent.

Taine estimated the creature's height at about three metres, and a length of around fifteen metres – it resembled a crumpled, mud-coloured tarpaulin thrown over a small caravan. A mane of knife-like spines rippled from its head and down the length of its back like a jagged fence-line on a craggy hill. Its tail was a fallen tree, its surface equally knotted and gnarled. Each stout leg finished in a spray of deadly-looking claws, the longest the length of a bread knife and shaped like a sickle. In an impossibly slow movement, the creature turned its bony, feathered head. It stared at Taine. Their eyes locked. Taine felt a frisson of fear. Not even in Afghanistan, where enemies had masqueraded as Afghan collaborators, had Taine felt anything like this. Men with rocket launchers and hand grenades he understood. Men like him. Men who bled. This – this was different.

An opaque eyelid blinked, the movement unhurried, languid.

While the lizard was immobile, Taine didn't shout a warning. Instead, he raised the Steyr, inching it slowly upwards, looked through the scope and took aim at the odd third eye in the centre of the monster's head.

Hadn't Odysseus taken out the Cyclops' eye? Its weak point?

Through the scope, Taine regarded the creature. It didn't flinch or shy away. Anaru's pierced and bloody corpse flashed through his mind. Taine had to keep the civilians safe. Already, the beast may have taken more than a dozen lives. It couldn't be left to roam the forest. He had no choice but to kill it. Taine steadied himself. Slowed his breathing. Squeezed. Fired.

But it was a bad idea, because as soon as he did, all hell broke loose.

The round hit home. Taine *knew* it had, but the creature charged across the campsite, catching a tent peg underfoot. Dragged it a step. Taine sucked in his breath. Miller dove out and rolled away. Taine breathed out as the creature carried the tent another step then trampled it underfoot. Was anyone…? Dropping to one knee, he prepared to fire again.

The creature ploughed on.

Where the hell were the sentries? Taine glanced to one side of his scope. Trigger and Eriksen were scrambling to respond.

"Fucking hell!" Trigger shouted, his voice carrying over the last of the drifting mist, and the frenzied barking of the hunter's dog tied to a nearby tree.

Taine lifted his rifle and fired again. Lefty and Trigger followed suit, rifles booming, while the rest of the section scrambled to gain a clear line of sight.

The monster thundered over the campsite, a moving truck, large and menacing. Taine glimpsed Ben's dive into the bush.

Good, that's one civilian out of the way. But Nathan, running into the camp, was taken unawares, picked up by his jacket with a casual flick of the monster's claw.

His scream echoed through the valley.

Taine raised his Steyr again, about to fire a third time, when something grabbed the creature's attention. Abruptly, it discarded the big man, then stepped over him, plunging forward.

On the ground, Nathan moved, but slowly, stunned by the force of the fall.

Taine was too far away to help him…

Read dashed in, firing at the monster – the noise infernal. With one hand, he dragged Nathan out of the way. No small task. Taine admired his quick action. The brute continued, ignoring Nathan and Read. The noise of the firearms had spooked it, sending it on its wild stampede? No, Taine could swear it had a purpose. It was heading to the opposite end of the campsite, intent on something. Fixed on... Taine plotted the trajectory. His face set hard.

Jules.

The doctor was frozen in place, her toothbrush in her hand, her face twisted in terror. Taine ran to cut off the animal. He had to do *something*. But what? He'd shot it in the head, and it had carried on.

Belting towards Jules, Taine realised his error. He'd fired at the skull. Solid bone! It was designed to protect. His shot had glanced away.

Taine sprinted, eyes on the lizard. It was going to be tight. Although Christ knew what he was going to do if he made it. Even shots aimed at the creature's flanks weren't slowing it down. But why? Trigger couldn't be missing *every* shot. Sure, the wretched beast was moving, but Trigger was no slug. He wasn't called Trigger for nothing.

Fuck.

Those Steyr rounds were as weak as weasel's piss. Hopeless penetration. Even with human targets they were more likely to maim than kill. And this thing was armour-plated. They might as well be firing at a tank, their bullets bouncing like rain off a corrugated roof.

They needed another way to stop it. Taine cast his gaze about for another weapon.

Any weapon.

At the same time, Trigger and Eriksen stopped their firing. They must have realised their Steyrs were useless, or they were worried they might hit a civilian. Or him. In the sudden hush, Jules let out a tiny gasp. The sound galvanised Taine, the image of a little girl in a hijab flashing through his mind. He put on a burst of speed.

"Boss!"

Read. Running parallel to Taine, ahead of the monster, he was unwinding a length of rope, twisting something around the end. A weight.

Hell's teeth! The newbie really did think he was Indiana Jones. But if Taine's guess was right, it was a bloody good idea.

"Yes! Here!" Taine called. "Trigger, help him." Quickly, Trigger dropped his rifle, the veteran sprinting up behind Read, fast in spite of his bulk.

"Lefty!" Taine yelled. "Behind me." With no breath to spare, Taine could only hope Lefty would cotton on.

Read launched the rope across the space to Taine, a hard flat pass that would've earned him the referee's whistle had he been on the rugby field. Taine stretched out an arm. Grabbed it. Twisted it in his fist. Immediately, he veered off, looking for a decent tree. There! A big tōtara. Thick and solid. Taine dashed around its trunk, keeping the rope high and tight, and taking two turns about its girth before handing it off to Lefty.

"Secure it! And make sure it's tight," he yelled.

Then he was running again, making for Jules while Trigger and Read tied the other end around a beech. The rope secure, Read stepped back. The monster charged through it. The rope pulled taut across its colossal thighs. It faltered, but kept coming. The nylon rope creaked with the strain. Taine swore under his breath. It was caught on the creature's scales, too high to act as a trip wire. It wasn't going to hold. That thing must have weighed as much as a loaded concrete mixer. Taine had only seconds before the rope broke and the creature reached its prey. *Not again.* He couldn't lose another person under his protection.

He needed more time! "Dr Asher! Run!" he shouted, waking her from her paralysis.

Dropping her toothbrush, she turned and fled, just as the first of the rope's fibres frayed in a sickening rip.

"Taine! It's gonna go!" Trigger shouted. He made a fist, a signal for Taine to make it fast.

Taine's chest tightened; Jules was glancing back at the beast. *No! Don't look at it! Run!*

The monster bore down on her. Not looking where she was going, Jules caught her foot in a protruding tent peg. Stumbled.

"Taine!" Trigger urged.

But already it was too late. They were out of time. Stretched to its limit, the rope snapped, the torn ends pinging backwards.

That's when Taine spotted the fire.

Fire! Animals hate fire. Taine scooped a burning log from the embers and threw himself in the animal's path while the doctor scrambled to her feet. Ignoring his scorching hands, he thrust the torch at the snout in an arc of orange sparks. Its muscles bunched, and the animal slowed. Taine's heart thundered with every step. It stopped, looming above him.

Jesus Christ, the thing was enormous. Its *eye* was enormous. Within reach of those sickle-like claws, Taine stood his ground, waving his torch, face-to-face with the beast's toothy grin, Jules Asher's blue toothbrush crushed beneath its claws. Rank breath hit him full in the face.

"Time for you to shove off now, big fella," Taine said quietly, brandishing the torch.

The beast swayed to one side, its eyes on Jules.

"Hey, over here, you overgrown gecko!" Taine shouted.

The creature seemed more bemused than perturbed. Ignoring Taine, it took a step forward, craning its head downwards for a better look at Jules.

"Get back," Taine warned her. "And you can get back too!" He leaped up then, forcing the burning end of the torch into the beast's yellow eye, jabbing hard. The torch gouged soft tissue, the smell of singed eye replacing the stink of its breath.

Blinded, the giant lizard bellowed, its tongue snaking out to swat away the nuisance. Taine jumped out of reach, Jules behind him. He struck again, this time hitting at the tongue, swinging the burning log like a baseball player at the plate. A sizzling hiss. Taine stepped back, panting. The monster roared again.

Shit. His bravado with the torch had only made it mad. It thrashed its neck and stamped a horny foot, trumpeting with all the fury of a bull elephant.

This was ridiculous. He was facing a wounded dragon, a damsel at his back, and armed with a burning toothpick. But the torch, stubbed in the creature's eye, and then dampened on its tongue, was close to expiring. Taine figured he had just seconds before it went out. He was going to need a plan...

INTO THE MIST

But, miraculously, mercifully, the frustrated beast, having told Taine what he thought of him, turned away, plunging headlong into the bush.

Trigger and Read leaped aside to let it pass.

CHAPTER 15

One by one the Task Force members assembled in the centre of the little campsite, Ben emerging from his hiding place in the bush, and de Haas from where he'd undoubtedly been shaking in his boots inside one of the tents. Taine resisted the urge to say, 'I told you so' to the geologist. He'd hardly believed Singh and Lefty's report himself until he'd seen the creature. The geologist sat down on a pack in the middle of the group and said nothing.

Taine checked out the rest of the party. Apart from a blanched look and some serious shaking, Jules seemed to be holding it together. Richard handed her a blanket, which she acknowledged with a nod, pulling it around her shoulders. Taine had lost sight of Foster during the skirmish. Looking at the mud on him, the man had taken cover in a ditch. He sat beside Jules now, patting her hand protectively, while Ira's dog sat at her feet.

Nearby, Singh was checking out Kerei's injuries, the medic clearly happier now he had something positive to do. Or perhaps it was relief the beast had shown itself, proving once and for all that he wasn't going crazy. Coolie and Trigger remained on alert, their guns off safety and their eyes on the bush, scanning the trees. The rest of the men were flopped on the ground.

"Trigger, Lefty, Eriksen, good work back there," Taine said. "And Read." His legs straight out in front of him and his head almost on his knees, the young soldier looked up. "What you did – pulling Kerei out of the way, the rope obstacle – was good."

His eyes directed outwards, Coolie lifted his rifle in agreement.

"Yeah, thanks, man," Nathan called to Read. "You saved my bacon."

Read blushed. "I saw the rope trick in a movie," he explained. "Ewoks trying to bring down the Imperial Transports. The image just jumped into my head." He gave a sheepish grin. "I'm not sure it worked in the movie either."

"You slowed it down, son. It gave us the time we needed," Taine said.

Miller butted in, "What the fuck *was* that thing anyway?"

There was a nervous silence.

"Some kind of dinosaur," replied Singh eventually. He'd had more time to think about it.

"A scaly fucking *tank* of a dinosaur," Eriksen said. He nudged at the remains of the fire with the toe of his boot.

"But that's impossible. There are no dinosaurs left," Miller said.

"Tell that to Winters," Lefty said. "Singh and me, we saw it take a bite out of him last night. And it doesn't do anything by halves either. That thing has two rows of teeth."

"Jesus, Lefty," said Eriksen.

"It's true!"

"Doesn't mean you have to scare everyone to death!"

"We're already scared to death," said Ben, who, bizarrely, was still clutching his mug.

"It's Temera's taniwha," Nathan said now, flinching under Singh's ministrations. "We should have listened to the old man."

"That was no taniwha. That was real. Nothing *mythological* about it," Eriksen said.

Tears welled in Jules eyes and she brushed them away. "If it killed Anaru, do you think it's killed Louise, too?"

"Shit," Lefty said. "You reckon it's got a taste for us?"

Coolie glared at him. "That's enough, Lefty."

"He's right though," Taine said quietly. "Before Winters, it probably killed the pig hunter."

Plus nine civilians and an army section.

"We should expect it to attack again at any moment. We need to be ready."

Miller fiddled nervously with the breast pocket of his vest. "Yeah, well, requisition some light sabres because standard rifle fire isn't going to cut it. Our bullets just ricocheted off its hide."

"The eyes and mouth are vulnerable," Taine said. "Aim for those areas. And light some fires. We know it doesn't like flames."

"Time to get out the rocket launcher?" Trigger said, and Taine nodded his assent.

"See if you can avoid setting the forest on fire," Coolie said.

Singh insisted on looking at Taine's burn. His left palm was black, soot scorched into the skin.

"How's Kerei?" Taine asked, trying not to wince while the medic cleaned out his wound.

"He's lucky. His jacket was torn to threads, but his skin's intact. He's got a bit of concussion and a wrenched shoulder, that's all. When you think what happened to Anaru..." The medic's voice broke. He coughed, then carried on, "In an ideal world, Kerei should stay quiet for a day, but he'll do if we have to walk out."

Taine nodded. "And Dr Asher?"

"Nothing serious. Grazed knee. She's bearing up."

Taine felt a twinge of admiration for her. Soldiers expected to come across adversaries. It was part of the job. They were trained for it. But a biologist? Their day-to-day tasks involved test tubes and trees, not running from monsters. And the beast had singled her out. Most civilians would be in a state of near hysteria.

He looked at his palm, the medic dabbing at it with an antiseptic swab. "What about you, Singh?"

The man's smile was grim. "I don't mind telling you, McKenna, I'm still trying to stop my teeth from chattering and my knees from knocking together," he said. "I hoped never to see that thing up close again. I *prayed* it was a figment of my imagination. This trip, it's not just the physical scars that'll need patching up. I'm no psychologist, but if even if we survive this attack by this... this... creature from the black lagoon, no one's going to believe a word of it. Whatever happens, we're all screwed." He placed a dressing over the wound and pressed the edges down firmly, taping it closed.

Getting up, Taine patted the medic on the shoulder. "Then let's start by surviving and leave the explaining 'til later."

"Richard. How is it even possible, this creature?" Jules said, her hands clasped around a cup of tea while her eyes followed the broad shoulders of Sergeant McKenna inspecting the ravaged campsite with Coolie.

"I'm not sure," Richard said. "It's hard to believe."

"We both saw it."

"I was trying *not* to see it."

"Do you think the soldiers could be right, about it being a dinosaur?"

Richard paused. "It's a reptile, but not a lizard. Judging from what I saw of the shape of its head and the ridge of spines over its back, I'd say it's a relative of the tuatara. And just now, Wright said it had two rows of teeth."

Jules tightened the blanket around her shoulders. "Two rows of teeth. So, from the Order Sphenodontia. That makes sense," she said, trying the idea out loud. "Except animals from that order tend to be the size a loaf of bread. Or a sesame bun."

"Do you think that this creature – let's call it *Sphenodontia gigantis* – has been here all along? I know it's the Ureweras, but living and breeding and foraging in the bush for a couple of millennia without anyone coming across them? No tracks or scats. No bones. It seems unlikely."

It was good to talk. The tremble in her knees was subsiding. Jules watched McKenna enter a tent and drop out of sight before replying. "There probably *have* been tracks, but we haven't recognised them. They might've looked like scuffs. But you're right. It does seem unlikely. Something aquatic like Nessie might've gone undetected, but not a terrestrial organism."

Richard paused to swipe hair out of his face. There was a smudge of mud on his cheek. "Wouldn't the tourism people love that?" he said wryly.

"It's possible bone fragments were here and we mistook them for the moa or the Haast eagle," she said. The blanket slipped again from her shoulders. Jules put her mug at her feet, taking a moment to give the dog a pat.

Richard brushed the dirt off his knees. "Did it look like a bird to you? It's too big. Bigger than a moa. I think if a fossil *had* been found, it's more likely to have been confused with a theropod, given its size. All we have of the Port Waikato Comsognathus is a toe bone, after all." Richard paused. "You know, this might sound crazy," he said, "but I think what we're dealing with here could be something extinct that's come back to life."

Jules pulled the corners of the blanket back up to her neck. "It's occurred to me, too. Only it's so outrageous, so *far-fetched*..."

"DNA *can* be stable though. What about the 2000-year-old-date palm seed found in Israel. Grew into a tree."

"Plant seeds wait for the right environmental conditions in order to germinate. The same can't be said for animals."

"What about water bears? They can survive desiccation for up to ten years."

"Water bears are practically microscopic, Richard," Jules said. "What we're talking about here is preserving a complex multi-cellular organism – a *large* one – in an ametabolic state, and not for just a few years."

Jules loved this intellectual sparring with Richard. Each of them playing the devil's advocate, asking questions and speculating. It made for some cracking good arguments over the years and, right now, the normality was comforting.

"But what if it wasn't about preserving the whole beastie?" Richard said, enthusiastically. "What if a fertilised egg were to freeze-dry under natural conditions? And then, when conditions are suitable, it's reconstituted in water. Voilà – instant living-breathing Sphenodon."

"Just add water?"

"Yep."

Jules shook her head. "The odds are too long. Lyophilisation is simple enough in theory, but in practise it's hard to get right. There has to be a simpler explanation."

Richard just shrugged, shifting his bottom on the pack next to her. "Doesn't mean it isn't possible. It's already been done in nature. Under the Siberian permafrost, with the woolly mammoth."

Jules frowned. "I'm not buying it. Those mammoths died slowly. They weren't snap-frozen like a packet of peas."

"Their DNA *was* preserved though. So what we're suggesting is plausible. What if our fertilised eggs dried out slowly in the nest? What if they were laid close to a geothermal area? And there might have been remains in the nest – proteins or sugars – that acted as cryo-protectants that spared the eggs from damage. Then, imagine if New Zealand – or what would eventually become New Zealand – suffered a cold snap? It's bigger than a chicken egg, but a desiccated Sphenodon egg wouldn't be so big that it couldn't freeze quickly. And what if it was mired in silt, say under a landslip – that would add pressure and contribute to the freeze-drying process."

There were rather a lot of 'ifs' in Richard's speech. "In any case, it's all just conjecture," Jules said.

Richard looked into the bush where the creature had disappeared. "No Jules, that's where you're wrong. It's reality. However it happened, that creature is out there."

Taine and Coolie surveyed the damage. The clearing looked like a bachelor's bedroom; clothes and gadgets scattered from one end of the campsite to the other. Taine stepped over an upturned boot, out in the middle of nowhere, as if it had been flung there in anger. Two of the hootchies were munted, the fabric torn, their ropes dangling forlornly. The radio was wrecked too, its face crushed under the animal's weight, the dials mangled. While

Coolie retrieved Read's end of the rope, picking the knot free, Taine stooped to examine Jules' toothbrush, buried bristle-down in the dirt where she'd tripped.

"Time to get everyone out of here, Boss?"

Taine nodded. "We better tell de Haas."

The geologist was in his tent. He scrambled out, pulling on a jacket. "I'm calling off the mission," de Haas said, getting to his feet.

Taine was itching to mention the creature, to say 'I told you so', after the pompous attitude de Haas had taken yesterday, but he noticed the geologist's fingers trembling as he struggled with his zipper and decided against it. Instead, he said, "We'll need to inform the authorities about what's going on in here. Until we know exactly what we're dealing with, we have to keep people out of the forest."

"What about us?" de Haas said. "How soon can the army airlift us out?"

"We haven't been able to contact anyone. The radio's smashed – trampled – and the forest canopy is interfering with our comms links."

And there's the small matter of our communications officer being dead.

"Richard Foster has a cell phone. We could try that," de Haas said.

Taine shook his head. "There's no coverage down here in the valley."

Coolie pulled his map from his vest pocket, his hands brushing over the tent fabric as he opened it. "If we can get high enough, we might be able to get a line on a cell tower," he suggested. He peered at the map. "There's a ridge here which might do. It'll be steep, but a small group could be up and down before dark."

Taine frowned. "I don't like splitting the group with that creature out there."

"I'll be the one to make that call, Sergeant," de Haas replied.

Taine raised his eyebrows. So, the rabbit had come out of its hole. "With all due respect, they're *my* men."

"And until we hear otherwise, I am still the appointed leader of this Task Force."

Taine was in charge. Arnold had made that quite clear: the minute they found anything untoward, *anything* that threatened the safety of their fellow New Zealanders, then the mission became army business. The problem was, until they made contact with the authorities, de Haas would continue to believe he was leading this entire shebang, and if they were to have any hope of making contact, Taine would have to put his men at risk.

"I like Coolie's idea," de Haas was saying. "He'll go. And those young ones. Read and Miller. They should be able to move fast. Nathan Kerei can go too, since he's familiar with the area."

"Nathan can't go. Singh wants to monitor him for concussion," Taine said, realising immediately he'd agreed to separate his section.

"Eriksen then," de Haas declared.

Taine clamped his lips shut. It didn't escape his notice that de Haas hadn't included himself in the line-up.

Taine crossed the clearing.

Sitting huddled in a blanket, Jules looked up when he approached. Her face was pale.

"Dr Asher? Are you okay? If you're hurt, Jugraj Singh will be happy to help."

Moving closer to Jules, Foster put an arm about her shoulders and hugged her to him. "She's fine. Made of tough stuff, our Jules."

Smiling weakly, Jules pulled out of his embrace. "I'm fine. Jug has already checked me over. I'm just a bit shaken. This morning wasn't your everyday wake-up call." She bent to stroke Ira's dog, and it promptly rolled onto its back, inviting her to rub its belly.

Taine turned to her boss. "Dr Foster, our radio was damaged when the…"

"Sphenodon. Jules and I have been discussing it, and we think it's a Sphenodon," Foster said.

"... when the Sphen-o-don..." Taine said the word slowly, "...charged through the camp. Do you have your cell phone? Is it still intact?"

Foster patted his shirt and, locating the phone, pulled it out and checked the screen. "Seems okay. I can't see it'll be much use though. I haven't had any coverage since we left the road."

"We'd like to take it, if you don't mind. Coolie's taking a couple of men up to one of the ridges to see if they can find a signal."

Foster handed him the phone, his fingerprints evaporating from the screen.

Jules' eyes widened. "But what about Louise?" she demanded. "And Ira? Aren't you going to look for them?"

Taine ran a hand over his chin, scratching his stubble. Last night he'd promised her they'd look for the technician as soon as it was light. "'I'm sorry. Looking for Louise and Ira will have to wait. I can't afford to split my section any further. I have to think of the safety of the rest of the group."

Pulling her to him again, Foster kissed the top of her head. "I'm sure she'll be okay, Jules," he murmured.

Taine gritted his teeth.

"She'll have found somewhere dry to wait until dawn," Foster continued. "If we stay put, I'm going to bet that she walks back into camp in the next hour."

"You think?" Jules said.

Unable to bear the look of hope in her eyes, Taine left them to it.

CHAPTER 16

Grasping the handgrips, Trigger shouldered the launcher – a Carl Gustave 84mm recoilless anti-tank weapon. He pointed it into the forest, testing its weight, before setting it down again – already missing the solid feel of the weapon on his shoulder. Then, he rose and moved the rounds closer, miming loading and firing the machine, reacquainting himself with it. The 'Charlie Gutsache' was usually operated by two men – one to carry the weapon and shoot, and the other to carry the ammunition and load. Trigger wasn't sure they'd have the luxury of two men, not if the creature returned while Coolie's group was off chasing cell towers. But after running through the breech-loading motion a few more times, he had to concede operating it solo wasn't ideal. He put the weapon down as Lefty approached.

"We should have brought M72 disposables," Lefty said.

"Yep. Didn't think we'd need them. Not here at home. And not in the forest. The only thing to point them at are people and possums."

"Until now."

"Yeah, until now."

"So, what do you reckon?" Lefty said, kicking at the ground with the toe of his boot. "Will the Charlie G kill it?"

"Should do. If it doesn't hit a tree first. It's pretty dense in here."

Lefty sniffed. "The Steyrs were fucking useless. Just bounced off."

"Yeah, be good when the DMW 7.62 rifles come in. Steyrs," he shook his head. "I reckon you get more penetration from a eunuch."

Lefty tipped his head at the grenade launcher. "The Charlie G might not be much better. It's a low speed projectile, right?" he said, pursing his lips and squinting into the bush.

"Close range target, though," said Trigger quickly, wondering just how close he'd be willing to let the creature get. "Can do a lot of damage."

Lefty placed a hand on a round, caressing its curved ogive. "What are these?"

"Soft target rounds."

"Fuck. Did that thing look soft to you?"

"Yeah well, we weren't expecting to see armoured tanks cruising around the Ureweras. But even with soft target rounds, it's an anti-tank weapon. It should do the trick. But how the fuck should I know? I've never had to shoot a dinosaur before."

"Take it from someone who's been up close and personal, it isn't pretty."

"Yeah, Lefty, about that. Sorry, I didn't believe you, mate." Trigger scanned the forest, catching Lefty's shrug from the corner of his eye.

"It's okay. It was hard to believe. I didn't really believe it myself, you know?"

Trigger nodded. "Not something you read about in the army brochures."

"Tell me about it."

"I'm going to do a circuit of the campsite before I take a break. You good to do a stint here?"

"Yeah."

"You okay to operate this?"

"On my own?" Lefty asked.

Trigger nodded.

"It'll be slow to reload."

"Want to go through it, in case?" Trigger said.

"Nah, I'm good."

"You see it, don't wait for an order. Just point and shoot. Go for the eyes, like the boss says."

"Okay." Lefty placed his rifle on the ground and, kneeling, lifted the rocket launcher. Bracing the stop firmly against his shoulder, he looked down the sight.

Jules was sitting by the fire, seemingly mesmerised by the flames. She looked up and smiled as he approached.

"Have a seat," she said. With Lefty and Miller patrolling the perimeter, and Singh monitoring Nathan, Taine could spare a moment. He hunkered on the ground beside her, a practice he'd picked up in the Middle East.

Jules pointed to the fire. "You've missed the show, but the credits are about to roll..."

For a while, they were both quiet. Taine picked up a piece of wood and turned it over in his hands. It was a nice shape, the grain rich and smooth. He took out his knife and started whittling, keeping his hands busy.

"Dr Asher—"

"Jules, please," she said, facing him. "You saved my life today, Sergeant McKenna. In my book that gives you the right to use my first name. I'd give you my firstborn, but I've only known you two days..." Colour rose in her cheeks, and she stopped talking, turning to fix her gaze on the fire once more.

"Jules," he said. "Taine." He glanced at her. She was troubled: her irises were dilated, darkened, and she was chewing on her bottom lip. For the briefest second, Taine wanted desperately to put his own lips there...

Coughing, he dragged his gaze away. What did he think this was? An episode of The-fucking-Bachelor?

He clamped his jaw shut. *Get a grip, McKenna. You're here to do a job.*

And that's exactly what he *was* doing: his job. Trying to keep this exploration party safe, while finding out what happened to the missing section. Jules had knowledge that could help him achieve both those objectives. It made sense that he talk to her. And for that he needed to gain her trust. It wasn't his fault she was so damned distracting.

Taine leaned in to place another branch on the fire, the ensuing sparks providing cover as he fought his way back to reason. This wasn't the time.

"Dr..." He corrected himself. "Jules. I was hoping you could tell more about the creature. Dr Foster said you'd been discussing it. What exactly is a Sphenodon?"

That's it. Steer the conversation to safer ground.

"A Sphenodon – it's related to the tuatara."

"I hope you won't take offence, but I've seen a couple of tuatara, neither of them much bigger than a school ruler."

Jules laughed. "I think we can safely say that this one will be called something like *Sphenodon gigantus.*"

"It's new?"

"Completely new. Or completely old, depending how you look at it."

Trigger joined them now, sitting on a mound the other side of Jules, his gun propped against his hip. He inclined his head in greeting, but didn't join the conversation, choosing instead to pick up a stick and draw in the dirt.

Taine turned back to Jules. "So, Singh and Lefty were right, then? It's a dinosaur?"

"Actually no, although Sphenodon were around at the time of the dinosaurs. Hang on, where did I put...?" She had a quick rummage in her backpack and pulled out a fork, which she held sideways. "If you imagine the flat part of the fork is a common ancestor, then these four tines represent: lizards and snakes; alligators and crocodiles; birds; and finally tuatara or Sphenodon."

He threw her a bleak smile. "Nice family."

"Exactly." Jules rolled her eyes. "Our beastie probably shares some characteristics of each of the other groups, particularly the squamata – that's lizards and snakes – but essentially it sits in a class of its own."

Taine said nothing. Even on its own, that thing was pretty formidable. He didn't want to imagine what they could be in for if there were more than one of these monsters in the forest. How was he going to keep her safe? How was he going to keep them all safe? He whittled some more.

"We need to know what we're dealing with here, Jules. Do you think you and Dr Foster could put your heads together and come up with some ideas about the Sphenodon's behaviour?"

Smiling, she said, "Of course. I'd be happy to. Quite frankly, I could do with the distraction. I'll go and talk to Richard now."

Getting to her feet, Jules brushed herself down and headed to the remaining tents, taking all the warmth of the fire with her.

"Jules, aye?" Trigger said when she was out of earshot. His eyes stay fixed on his sand picture.

Taine clenched his teeth. "You didn't have to listen."

"I could hardly help it."

"Just gathering some intelligence," Taine said, slipping the roughly carved wood in his pocket.

Trigger nodded. "Makes sense." He gave a small shrug and went back to his scribbling.

Grunting, Taine stalked off to check the camp perimeter again.

Rotorua township
Temera flicked through the pages of a *Woman's Weekly* while he waited to see the doctor. Apparently he'd been lucky. There'd been an unexpected cancellation at the surgery, so Pania was able to get him in at short notice. "It's just a routine check-up," she'd said, but Temera hadn't come down in the last shower. Wayne had brought him in for his annual wellness check back in November. Temera didn't call her on it. Pania had his welfare at heart.

But she wasn't his daughter, so he made her wait in the waiting room.

"How have you been, Mr Temera?" the locum asked. He was so young. He couldn't possibly have spent seven years at medical school.

"How old are you?" Temera demanded.

"Thirty-two. How old are you?"

"Isn't that in your notes?" Temera waited while the locum clicked his mouse, then examined the screen.

"It says here that you're eighty-three, Mr Temera. Is that right?"

"Must be, if it says so there."

"You look in pretty good shape for your age. Get plenty of exercise?"

"I work in the garden."

"Good for you." The doctor glanced over Temera's head. Temera knows from previous visits it was where the clock sat. "Your niece – Pania isn't it? – she tells me you've been having a bit of trouble sleeping lately? How long has this been a problem?"

"Since I was nine years old."

"Since you were nine?"

"Yes, but I think Pania wants me to talk about the last month."

"Is there something special about this last month?"

Yes, there was something special about this month! A taniwha had returned to Aotearoa – the monster, no benevolent protector of the land and its people. He was vain and arrogant and meant to challenge the forest god himself. Even Temera, who had the gift of foresight, couldn't tell who'd be the victor, only that the battle would be intense. He was worried for his people…

The doctor didn't notice Temera's hesitation. His eyes were on his computer screen. Temera wondered if maybe he was checking his face-page thingy.

"Like Pania said, I'm having a bit of trouble sleeping. Nightmares. They keep waking me up."

The boy-doctor looked up. "Nightmares?"

"I shout in my sleep. Sweat. Pania says it's like I'm terrified. Twice I've woken myself up, sitting up in bed. I've been waking Wayne and Pania, too. I'm so tired during the day that sometimes I fall asleep out in the potting shed."

"Uhuh. I see. Has anything been bothering you lately, Mr Temera? Anything that might cause you stress or anxiety?"

Temera snorted. "Only the usual demons."

"The usual demons?" the doctor repeated. "What do you mean by that?"

"Nothing. Just the usual stuff. Getting old. Life." He shrugged.

"Have you noticed any out-of-character feelings of aggression?"

Now why would the doctor ask that?

Temera felt a prick of shame remembering his outburst on the side of the road the other day. Luckily, Wayne had been there to stop him doing something stupid. Perhaps Wayne had mentioned it to Pania? Mind you, that de Haas fellow deserved it; insulting other people's beliefs and behaving like he was God's gift. It wasn't the first time Temera had felt the urge to lash out at someone, but he'd never actually acted on it before. Unnerved, he felt in his pocket for the packet of smokes there. He did it automatically, the way an infant reached for a cuddly blanket. Then remembered where he was.

"I might've been a bit grumpy. Hardly surprising, since I'm not getting enough sleep."

"I see here in your notes that you smoke."

So he hadn't missed *that* then.

"Are you still at half a packet a day?"

"Yes."

"Not increased it any?"

"No."

"And you're not smoking anything other than tobacco?"

"Weed, you mean?"

"For example."

"Nah." Temera laughed. "Where would I get that?"

More clicking, this time on the keyboard.

"What about alcohol?"

"No."

"Okay, good. Well, I'm going to send you for a couple of blood tests, Mr Temera, and perhaps a peak flow test just to be on the safe side. But I suspect what we're dealing with here are night terrors. They're more typically associated with children, but adults can get them too, particularly if they're depressed or anxious. They're usually not too serious. Mostly, they go away of their own accord. But I'm going to suggest that you keep a sleep diary anyway. That'll give us an idea of your patterns of sleep. Do you drink tea?"

Temera gave a grunt for yes.

"Then you might try a cup of St John's Wort before bedtime. If in a week your nightmares are still disrupting your sleep, I'd like you to make another appointment."

When Temera exited the doctor's office, Pania uncrossed her legs, and replaced a dog-eared magazine on top of the pile.

She stood. "Everything good?" Her expression was full of concern. She was a good kid, Pania.

"Got to go for a few blood tests," Temera said, waving the form at her.

"What for?"

Temera squinted at the computer printout. "No idea. Can't read it."

"Well, the Medlab should be open," said Pania. "Let's go now, shall we?"

CHAPTER 17

Te Urewera Forest, Day Three

After five hours, Coolie's group returned. Read and Eriksen emerged from the bushes first and flopped to the ground, exhausted. Behind them, Miller, his shoulders slumped, sloped off to one of the tents – gone to have one of the fags he thought no-one was aware he hid in that top pocket of his. Taine considered stopping him – army regulations forbade smoking while on an op – but changed his mind. Let the kid have one if it helped to calm his nerves.

Coolie was last to enter the campsite. Taine strode over to meet him, questions already forming on his lips, but Coolie cut him off with a shake of his head. "No luck," he said. "Even with a clear view over the mountains and valleys, we couldn't pick up a signal. Then the mist closed in on us like something out of *The Hound of the Baskervilles*. We could've been standing in the middle of a fucking cloud. Miller bloody near stepped off a ridge. Read grabbed him by his jacket; only just managed to pull him back in time. We waited a bit for the fug to clear and then tried the phone again. Even climbed another peak, although it cost us half an hour. Got nothing."

"So we're on our own."

Coolie swallowed hard. "No, Boss. It would be a mistake to think that. That thing, I swear it followed us all the way, stalking us like a cat hunting a bird."

"You saw it?"

"No, not as such," Coolie said, shifting uneasily. "A couple of times, I thought I heard it, rustling and scratching on either side. I told myself I was being paranoid, but the longer we carried on, the more convinced I was that it was tailing us. You'd think something that big would make a lot of noise, wouldn't you?

Like a herd of elephants. It was nothing like that, it was quiet, canny. Then, when we made it to the summit, it was worse, because there was no noise at all. Just silence. We were sitting up there in fog as thick as porridge. King Kong could have been just centimetres from us. Fucking creepy. Made the hairs on the back of my neck tingle."

Taine knew that feeling. He'd felt it more than once himself, crouched in the dusty ruins of bombed buildings, homes that had once housed families, trying to shake off the feeling a sniper had his weapon trained on the middle of his back, his last breath about to be drowned out in the crack of gunfire. If his corporal said the creature was there on the summit, then odds-on it was. Coolie wasn't prone to exaggerating.

Taine had a chilling thought, and raised an eyebrow. "It followed you back, didn't it?"

The smallest nod.

That explained why Coolie was the last to arrive. He'd been playing sweeper, watching their backs. Taine swivelled on his heel, ready to tell everyone to pack up, they were moving out, but Coolie grabbed his arm, holding him there a second longer. "There's something else."

Taine nodded for him to continue.

"I got the feeling it was deliberate, like the creature *wanted* us to know it was there."

"Unfortunately, we weren't able to get any cell coverage at the top of the ridge," Taine announced to the little group standing around what remained of the campsite.

"I suppose that means we can't count on the cavalry charging in on their white horses to save us then," Eriksen said, morose.

"We've only been offline a few hours," Read said. "They won't know we're in trouble yet. We need to give them a chance."

"They're never going to guess there's a fucking *dinosaur* in here though, are they?" Eriksen retorted.

"It's a Sphenodon, a relative of the tuatara," Foster corrected.

Eriksen forced air between his lips like a horse snickering. "Makes no difference what it's called, a Fenneldon or whatever, they're not going to guess."

"But the army know *something's* up, right? After last night? So it's only a matter of time until they send someone, right?" Ben said.

"Once they realise we're in difficulty, yes, the army will send help," Taine reassured Ben. "But that could take a while. We should try and get out of here before then."

"Hmm," Coolie said under his breath. Barely there, his murmur was just loud enough for Taine to hear. A reminder this was an off-record mission and theirs already the second section sent in to investigate. Coolie knew, as Taine did, that even with the civilians in the group, the army wouldn't be in a hurry to risk more soldiers.

"Let's hope when they come, they bring a tank," said Eriksen.

"Tell them to hurry the fuck up…" Miller murmured.

Taine let their comments go. "Dr Foster," he said, holding the cell phone over his head. He tossed it to Foster, who caught it clumsily with both hands. "Thank you for the use of your phone. Would you mind keeping an eye on it, in case we hit a pocket of reception? I'd like to get word out if we can." The phone's battery was almost flat, and Taine doubted there was any reception in the entire park, but there was no point telling the civilians that.

Nodding, Richard pocketed the phone. "I'm on it."

"Right, in the meantime, we're on our own in here. And with a singed Sphenodon in the vicinity. We've got no choice but to abandon the mineral investigation," Taine said. "Nathan'll lead us back to the safety of the road. But before we go, we're going to look for Louise Hemphill and Ira Bidois. We'll give it two hours, while it's still light…" Trigger nodded his approval. "… and hope we find them. Whether we do or not, we'll be leaving the area at 1500 hours, hiking back the way we came. I don't want to be here at daybreak tomorrow."

De Haas got to his feet. "I disagree, Sergeant. I propose we leave *now*."

LEE MURRAY

"You mean, not look for Louise?" Jules said as she turned to de Haas. "But we have to!"

"That thing will have eaten her," de Haas said with an offhanded flick of his hand. "We'll just be putting ourselves at risk."

"What if it was *you* lost in the bush?" Trigger growled. "Would you want us to leave you?"

"Ms Hemphill might not be dead," Read said. "She might have taken shelter, hidden herself somewhere."

"Well, if she is alive, she should've come out by now," de Haas said.

Taine seethed at the man's insensitivity. Louise was his assistant! Someone he worked with every day. Taine kept his voice even. "Except she may be injured and unable to come out. Even if she isn't, we have to remember that she not only saw the creature, she may have watched it kill a man. In those circumstances, anyone would be traumatised."

"We'll wait here then, while you send a couple of your men to look for her," de Haas said hurriedly.

"We'll stay together."

"You split the group when your men went to the ridge," de Haas said. Taine couldn't believe he hadn't noticed the whine in de Haas' voice until now.

He grit his teeth. "That was against my better judgment. I don't intend to risk it a second time."

De Haas puffed up his chest. "It doesn't matter. It's not your decision. I'm in charge here."

Taine couldn't back down. Not again. Not in front of his section. He folded his arms across his chest, the movement slow and deliberate. Then, dropping his voice, he said, "Not anymore."

Coolie and Trigger moved to stand on either side of Taine.

"Excuse me," Jules said. She approached de Haas. "I agree with Sergeant McKenna. We should stick together."

De Haas sneered. "Yes, yes, we know you liked Louise, and I expect you're all starry-eyed about the sergeant now after he dashed in to save you this morning—"

144

Jules' eyes flashed. "Yes, I like Louise, but that isn't the reason," she said.

"We're really not interested—"

"Shut it!" Taine said sharply, cutting off the geologist. "Go on, Dr Asher."

"I was going to say that what we're dealing with here is a predator, and predatory animals tend to be wary of large groups. Take lions, for example. They'll skirt around the edges of a herd and pick off stragglers, so us staying together in a larger pack would make sense. Also, if this creature *is* a Sphenodon – our best guess at this stage – then it's likely its ecology is similar to the tuatara's. Which would mean it typically feeds at night, from dusk through to midnight. It's just a theory of course, I don't really know for sure, but while it's daylight, odds are the creature will be asleep."

"But Dr Asher, aren't tuatara cold-blooded?" Coolie asked quietly.

"Well yes, technically tuatara are ectotherms."

"So, wouldn't they get cold and freeze up at night?"

"You would think so, but tuatara are exceptional in that they're able to function at very low temperatures, lower than any other reptile."

Richard Foster piped up. "Plus, our guy is gigantic. These days the consensus is that prehistoric megafauna, large dinosaurs like our Sphenodon, were actually mesothermic, behaving more like mammals than cold blooded lizards—"

Taine butted in. "I hate to break up the science lesson people, but we need to get going. Stick together. No stragglers. We have two hours."

Ben shifted the foliage with his hand, searching beneath the paddle-shaped ferns for any sign of the girl. There was nothing. Not even a lost sock or a hair scrunchy. Not that he'd expected they'd find anything.

Ben almost laughed. Kiwis were always going on about New Zealand not having any dangerous species. Unlike Aussies, where people *expected* the bush to be full of nasties: snakes, crocs, spiders. But Australia had nothing on this. A bloody dinosaur. Poor Louise Hemphill. A woman on her own running from that? And in heavy rain? Of course, she'd be dead. It would've killed her. Eaten her. This search would be about filling the gaps in the sergeant's report, because they'd be lucky to find so much as a toenail.

His nerves frayed, Ben checked his watch. 2:40pm. Just another twenty minutes. Twenty minutes until McKenna called off the search and they'd be heading back to the road, to civilisation and safety. The sooner, the better.

But what was he going to do about Murphy?

He snorted quietly. *So-fucking-what about Caren Murphy! The woman can get stuffed.*

All the money in the world, he wouldn't be able to spend it if he was dead, would he? Still, he wondered what Murphy would do. Would she follow through? Ben shifted another frond with his foot and waved his hands in the space underneath.

What's that?

Ben spun, his heart in his throat.

But it was just the dog passing him in the brush, its nose to the ground and tail high. It hadn't run away then. Earlier on, Jules had it tied up, but one of the soldiers had suggested she let it loose, give it a chance to catch a scent of its master, or of the missing woman. And although no one had said so out loud, they'd hoped it would bark a warning if the creature turned up, too. But ever since Jules let it off the rope, the mutt had been dogging them – literally – slipping in and out of the group, getting underfoot and generally putting the wind up everyone.

Except it had done him a favour because, now he was upright, Ben realised he'd strayed a few metres from the others. Not too far, but enough to make him uncomfortable. Jules had said to keep together in a group. She'd said a predator like this one would look for stragglers, pick them off. Ben had no intention of being a straggler. He jogged to catch up to Singh, slowing only when he reached the medic.

Jug whirled, bringing up his gun as Ben approached.

"It's me!"

Jug exhaled. "Geez, you gave me the willies."

Ben shrugged an apology and Jug lowered his gun. They returned to their searching, this time keeping only a couple of arms' lengths from each other.

Ben checked his watch. Great. Just a few minutes left now.

There was more rustling, like a chip packet being opened, and it wasn't coming from Jug.

Again, adrenalin coursing, he felt a stab of panic. He swung about, checking for the source of the noise. Holding his breath, Ben strained his ears and his eyes, all his focus on the surrounding bush.

A movement. It was coming from over there...

That bloody dog again. Nearly gave him a heart attack. At the rate it was going, ducking in and out around his feet, Ben would die of fright without even seeing the creature again. Exhaling, he glimpsed a flash of white – the dog's tail – as it darted away, disappearing in the greens and greys of the forest floor. Ben took another slow breath, and checked his watch, before resuming his searching, stooping to search the gap between a rock and a tree.

More like a rock and a hard place.

More rustling again.

For goodness sake. That damned dog. Jules needs to tie it up.

Ben poked his head around the tree trunk, so close it scraped at his beard.

It was the dog again. Only this time, it was in the creature's mouth.

Stock still, the dinosaur had the dog clasped head first in its jaws. The dog whimpered, the sound muffled in the beast's mouth.

Fuck.

The dog was as good as dead. There was no getting out of that. Ben stepped back slowly, *slowly*, his hands outstretched behind him. He had to get away. His body screamed at him to run, but his brain, not wanting to attract the beast's attention, told him otherwise, forcing him to move in millimetres.

At least the creature wasn't looking at him. Like an art feature in a hotel lobby, it didn't move. It didn't even blink. You'd think it was dead, only Ben wasn't that stupid.

He took another backward step.

The dinosaur threw its head back, half-gulping the dog down.

Ben held back a scream.

He wanted to run, but Louise Hemphill ran and where the hell was she now? Probably the same place as Ira's dog.

I've got to get out of here.

Ben took another step back, keeping his movement slow and quiet, cold sweat pricking his forehead and trickling down his back.

Don't see me. Don't see me. Don't see me.

A stick cracked beneath his boot. Ben froze. Held his breath. But intent on its meal, the beast gulped again, a lump appearing in its throat. Almost devoured, only the dog's legs were visible, protruding from between the rows of razored teeth.

Frantically, Ben looked around. Where the hell was Jug? He was right there just a second ago. They were supposed to keep together! Where were the others? McKenna. The soldiers. *Anyone* with a fucking gun!

There was something at his back. Ben gave a tiny start, his heart pounding out a heavy bass.

But the beast was *in front of him*. Eating the dog. The hairs on Ben's neck rose. Was there another one?

McKenna's voice came low in his ear. "Get behind me, Ben."

Flooded with relief, Ben moved to one side, about to step around the sergeant when the creature looked up, fixing them both with that creepy eye in the centre of its head. Ben's blood ran cold. The beast extended its neck in their direction. Could it smell them?

It planted a taloned foot.

It was coming closer!

Ben couldn't bear it. He didn't want to die. Didn't want to be dinosaur fodder.

The creature hissed, and even from this distance Ben could smell its sour breath.

It was too much.

Ben bolted.

Taine found himself facing the monster once again. The dagger-like spines on its back were raised, and the green-brown feathers around its face stiffened like a porcupine's quills. One of its eyes was raw, scorched and blackened where Taine had jabbed the burning log.

Good. I hope you hurt, you greedy son of a bitch.

Taine raised his gun, more through bravado than anything else. Maybe the Sphenodon knew it too, because, through the sight, it looked at Taine, its expression almost quizzical.

Then it took off, thundering through the bush after Ben.

"It's here!" Taine shouted. "Over here!" He sprinted after the creature.

Taine hadn't a clue what he'd do if he caught up, but he kept running, batting away branches and leaping over fallen logs. The Sphenodon changed direction more than once. Was Ben weaving, forcing the creature to slow and turn? Attempting to shake it from his tail? Good. Taine hoped he was making ground because this thing was *fast*. Taine put on a spurt of pace himself, dodging trees and following the furrow the creature left in its wake as it crashed through the forest.

"Ben!" Taine shouted. "Keep moving. I'm going to try and draw it off you."

But abruptly the noise stopped.

Ben glanced around wildly. Where was it? Had he outrun it? Maybe it had gone after McKenna instead? He hadn't heard the sergeant for a while, not since the man had yelled to alert the others. Did the dinosaur have him? Remembering the wet sound of the dog being devoured, the animal's pitiful whimper, Ben shuddered. But if it were a choice between McKenna and him, Ben would rather it wasn't him.

He looked around again. No sign of the creature. Maybe it was listening for his footsteps. He slowed to a stop and concentrated on listening, straining to hear over the thundering of his own heart. The forest was eerily quiet. Only the murmur of leaves and the creak of tree trunks. But then Ben had thought that earlier, hadn't he, and the creature had been standing right there beside him with the dog in its jaws. It could be behind him now for all he knew.

Don't let it be behind me.

Slowly, hardly daring to move, Ben turned his head to check behind him, every impulse screaming at him to run again, to go, get the hell out. And he would, if he had half a clue where to go. The truth was he was lost. One look from the Sphenodon and he'd panicked, charging off, running for his life, desperate to put as much distance as he could between him and those teeth.

Ben let out a breath. The forest behind him was empty. It looked like he'd shaken it off. He listened again. Nothing. It must have gone. Given up. That big, it'd use a lot of energy just moving about. Thank God, he was safe, for the moment at least. But how was he going to get back to the others? One bit of this forest looked surprisingly like the next. And it was so dense. On his own, he could wander around for days and not find his way out. That was, if the creature didn't find him first. Should he shout? No, no shouting. The Sphenodon might hear him. Well, he couldn't just stand here, hoping the others would come for him. McKenna had said they'd pull out at 15:00 no matter what. Ben needed to get back.

He forced himself to think. They'd been heading south, and the road out was behind them, so he needed to go north, maybe north-east. Ben checked the trees for the side with the most moss, but this part of the forest was so dense that moss grew everywhere. Just as well his parents had sent him to Land Cadets. He took off his watch and laid it across his palm, angling it so twelve o'clock was pointed at the sun. Only with the light fading, and the canopy towering over him, the sun was difficult to locate. Ben took a step to one side. There. Now all he had to do was bisect the angle between the hour hand and 12 o'clock, and he should—

A twig snapped behind him.

Ben almost dropped the watch. His legs went warm. Urine seeped into his socks.

He forced himself to breathe.

It's just my nerves overreacting. Listen. The forest is still quiet. I already looked behind me. There was nothing there.

He looked anyway.

The creature lunged, all teeth and claw. Ben stared in horror. The truth dawned. Upwind, it had stalked him.

Run!

But he could only gape as a talon sunk deep into his chest, pink froth bubbling around the nail. Skewered like a prawn on the barbie, he thought, tumbling backwards. Odd that it didn't hurt. But his nerves weren't dead yet. All at once, every cell flared in pain, searing pitiless pain, as if he'd been doused in petrol and set alight. Ben screamed. No sound emerged, but more foam billowed from his chest.

Ben was aware of being lifted off his feet before he plummeted into darkness.

CHAPTER 18

Taine crept away on the sides of his boots. Then, when he was far enough away for the sound not to carry, he sprinted, racing back to find the others.

Trigger and Coolie had them herded together, not far from where he had last seen them, Trigger with the rocket launcher on his shoulder, the civilians inside the huddle, and the rest of the soldiers facing outwards.

Seeing him coming, de Haas pushed through the soldiers. "You're alone."

Taine nodded as he caught his breath.

"Fogarty's dead, I presume?" de Haas said.

"The Sphenodon took him. The dog, too."

De Haas blanched. Jug fiddled with his watch, and Trigger closed his eyes for a second.

"But that can't be right," Jules said, shaking her head. "It's *daytime*."

"I'm sorry. I saw it take both of them," Taine replied.

"It hunts during the *day*..." she said, and Taine recognised her response; faced with the enormity of what had happened, her brain has chosen to focus on the technicality.

"We're leaving this area now," he told his men. "Get ready to move out."

"No!" Jules protested, pulling herself out of her stupor. "We can't leave yet. You promised we'd look for Louise."

Foster stepped towards her and snaked a hand around her waist. "Jules, we've looked for her. If she were here, we'd have found her."

But she twisted out of his embrace, turning to Taine, her eyes flashing. "You said we'd search for her for *two* hours."

"That was before it killed Ben," Taine said.

"All the more reason for us to stay!" Jules said, her voice shrill. She stopped then, her eyes wide, and clapped her hands over her mouth. "Oh God, listen to me. What must I sound like? I'm really sorry about Ben, I truly am, but don't you see? Louise might still be alive. And if she is, we can't just abandon her. We can't let the Sphenodon get her too."

Holding her close, Richard dropped his chin on her head. "I agree, it's cruel," he said. "But given a choice between you and her…"

Foster stepped back. Hands gripping Jules' shoulders, he forced her to meet his gaze. "Jules," he said, wiping a tear from her cheek with the back of his hand. "We need to get you to safety."

Taine looked away. "We leave now," he barked.

Jules looked around for support. No one was keen to hang around. Within minutes they headed out, back the way they'd come. Taine pushed them, forcing the group to run as hard as they could. It didn't take long before they arrived at their original campsite.

Not far enough away. They can't stop yet.

"Leave the science equipment," he said. "Weapons and survival gear only."

"What about Winters?" Singh asked.

Taine shook his head. "We leave him."

"We can't just leave him," Lefty protested.

Singh didn't look too chuffed about it either. Taine understood. It went against the grain for a soldier to leave a mate behind, even a dead one, and the pair had witnessed Winters' death.

You don't always get what you want. They'd left Louise Hemphill.

"We can't carry a body bag out of here. It'll slow us down," Coolie said.

Taine had another thought. What if the Sphenodon used the scent of death to track them? He couldn't take the risk. "We'll weigh the bag down with stones, and leave it in the stream," he said. "The cold should preserve the body until we can come back for it."

He didn't say the water would also cover the smell of decay.

While Lefty and Singh submerged the body, Taine pulled Nathan aside, aware the guide had had precious little time to recover from his concussion. There was nothing else Taine could do. They needed his expertise.

"You know this land. What do you think? What's the best way out?" he asked, pulling out his map.

"There's this trail here," Nathan said, pointing out a route on Taine's map. "It'll take us a bit longer, but it might be safer. Keeps us out of the area Ira warned us about, where he said weird things were happening."

"You think that's where the creature lives?"

Nathan shrugged. "Just a guess."

"Coolie's pretty sure it can track us, Nathan. I'd just as soon get us out quicker if we can."

Nathan rubbed his nose between his finger and thumb. "So, we take the more direct route? Risk running into it?"

Taine gave him a terse nod. Their eyes met in unspoken understanding; maybe Ben and the dog had bought them some time. Folding the map, Taine returned it to his pocket. "Let's move!"

An hour later the group were sandwiched in a narrow fissure between two banks. Taine needed to get them out of this gully. If the creature were to corner them here, they'd be exposed. It could sit over the cleft and scoop them out with its talons, like popcorn from a box.

Nathan clambered up the slope, followed by Trigger, while behind them, de Haas took advantage of the bottleneck to rest. Hands on his knees, puffing, his bald head like a pink bowling ball, he waited his turn.

Uneasy, Taine looked back over his shoulder at the trees, squinting into the shadows, which were deepening to purple in the fading afternoon light. For the umpteenth time, he flared his nose for the musky metallic smell of the creature, relieved to detect only the fresh scent of leaf rot.

"Keep moving," he said, facing the group again.

When de Haas had reached the top, Foster used a branch to hoist himself up the slippery grade and out of the funnel. Read went next, darting up, making it look easy. Then Coolie. When it was Eriksen's turn to haul himself up, Taine stole a glance at Jules. Her hair had worked itself loose from its pony tail and fell about her face in wisps. Her face, though, was grim, lips tight.

"Thanks," she said, as Eriksen turned, bracing his back against a tree, and extended a hand to Jules. Taine picked up the weariness in her voice. She was tired. They were all tired. But Taine couldn't let them stop. Not yet. Tired was better than dead. Another hour, and hopefully they'd be out of the Sphenodon's hunting grounds. Another hour of travelling up and down the line checking on each party member, doubling the distance of everyone else and straining his senses for signs of the creature. Punishing himself for Ben's death, and for failing to find Louise.

The last to climb out of the gorge, Taine grabbed at a tree trunk and heaved his body over the lip. At least that way he could keep the group close.

Te Urewera Forest, East of the Cell HQ
Mist cooling at his neck, Jason hugged his knees. He pulled his jacket around his shoulders and leaned closer to the rock out of the wind. Beside him, Danny did the same.

Well, this sucks! At first, becoming part of the new Tūhoe revolution had been great, an adventure worth dropping out of his economics degree for. What was the point of squinting over textbooks reading about scarcity, externalities and output gaps when you could actually *do* something about it, make a difference, standing up for what was important? Jason hadn't needed much convincing. And mostly, the past four months had been awesome, making him feel like a real-life Che Guevara, waging protests against government theft, its collusion with big business in order to oppress the poor, and especially the white patriarchal gits lording it over his Māori brothers. But no one had told him he'd be sitting in the middle of the forest freezing his balls off for days at a time. And the group's leader, Te Kooti – not his real name – had insisted they be armed.

"You can't have a revolution without guns," Te Kooti had said. "What this country needs is a strategic show of force. They need to know we mean business."

The new Te Kooti divined that, like before, the Tūhoe would lead the way, rejecting injustices against the people, just as the tribe's elders had rejected the Treaty of Waitangi nearly two centuries earlier.

"Patriarchal document!" Te Kooti had spat. "Common thievery. Not worth the paper it was written on." It was parchment, but Jason liked Te Kooti's vision. A return to simpler things. Creating a self-sustaining nation on traditional Tūhoe tribal lands. Giving their people a share in the wealth. But hunkered here in the bush, his toes cramped, cold seeping through his clothes, and holding a gun, Te Kooti's strategy felt more of a hark back to the musket wars, than a step toward the future.

"You okay?" Danny murmured.

"Yeah. Bit cold."

"Yeah, it was better when we were moving. How long you reckon we've been holed up here?"

Jason checked his watch. "A few hours."

"Do you think they'll even come this way? It's a big forest. We could wait a year and never see them."

Jason shrugged. "Te Kooti and the others must know something." Using the sawn-off shotgun as a support, he stood, his jacket scraping on the rock, and stretched his muscles.

Danny stood too, dancing on his toes like a boxer, and blowing on his hands. "How many of them are there, you reckon?" he whispered.

"Dunno."

Danny had already asked him those questions. Jason didn't know the answers any more than the last time, but he did his best to tolerate Danny's chatter. Everyone knew Danny wasn't the sharpest tool in the box.

"That Nathan Kerei, though," Danny said. "He takes the cake, doesn't he? Betraying his own people, bringing the army in here. I'd like to bring that guy down a notch or two."

"He probably needs the money, Danny. It's how they do it, keeping a brother poor so he's got no choice but to take on the government's dirty work so he can support his family."

Danny blew on his hands again. "Yeah. Fucking government."

"Shh," came the whispers down the line. "They're coming."

"Stop right there."

Startled, Nathan pulled up. A gun, its barrel like an upturned nostril, was pointed at his face. "What's going on?"

Behind the rifle, a wild-eyed man, flanked by two other men, stepped into view. Flashes of colour to their rear told Nathan there were more hovering in the trees.

"I could ask you the same thing, Nathan Kerei. You've got a nerve, bringing the army in here. What for, aye? What are they up to on our land?" the wild-eyed man said.

"You know my name? Who are you?" Nathan said. The voice was familiar, but the man's face was obscured behind a woollen scarf. Someone he knew? Would someone he knew take a shot at him? Unsure, Nathan shifted to one side to be out of the line of fire, but the other two, the fellow's right hands, trained their guns on him instead.

Reaching up, the leader pushed the scarf further up his face. "You can call me Te Kooti," he said from behind the weave.

"Te Kooti, huh. Nice alias. What's your real name?" Nathan said with a boldness he didn't feel. The guy was probably high. Who knew what he might do?

McKenna pushed to the front, Nathan almost missing the slight lift of his chin as he strode through the group, and came to a stop in front of Jules Asher.

"Why have we stopped?" he demanded as Trigger and Coolie slipped quietly into the forest on either side of the track.

Nathan waved his hand at the newcomers. "We've got company."

McKenna turned. Te Kooti and his men trained their guns on him.

"Do you have a radio?" McKenna demanded.

"No, we don't," one of the flankers said.

"Shut up, Eldridge," said Te Kooti.

"Fuck, don't tell them my name!"

"What about phones?" McKenna goes on, ignoring their squabbling. "Do you know where there's coverage?"

"In here? You're kidding, right?" Eldridge said.

"Eldridge, shut your damned pie hole!"

Taine turned to Nathan. "You didn't tell them what's going on?"

"Not yet. So far, this one in the middle – calls himself Te Kooti – has been doing all the talking."

"Tell me what? I'm listening now. What's going on?" Te Kooti demanded.

"We have to get out of here," McKenna said, cool as a cucumber, although the barrel of the gun was just inches from face.

"Why have we stopped? We need to move," de Haas said, at Nathan's shoulder.

"That's where we agree," Te Kooti said. "*You* have to move. These are our lands. Tūhoe lands. You people have no right to be here."

"Good, we're all in agreement, then," said McKenna briskly. "It's our intention to leave the area immediately. If you and your boys could stand aside, we'll do just that."

"Now hang on a minute, McKenna," said de Haas.

Nathan groaned inwardly. The geologist was a complete pill. Did he want to start a fight with Te Kooti and his guerrillas? The other day he'd gotten Rawiri Temera so riled up he'd taken a swing. Temera was as old as Methuselah and could hardly hurt a fly, but these guys were another story.

"These men have no right to tell us where we should and should not go," de Haas went on in that pompous South African twang of his. Nathan cringed. "I'll have you know that the minister himself appointed this team. We have every right to be here."

Who cares? Nathan wanted to shout. There's a dinosaur behind us and you're arguing about who has the right of way?

Smirking, Te Kooti glanced left and then right at his henchmen. "Government minions," he said. "I thought as much. What have you come to steal?"

"Steal? We didn't come to *steal* anything!" De Haas was indignant. Another time, Nathan might have been tempted to say 'yeah right'. "I'll have you know that this is an official mineral exploration. We've been tasked with investigating the prevalence of gold in the park," de Haas expounded.

"That mission has been aborted. We're leaving the forest now," McKenna said, cutting across de Haas, and gesturing to Nathan to move on.

But Te Kooti, his eyes gleaming, pressed his gun to McKenna's chest. "Hang on." Turning to de Haas, he missed the tiny movement of McKenna's head. "Gold, huh? I reckon you're lying. There's no gold. There can't be. If there was, the government would've already confiscated the land."

"There is…" de Haas trailed off.

"There is what?" Te Kooti's eyes flashed.

"Nothing," de Haas replied. "We didn't find anything." He slipped a hand into his coat pocket.

Te Kooti frowned. "Eldridge, take a look in that pocket," he ordered, his gun still trained on McKenna.

Nathan caught sight of the sergeant, who shook his head.

Eldridge thrust his hand inside de Haas' pocket, pulling out the nugget he and Fogarty had found in the stream bed yesterday. The henchman held it up.

"Let me see that," Te Kooti said, his rifle held wide while he snatched at the nugget.

"Give that back. It's not yours," de Haas whined.

"It's not yours either," Te Kooti retorted. "Not if you found it on *our* land."

"Let him keep it," McKenna said, putting an end to it by grabbing de Haas by the shoulder. "We're leaving this area *now*." He looked at Te Kooti. "You and your men would be well advised to join us."

"Join you? You're joking, right? Why would we want to join you? You think we don't have our own guides?" He stared pointedly at Nathan. "Men who aren't traitors to their people."

Nathan glanced at McKenna. Raised an eyebrow. Should they tell them? The sergeant only shrugged. Te Kooti and his men weren't likely to believe their story, but to run right past them and not warn them? Nathan didn't want that on his conscience. "Look, this is going to be hard to believe," Nathan said, his palms open, "but there's a taniwha in the forest."

"A taniwha?" Te Kooti laughed, the men on either side of him following suit, like the canned laughter from one of Paula's sitcoms.

"It's true. Rawiri Temera warned us about it. It's already killed two people," Nathan insisted.

Te Kooti raised his gun again, pointing it first at Nathan and then at McKenna. "Good try that. You almost had me convinced, using Temera's name," he said, his tone sarcastic. "Well, taniwha or not, we're going to have to detain you for trespassing on Tūhoe lands."

Now, McKenna lifted his weapon. "Wrong. We're going. If you want to have a gunfight, that's up to you, but my men have your group surrounded and I think you'll find they're better trained."

Te Kooti's henchmen looked wary.

One of them whispered in their leader's ear, so low Nathan barely caught the words. "This is stupid," the man said. "Let them pass. They're leaving anyway."

"Why'd he let them go?" Te Kooti heard one of the kids ask after the soldiers had passed by.

"You want to be dead, Danny?" his friend retorted. It was the bright one. What was his name again? Jason? "The soldiers had guns. They're trained to fight," he explained to Danny.

"But—"

"Exactly," Te Kooti butted in. He turned to face them. "I wasn't prepared to have any casualties on our side. Face-to-face confrontation with the army isn't the way."

"So that's it? We just let them go?" Eldridge said, and Te Kooti frowned. He was going to have to have a talk with Eldridge. Fine for his inner circle to question his decisions in private, but Te Kooti couldn't have Eldridge nay-saying him in front of the troops. It wasn't good for morale.

"No, we follow them," Te Kooti said. "See where they go. They'll have to set up camp eventually. We'll wait until night and ambush them while they're sleeping. Confiscate the guns. Take them hostage."

"Hostages!" Eldridge said. Te Kooti hid his annoyance.

"Hang on." Jason pushed to the front. "What if they really are leaving the forest, like they said?"

"They shouldn't've been here in the first place. Trespassing on our land," Eldridge said.

This time, Eldridge had the right of it. That bald guy with the big mouth and his soldier friends had no right to be here.

"But if we kidnap a government expedition and a bunch of soldiers, we'll have half the country after us," Jason said.

"Then we hole up where they can't find us… in one of the caves. We'll make some films to leak to the media, maybe threaten to kill the members of their party unless the government adheres to our demands. That ought to get us some attention."

"We won't actually kill them though, right?" Jason asked nervously.

Te Kooti smiled at that. Like many of his followers the boy was an idealist, so it was important he treaded carefully here. Now wasn't the time for dissenters.

Te Kooti straightened his back. "You know I don't condone violence, Jason," he said, hoping he had the kid's name correct.

INTO THE MIST

"I have no intention of harming anyone. Our cause has always been about protecting the people's rights." He paused for effect, making sure he looked the kid directly in the eye. "But let's not forget that this is a war. In any war, collateral damage is inevitable." He clenched his fists, for the right level of intensity. "Remember, we're warriors, warriors fighting for the betterment of our people." He stared past his followers into an unknown future beyond the trees.

Dropping his gaze from the horizon, Te Kooti took one look at their faces and knew he had them.

CHAPTER 19

Te Urewera Forest, Third Campsite

"Knock, knock," Jules said. She ducked into the tent. "Richard, there's something I want to ask you..."

His back to her, Richard had his shirt off, his left hand squeezed down the side of his pack, rooting around for a clean t-shirt.

"Oh," Jules said, backing out of the cramped space.

Richard turned to face her. "Jules, it's okay. It's not like I'm naked."

Jules checked herself. He was hardly about to jump her just because he had his shirt off. She crawled into the tent and sat cross-legged on Richard's bedroll.

Abandoning his search, Richard sat opposite her. Their knees were almost touching. His skin was pale and hairless, and, while he wasn't exactly fat, his belly was showing the first signs of softness.

"I meant to thank you for backing me up before," she said. "You know, about Louise."

"I'm sorry we didn't find her."

She blinked back tears. "Me too. Poor Louise. It must be terrifying for her, out there in the forest with that creature."

He leaned towards her, his hair flopping. "You're welcome to share my tent, Jules. I'll make some space. No one would blame you for not wanting to be alone."

Jules gave a weak smile. He thought she was here on a pretext; afraid to sleep by herself. She was tempted to take him up on his offer. It would be nice to be able to hear someone else's breathing and know she wasn't entirely alone... but that wasn't why she was here.

"Actually, I came about Taine... Sergeant McKenna."

Richard's brow furrowed. "Overbearing, isn't he? Shouting orders at everyone."

"No, no, it's not that. It's just that I got it so wrong when I told him the Sphenodon wouldn't hunt during the day. And then, because of me poor Ben got…" She trailed off, shaking her head.

Putting a hand on her forearm, he said. "It's not your fault, Jules. No one could have known."

"I should have, though. Adult tuatara don't hunt during the day, but juvenile tuatara do. If I'd given McKenna's soldiers better information… Anyway, I thought you and I should discuss the creature. Maybe make some better guesses about its physiology, its behaviour."

Abruptly, he pulled his hand back. "I see. Know thine enemy," he said, his voice hard.

"I beg your pardon?"

Turning away, Richard resumed his tussle with the contents of his pack. "The sergeant plans to kill it, Jules."

"That's not true! Taine's trying to get us out of here."

"I don't mean right now, but later, when we're out of here, he and his army friends will come back. It's all those guys ever think about: killing and butchering." At last, he yanked out a crumpled t-shirt. He gave it a quick shake and pulled it over his head.

Jules frowned. "I don't really think—"

"Oh, I know his type. Seen plenty," Richard said, tugging the shirt down. "He would've started with picking the wings off flies then progressed to being the school bully – pinching kids' pocket money and pushing their heads down toilet bowls. Later, he'll have moved on to tweaking girls' breasts…"

"Richard!"

"…and slashing the teachers' tyres. And when persecuting school underlings wasn't enough, that's when his fascination with firearms will have started, leading him to the army where taking a life gets you a bunch of medals and citations."

Richard grasped Jules' hands with clammy fingers. "We can't

let them do it, Jules. That Sphenodon is magnificent, possibly the only specimen of its kind."

"That *specimen* has killed people, Richard. Anaru was *bitten in two*. Severed. Only yesterday he was sitting next to me reading a book!"

Snorting, Richard shook his head. "It doesn't kill out of *malice,* Jules. It's an animal. It was simply displaying its normal predatory behaviour. Trying to stay alive."

Now it was Jules' turn to pull her hands from Richard's grasp. "Yes, and somewhere out there, Richard – probably not too far from here – that predator is foraging for its next meal. This might surprise you, but I don't like the idea of being eaten. I think we should help the sergeant. He's trying to keep us safe!"

Richard ran his hand through his fringe, pulling it off his face. It immediately flopped back. "Look, Jules," he said patiently. "I get McKenna's reaction. He feels threatened. The guy knows nothing about science, so his first response is to fight back. But we're different, you and I. We're conservationists. That's why we joined Landsafe, and why you were put on this Task Force in the first place. To protect and conserve New Zealand's native species. We should be doing everything we can for that animal."

"What do you mean?"

"I think we should capture it."

Jules went cold.

Capture it!

Stunned, she said nothing as Richard, his eyes ablaze, went on and on about capturing the animal, the papers it could generate, the accumulated knowledge, its value to science, to *humanity*...

"Richard. Stop. Please. It would be great to be able to study the animal. Of course, it would. But we have to remember that it's *killed* people. It could kill again."

Richard grunted. "You're upset about Louise. Otherwise, you wouldn't see things this way. That Sphenodon is one of a kind."

Jules' ire rose. "Yes, I'm upset! Of course, I'm upset. Who

wouldn't be? But that doesn't give you the right to flip me off as some hysterical woman who doesn't know her own mind!"

"That wasn't what I meant, Jules, and you know it. I only meant that you're frightened."

"You're damned right I'm frightened. Your precious Sphenodon killed Anaru and Ben, and now you want to go after it?"

"Some things are worth the risk."

"Yes, but not for you. Not for us! You helped Jug Singh with his report. You *know* what it can do. We can't capture it. Not without getting ourselves killed."

"I wasn't proposing that we go looking for it *ourselves*." He laughed heartily. "Against that thing? No, thank you. I was talking about sending in a team later. When we're out of here. It's the right thing to do. The only living specimen of its kind, it has to be saved."

Jules could have sworn his eyes narrowed, but the next minute he smiled, his hair flopping forward, and she wasn't sure if she'd imagined it or not.

Hamish Miller leaned in the lee of an ancient beech waiting for his watch to be over. His parents warned him army life would involve a lot of waiting round. Fucking oath, they were right. One training exercise had him and three other guys doing surveillance on an imaginary guard post. The guys up the line fucking left them out there, bivvied up, watching a concrete bunker for an entire week! In those kinds of conditions you're likely to shoot each other out of boredom. Up until now he'd never really regretted enlisting. It saved him listening to more of his parents' speeches about how the decisions he made now would affect his entire future. They weren't wrong. There weren't too many jobs on civvie street for a guy whose best subjects at school were playing X-Box and chasing girls. Not paying as much as NZDF and with six weeks paid holiday. For bugger-all work, too. But now, with Winters and that Australian consultant dead, he wasn't so sure. Maybe he should have focussed more on graphics and he might not be sitting in a goddamn forest while a fucking velociraptor fancied them as hors d'oeuvres.

Shit.

This waiting was deadly. He was too freaked to put his gun down. His knuckles had gone white from holding it so tight. Nothing in the training prepared you for looking death in the eye. All the psychological tests, all the situational training... in the end whether you fought or fled came down to character and balls. Hamish wasn't too proud to admit that he wasn't the natural hero he imagined he might be. In fact, he was so jittery, Coolie had made him switch the Steyr to safety, scared he might pop one of the others by accident. He'd made an ulcer on the end of his tongue from rubbing it over his teeth. His gut was dodgy. He was close to nausea.

He could take a little something to soften the edges. He brought his hand to his chest, where in his vest pocket, carefully wrapped in a tiny piece of kitchen foil and sealed in a plastic bag, was his first ever dose of meth. One hundred milligrams of pure white crystalline powder – the recommended starting dose. And for the last wretched hour that little packet had been calling him.

Fucking nerves!

Hamish knew other guys who'd taken meth. His mate Chris had been taking it on and off for months now. Chris reckoned all the hype about it being addictive was crap. Use it sensibly and you can take it or leave it, was what Chris said. Sure, you crave it while you're tweaking, so it was important not to have any more available nearby – in the house or anything – otherwise you'd be crawling on the floor like a cockroach, trying to hoover up the crumbs. Chris was convinced that was how he got those sores on his lip and around his mouth. Hamish reckoned Chris probably shouldn't pick at them. It'd made them worse. Weepy and shit. Anyway, it was just another reason why it was a good time for him to try it now because where was he going to get hold of more out here? But mostly Chris said being on meth was like a total mind-fuck. Said you felt like a giant: ten foot tall, productive, creative, and full of confidence. *Pure energy* was how he'd described it. A 12-hour rush of pure positivity.

A damn sight better than sitting here twiddling his thumbs and waiting on a monster that'd taken a shine to human meat. Hell, if he took it, Hamish might even be able to come up with a decent strategy for getting them out if this shit. But meth could be dangerous. Not everyone reacted like Chris. You heard stories. He'd wait until tomorrow. If he wanted it tomorrow, he'd take it then.

Jason was lightheaded with excitement.

They were doing it. Actually doing it! So radical!

He and Danny walked a few steps behind Te Kooti and his right hand men – Eldridge and Smith – as their band of fifteen crept through the gloom, approaching the edge of the soldiers' encampment.

Jason plucked a frond away from his leg, ignoring the niggle low in his gut, the voice telling him that this was wrong, that people could get hurt. *Well, if they do, it'll be the government's fault.* They should've thought harder before sending the army into the Ureweras, before sending a mineral team to steal the Tūhoe treasure from under their feet. Te Kooti was right; their actions tonight would teach those suits in the Beehive not to mess with the Tūhoe. And it'd show people that when they banded together with their neighbours, they could be a force to be reckoned with.

In the grey light, Danny stumbled forward a few steps, bumping Jason's shoulder with his gun.

"Careful! You want that thing to go off? You could kill someone!" Jason hissed.

"Sorry."

The men around them glowered.

"Keep it down you two," someone muttered.

Jason clamped his mouth shut. They were counting on the element of surprise to capture the government party. There'd be sentries, of course. But with only eleven in the expedition group, it was likely they'd only post one or two and let the others sleep. That sergeant was pushing them pretty hard. By now they'd be well into the Land of Nod. Jason chuckled.

Just two sentries.

Easy enough for Te Kooti's guerrillas to overcome. Once they'd been taken down. The whole operation should only take a few minutes.

The man in front of Jason put a hand in the air, causing the line behind to slow and halt.

"What?" Danny asked. Jason shook his head at him, reminding him to keep quiet. They'd find out soon enough.

There was some jostling at the front.

Next thing, the leaders – Te Kooti included – were pushing between them, heading back the way they'd come.

What's going on?

Eldridge motioned with his hand to indicate they should follow. The leaders were withdrawing! Eldridge's eyes darted about nervously, perspiration making a glossy patch on his forehead. Jason heard the word 'taniwha' whispered as Eldridge passed.

Taniwha? What was all this bullshit about taniwha? Jason swivelled. He jogged forward a few paces towards the soldiers' camp.

"Jason! Where are you going?" Danny said.

"Don't wait. Go with the others. I'll be there in just a sec," Jason replied. "I just want to take a look, see what's happened."

He crept forward the last few metres, careful not to kick up stones or break twigs. He dropped to his belly. What could have sent Te Kooti running like that? Jason raised his head above the ground cover and took a look.

There were five tents in a cluster. Two sentries on either side, one of the soldiers tucked behind a tree-trunk where the other man couldn't see him, taking time out to suck on a fag, the tiny red bead signalling each intake of breath. Idiot. Even if his colleague couldn't see the fag he could surely smell it. What the hell is he smoking? It stunk of the abattoir Jason worked in over the varsity holidays.

But then Jason caught a glint of light. Someone else watching? A possum high up in the trees, its eyes gleaming? Jason strained to see.

It can't be. *Now* he understood what made Te Kooti run. He closed his eyes, opened them again.

It *was* a fucking taniwha.

Its elongated snout and crest of spines protruded from the bush. It was watching the campsite, so motionless that Jason wouldn't have picked it out had it not been for the glint of its eye, and that horrendous smell. This was not a story-book taniwha. This was real. Flesh and blood and nail. A living breathing monster. Upwind from the soldiers, they had no idea it was there. How long had it been there? A chilling thought struck him. Had that thing been following *them*? They'd been quiet, trying not to be heard, running hard to keep up with the soldiers. If the creature had been following them, it had been silent and swift.

Right now though, it stood on the edge of the camp, watching the humans, stalking them, like a big cat creeping slowly, slowly across the plains, keeping to the grasses, barely visible, ready to pounce. Jason raised his head and decided he was being paranoid, the beast was only being inquisitive. It didn't look like it was about to attack.

The taniwha moved off, slipping slowly through the shadows, staying upwind of the campsite, and coming towards Jason. Not about to attack? Now, that it was heading his way, Jason wasn't so sure.

Enormous, it loomed over him, encrusted with bony scales and talons like scimitars. The sentries didn't see it. In spite of its size, it was uncannily quiet. It paused.

Jason froze, played rabbit. Thankfully, the creature was fixed on the campsite, its head turned away from him. Something there had caught its attention.

INTO THE MIST

Better them than me.

Jason flattened himself to the ground, making himself small as the lizard continued its approach. His hair stood on end. The animal was a few metres away, perhaps nearer. His eyes closed, Jason drew a shallow breath, willed his pulse to slow, and prayed the creature passed him by.

The ground trembled…

Jason didn't move.

The stink eased when it was gone. Jason crawled backwards, away from the campsite.

Danny was waiting for him just twenty metres back down the track.

"What did you see?" he asked.

Jason didn't answer. He ran. Danny scurried along in his wake.

CHAPTER 20

Hidden in the Urewera Forest

Hawera wiped a smear of sausage fat from his chin. He'd fallen on his feet here, although he wouldn't mind a shag. The last time he'd got any was three months ago, a few days before his old lady had filed the complaint and he'd ended up on the assault charge. She'd had it coming; always banging on about not having enough money for the kids, when *she* was the one with the job. Going on and on with that whiny-shit voice of hers calling him useless and bringing him down. He'd broken her jaw, only not well enough, because the tart had run, lips flapping, to the pigs. But a friend gave him a heads-up and Hawera had shot through before they'd come to pick him up.

He chuckled. Not so useless now, was he? Safely hidden in the backwoods of the Ureweras, and raking in the cash, none of which would be wasted on stupid school shit. When things had quietened down, he was going to take his money and hide in a big smoke somewhere. Maybe go to Aussie if he could pull some strings, get his tattoo removed and rustle up a passport.

His back against a tree, Hawera watched the head guy, Grant, come out of the drying shed and cross the clearing to the accommodation lodge. Grant paid no attention to him, sitting in the shadows. It wasn't just Hawera who was hiding; the whole plantation was invisible, tucked in here for close to a decade, hectares of weed concealed by the distance, the forest, and the mist. Grant'd been running the gig for the last five years. It was so fucking bold, hauling dope out of the Ureweras right under the noses of the authorities, and the Tūhoe. Since that separatist-terrorist shit, the police were too scared to step over the Aukati border. So easy. For all Hawera knew, there could be fifty or a hundred set-ups like this operating out of the forest.

As the boss-man slipped inside the lodge, Hawera slapped at an insect on his neck. Maybe he should grab another sausage off the BBQ. Later. He picked up the mug of home brew at his feet and took a long draught. Might as well enjoy the downtime while he could. Soon, when the weather got warmer, they'd start planting out the new seedlings. This time of the day, the last couple of hours before sunset, was the best time for planting. He'd learned heaps since he got here. Before he learned how to sex them, Hawera thought a plant was just a plant. Turned out the female plants were bigger, coped better with the cold, and their leaves had more THC – the stuff that gave you the buzz – than the male plants. Hawera took another sip of his beer. Maybe one day he'd think about going back to school. All the shit he'd learned, he would make a pretty good scientist. Yeah. He snorted. Like *that* was ever going to happen.

Wearing his ZZ Top t-shirt, Alex came around the corner of the lodge, puffing on a joint – perk of the trade. The man reminded Hawera of a toilet brush, stiff and lean at one end and his beard a mass of bristles at the other. Not for the first time, Hawera wondered what brought Alex here. Not that he'd asked. Didn't plan to either. Alex caught sight of Hawera under the trees and acknowledged him with a flick of his head. He loped over and sat down, bony elbows on gangly knees.

"Freeze your arse off out here, eh?" Hawera said. "Any sausages left?"

"Nah. Slasher just ate the last one." Alex nodded at Hawera's coffee mug. "Beer's gone too. Swap you my joint for the rest of your mug." Everything was a negotiation with Alex. He'd sell his dick if he thought he could make good on the deal. At least you knew where you stood with him. Some of the others here, you didn't want to fuck with.

"That joint? But you've already smoked half of it."

"You've drunk half the beer."

Hawera sighed. "Pass it here then."

The transaction complete, Alex took another joint from his back pocket, smoothed it flat over his knee, then lit it.

"Aw shit, you didn't say you had a whole one."

Alex grinned. "You didn't ask."

"You're an arsehole, you know that?"

"Yeah, so they tell me."

Polishing off the last of the beer, Alex tipped the mug upside down and shook the remaining drops on the leaf litter. Then he sloped off, leaving Hawera to smoke his half joint in peace.

Rotorua township

Outside, the morepork hooted, calling Temera to wake into the spirit world. Temera understood that he should follow, but he was heavy with dread. He contemplated staying here, outside the dream, cosseted in the warm cocoon of his blankets, listening to the up-and-down drone of Wayne's television – left on to cover the sound of intercourse from the room next door. If he tugged the sheets up over his head, if he could just allow himself to drift off, maybe he could slip into some other dream, perhaps even dream-visit Hera, his old lover...

It called again, insistent. The morepork never dragged him from his bed without good reason. Temera forced his creaky body from the bed, and stepped into the spirit world, into the Urewera forest, not far from home.

From high up in the boughs of an ancient beech, his friend the morepork repeated his greeting.

"Hello old friend," Temera said, scanning the branches for a glimpse of the little owl. "Are you calling for me?"

The owl hooted again. This time the sound was sorrowful, the notes as thick and gloomy as the night that carried them. Temera caught a glint of golden eye overhead.

There you are.

But the owl flew off – the tree limb lightly catapulting it somewhere deeper into the bush, and Temera understood that he should follow.

Somewhere in the Urewera Forest

A shout, a pure note, echoed back from across the valley. The four men in the lodge were instantly awake.

"What the fuck?" Alex cursed, and tumbled from his bunk.

"It's one of the sentries," said Slasher. "Maybe a wētā crawled up his daks."

"Shh!" Grant hissed. "It could be a raid. Get dressed." Against the tiny window, Hawera could see Grant's silhouette, pulling his jeans on. He scrambled for his own clothes. About him, the other men did the same.

When he straightened, Grant threw Hawera a gun: a rifle.

"Know how to use it?"

"No."

"You see a cop, you point it and pull the trigger. If he doesn't fall down, you do it again. Got it?" He leaned across, and with one hand clicked something on the gun. "There, it's on auto."

Hawera looked down at the weapon in his hands, frowning. It was made of plastic, like a toy. He held it away from his body, and shook his head. "Uh-uh. I didn't sign up to shoot anyone."

Grant rounded on him then, his night breath fetid in Hawera's face. "Look, the police don't give a rat's arse who we are. Drug dealers, pig hunters, gang members, they're gonna say we're a bunch of separatists and shoot us on the spot. Who do you think's going to come and check? No such thing as due process up here."

"Come on, stop blathering for fuck's sake. We gotta get out of here." Slasher's voice was tinged with panic.

"I'll take the gun," Alex said, grabbing it from Hawera. He opened the door a crack and peeked out, sniffing the air. Pushing the door to without closing it, he looked back over his shoulder. "Can't see anything."

"Dogs?"

Alex shook his head. "Dunno. If they're out there, they're quiet."

Alex was about to slip through the door when Grant pulled him back, yanking on his ZZ Top shirt. "Don't all of you head for the road," he warned. "The police'll be watching it. Spread out. We might get through. And if you get nabbed, keep your fucking mouths shut."

Twisting out of Grant's grasp, Alex disappeared into the night.

"What about Dave and Brew?" Hawera said.

Grant shrugged. "Not my problem."

A few minutes later Hawera was the only one left in the hut. Suddenly, there was the crack of a rifle. A long screech pierced the night air. A sound to freeze your blood. A man – could have been Slasher – screamed for help.

Bastards.

Grant was right when he'd said there'd be no due process. The cowards must have shot Slasher and left him lying wounded. They'd be hiding behind the trees with their Kevlar vests and their badges, ready to pick off the rest of them. Well, Hawera didn't plan to end up in a tin of dog food. Not tonight. Steeling himself against the screams, he opened the door and stepped into the parting mist.

Hawera sprinted into the drying shed, slammed the double doors and threw the lock. He wedged a spade handle across the door. Then he crouched low, slinking to the back of the shed where he hid amongst the racks of weed, its scent sharp in his nostrils. His blood coursed, his lungs heaving. He focused on making his breathing shallow and quiet, squeezing himself into the smallest space possible. *Don't touch the weed. It'll rustle.* And it had that sweet smell. Who knew what that thing could smell? What it could hear?

Outside, the moans of dying men punctuated the air. Agonised shrieks. Hawera put his hands over his ears. It didn't stop the image of Alex crowding his mind, the dark contents of his stomach spilled on the ground while he'd tried to scoop it back into the hole with blackened fingers. It was a waste of time.

Alex's intestines had ruptured. You didn't have to be a fucking medical expert to work that out. The smell was enough. Their eyes had locked, Alex's full of horror, knowing he was as good as dead. No point negotiating with a dead man. Hawera had grabbed the gun and run straight on. Hunkered in the shed, he wiped the sweat from his eyes, clamped his mouth shut and concentrated on getting his breathing under control.

Outside, the night was quiet, the death screams of the others long gone. Hawera's muscles were cramped and cold. He had no idea how long he'd been crouched in the shed. Minutes? Hours? He'd never felt so alone. He strained to hear, but even the morepork and the possums had stopped their scratching. Everything was silent. Maybe the creature had gone? The timbers of the hut creaked, making Hawera jump. A tiny rustle came from the weed to his left.

Shit a brick!

He had to stay calm. It'd be a rat that'd built a nest in the leaves. Yeah. Just a rat. But the noise came again, soft and ominous.

"Who's there?" Brew's voice. Shaky, like a kid on the first day of school.

"Hawera." Hawera kept it to a whisper, barely louder than the thumping of his heart. He scanned the shed with eyes accustomed to the dark, but still he couldn't see Brew.

"When I heard you come in, I nearly died," Brew rasped. "I thought everyone was dead." He paused. "Or dying."

"Yeah." A mound of leaves shifted. Hawera caught the movement. Brew had been hiding under the pile of drying leaves.

"It killed Dave," Brew said.

"Alex, too. His guts were all over the place."

Brew threw off the last of the plants, and stole over to join Hawera at the back of the shed. He mustn't have had time to get dressed—he was wearing a pair of long-johns. "It's just us then, isn't it?"

"I reckon."

"What the hell was that thing?"

Hawera didn't reply. What was it? He didn't have an answer.

"You think it's gone?" Brew said.

"Dunno."

They were quiet for a while, contemplating the alternatives.

"I reckon it's out there," Brew whispered eventually.

"I can't hear anything."

"Maybe it's eating them."

Hawera's stomach clenched. The evening's sausages rose in his gorge. He fought them back down. "Poor bastards," he whispered.

"I gotta tell you, Hawera, I reckon I'd be happy to see a policeman right now." In the gloom of the shed, Hawera nodded. "What'll we do?" Brew said.

"Wait. Stay hidden."

"Yeah. Maybe it'll go away." The way Brew said it, it was like a special Christmas wish. Hawera thought of his kids. For a second he wished he'd been a better dad, the kind that didn't gamble away money meant for new shoes. Behind the door, the night was still.

Not a creature was stirring... not even a mouse...

"Hawera, that thing, did you see the size of it? If it finds us, if it can sniff us out in here amongst the weed, how long do you think that spade will hold? All it would have to do is lean on the doors..." Brew whispered.

"Yeah."

The ground outside quivered.

Hawera's heart lurched. The creature was near – just outside. Had it been there all along? Sitting faithfully by the doors, like an old dog, just waiting for them to reappear?

Desperate, Hawera looked around for an escape. Maybe if they lifted a board from the back of the shed? Emerging from his hiding place, he moved to the back wall, running his palm along it, searching for a flaw, a gap, anything that he could prise his fingers into.

"Help me!" he whispered to Brew. "We've gotta find a way out. Look for a loose board."

Finally, they found one, the tiniest slit between two boards buckled and warped by years of water and sun. Hawera slid his fingers into the space and pulled. Some of the board came away rotten, but the hole was barely big enough for a rabbit.

Again, the ground vibrated. The animal pacing in front of the shed? Searching for a way to get in? Hawera hoped the fucking thing wasn't too evolved. Maybe it'd be too dense to work out how to get them. Now who was being dense? Even his uncle's Labrador could work out how to get into a bag of chips.

Something scraped the door.

Hawera imagined the creature's sharpened talon slipping between the gap, and ripping the doors open. His adrenalin spiked. Sooner or later, it was going to get in. Frantic, he scratched at the dirt floor with his nails to expose the base of the board. Brew did the same, both of them scrabbling feverishly at the packed earth. At last, Hawera was able to slip his fingers underneath the timber. He tugged at the board with raw fingers, pulling and straining. At first, it seemed the board might give, but after a few minutes his body sagged.

"It's no good. It won't move."

"It has to!" Brew hissed, shouldering Hawera out of the way. He bent his knees, grasped the board and heaved, ropey tendons standing out on his thickened neck.

No chance.

But Hawera hadn't given up yet. He searched the shed for something to use as a crowbar. His eyes stopped on something, but Brew stayed his hand.

"No, not the gun. You'll mangle it, and it'll be useless."

"But…"

"I said, no." Eyes flashing, Brew snatched up the gun, cradling it close to his chest.

Hawera was about to argue, when he remembered the spade. He turned to look at it, wedged snug against the door. With the spade, they could lever up the board and slip out the back of the building. It was a risk. What if that thing could sense him? What if Hawera removed the spade and the thing tested the doors? Would he have time to get to the back of the shed, pull the board off, and get away? Hawera didn't know. He looked again at Brew, who tightened his grip on the gun. It had to be the spade.

Softly softly, like a mother checking on a sleeping baby, he edged towards the end of the shed. Gently, he removed the spade wedged across the doors.

He stopped, spade in hand, listening, but there was no sound outside. No vibrations. He crept back the length of the shed. With Brew watching, he prised off the partially-rotten board. A crack of timber resonated in the quiet of the night.

Both men froze.

The beast pushed down the doors. They fell with a whump, their rusty hinges broken right off. The doorway was filled with rows of sharpened teeth. The shed, with the stench of blood and bile.

"Shoot it, Brew," Hawera said, his eyes not leaving the monster. But Brew was edging away, making for the hole. "Shoot it, goddamn you," he insisted. "Shoot!"

At last, Brew fired, the blast deafening in the confines of the shed.

Hawera crumpled to the ground.

What?!

Puzzled, he looked down. Half his lower leg was missing – blood pumping, pooling on the floor. Hawera knew it should hurt, but strangely he felt nothing.

"Sorry, man. Need to buy myself some time," Brew said. He turned and threw himself through the gap in the boards. Hawera stared in horror as the creature squeezed itself through the door frame.

CHAPTER 21

Rotorua township

As always, Temera was nine again – the age he was when he first ventured into the world of spirits, when he first understood his gift. Joyous, he ran his fingers through his own black hair, revelling in its youthful softness. His lungs, free of decades of smoke and tar, threw open every tiny cavity to let in the damp night air.

The morepork called from up ahead. Urgent now.

He recognised the curve of this hill, the gentle sway of the trees and the damp odour of decaying leaf-litter. He set off, following his friend into the dark beech along the tracks of his boyhood. Jumping a trailing root. Scrambling down a bank. Up a rise. Weaving through a stand of tōtara. He ran for what seemed a long while, tireless on his nine-year-old legs, chasing the hoots of the owl, his fears already forgotten in the intrepid freedom of youth.

Near dawn, when the other birds were stirring, the tui and pīwakawaka beginning the first of the day's conversations, Temera came across a body. The man was clearly dead. His ZZ Top t-shirt was torn, exposing intestines that spilled like a string of sausages along the ground.

Temera pulled up sharply. Swallowed hard.

It was a shock. Even though his inner-self knew he was still in his dream, that his own body was safe and warm in his bed at Wayne's house. This death had already happened, or perhaps was about to happen in the days to come, but it wasn't happening now. Temera took a moment to calm himself, his shoulders heaving from the shock of seeing the man, and from the effort of running.

The dead man was forty-ish with a bristly beard. He wasn't anyone Temera knew, although you'd have to be truly callous to wish such a death on another human being. Temera could see the scuffs made by the man's boots as he'd hauled himself into the lee of a small hut, the body slumped against the wall as if he'd attempted to close the wound by folding himself in half.

The owl called anew. There was nothing left to learn here, so Temera ran on.

In a clearing not too far away, Temera came across a collection of small buildings. More bodies were scattered about, like the chip packets and popcorn boxes left on the seats after a movie. A massacre. It was as if a ruthless war party with bloodlust and slaughter on their minds had descended upon these men while they slept. The victims had only enough time to rise from their sleeping bags, one pulling on his trousers.

But they aren't all dead!

In a drying shed he found a man, his throat torn open, laying drowning in his own blood. On his right side, the man's lower leg ended in a raged stump. He stared at Temera with frightened eyes, blood frothing down his body. Did he detect the seer's presence? No, the man's gaze passed right through Temera to the forest beyond. Temera couldn't save him. How could he when he wasn't actually there?

Even so. A man is dying.

Temera-the-boy grasped a nearby leafy twig and, holding it in one hand as a sign of mourning, crouched, placing his free hand over the stranger's grimy fingers. Temera spoke respectfully to the man's spirit, urging it on its way to the stepping-off place, the magnificent 800-year-old pōhutukawa tree at the northernmost tip of the country. Only there could his wairua slip into the ocean to begin its voyage north to the spirit world.

Yet, in spite of his pain, Temera sensed the dying man's spirit wasn't ready to leave. It was troubled. Angry. As if there was something to be resolved. Perhaps it preferred to leave this life with a proper burial; the company of a loyal brother, a tearful wife, and a handful of children. But there was just Temera – only there in spirit – to bid this soul goodbye. Temera whispered a gentle encouragement. Soon the man's eyes fluttered for the last time and Temera murmured a farewell, wishing the spirit well on its final journey to the island of Ohaua. Above, like a bugle call from afar, the morepork marked the moment with a desolate cry. It fell silent.

It was dawn. Temera was alone. From somewhere close came a quiet hiss.

At last. Here was the reason he'd been summoned.

Releasing the dead man's hand, the boy-seer rose and made his way toward the sound, pushing through a clump of mānukā. It scratched at his arms and legs and clawed at his face. Exasperated, he dropped to his hands and knees, and crawled forward on his belly. Another hiss. Finally, through the grey trunks and thick brush, he spied it.

The taniwha.

This time there was no kind, concealing darkness. The creature was terrible and magnificent.

And big!

Temera couldn't tear his gaze away. But if he was going to encounter a taniwha, best to do it at full height, not down here snuffling about like a little brown kiwi. Temera forced himself to stand on shaky legs. He poked his head through the thicket of branches.

The taniwha stared at him. Greeted him with a hiss. Then it continued tearing at its meal – another body. The taniwha held a human arm in its curled talons and shredded the clothing through its two rows of teeth, the way a child shredded the seeds off a sedge grass.

I'm not really here, Temera-the-boy reminded himself as the taniwha chewed the arm like it was a Snickers Bar.

It can't hurt me. It might not even see me. I'm not actually *here.*

But the taniwha's spirit spoke to him anyway. The words – not really words – resonated deep in Temera's chest. Like the circles that spread outwards when rain dropped into a pool, the ideas seeped quietly into his being, reaching out to every part of him and settling in his understanding.

"I expected you sooner, little matakite. I sent a bird-messenger," the taniwha rumbled. "The day is here. The sunlight pains me. I would regain my lair."

Temera nodded. "The morepork called and I came. What do you want? Why did you call me from my bed?"

"To remind you that this is my forest."

"It is not." The words only sounded brave. Temera had to concentrate to keep his teeth from chattering. "It belongs to the forest god, Tāne Māhuta. It's for all creatures to use with respect."

"Not while I'm here."

Temera pushed through the branches now. He stepped over the corpse and stood before the taniwha. The creature towered over him. Temera felt the warm stench of its breath on his cheek, but he straightened his back, and with all the bravado he could muster, looked it in the eye. "Why are you here? Why did you come?" he demanded.

"Rūaumoko, the earthquake-maker, fashioned me from a lump of cold earth in his home under the ground. He nurtured me in his warmth and raised me up."

"Rūaumoko? Why should he do that?"

"To protect the forest."

Temera burned with anger. "By eating my people?"

"I was hungry and they are so easy to catch. Not like fish, which are slippery and clever. Or birds, which are hard to trap. Besides, birds are too small, all feathers and bones."

"But killing humans is dangerous. Surely you know that. Your kind—"

Its head jerked up and a morsel of flesh tumbled from its mouth. "There are others of my kind?"

Temera considered this. Perhaps he'd said too much? But Mātua had counselled Temera to be honest in all things – and especially when dealing with spirits. Even the smallest lie could come back to bite you, Mātua had warned.

Temera said, "There were others. Once. It was long ago, in the past."

"Where are they now?"

"Dead. Gone. When beloved members of the tangata whenua are killed, their friends and family won't stand for it. My ancestors sent their best warriors. Brave men who were not afraid to die. They defeated your kind." Temera thought of the army sergeant he'd met that day on the road. There'd been a quiet strength there. A true warrior. Would he have the skill to overcome this creature? Temera wasn't sure.

Nevertheless he lifted his chin and said, "Already, a powerful chief has sent his best warrior into the forest."

Temera hoped it wasn't a lie.

"A man?" The beast slipped a talon under the jersey of the corpse and picked up the torso. It waved the body before Temera as if it were nothing more than a piece of toast. "I am not afraid of these spindly little things." Bits of dried leaf fell from the corpse like a sweep of crumbs. "I gave you a chance. You should have warned them. The forest is mine now."

"I already told you. This forest belongs to Tāne Māhuta."

The taniwha shredded the clothing from the torso, tearing its head off in the process. The head rolled across the ground and came to a stop. The dead man's face stared wide-eyed from the undergrowth.

"The warrior will kill you."

"Is that a challenge, little seer?" The taniwha dropped what remained of the body. The creature thundered forward. Opened its maw. Hissed. Had it been human, Temera would have sworn the monster was smirking. Trembling, he took an involuntary step back.

"He *will* come."

"Then let him come," the taniwha rumbled. "Let him come."

Te Urewera Forest, Cell HQ

Sitting on the edge of the crude wooden deck beside him, Danny picked at his laces, trying to tease the knot open with his nails. "But Jase, why did we run away?" he asked.

Jason stripped off his boots, removing his wet socks and wiggling his toes. They'd been running half the night. "The timing wasn't right," he replied.

"But why? We could've taken them. There were more of us."

Jason emptied a pile of tiny stones from his boot, giving it a brisk shake in case there were any left in the toe. "Something made Te Kooti think the better of it."

"But we had a good plan."

"You know what they say, even the best laid plan needs to change according to the circumstances."

"Yeah, but what circumstances?"

Jason put the boot on the deck, twiddling the end of the lace in his fingers. High up in the branches of a beech, a tui's dark feathers caught the first rays of sunlight. "Te Kooti saw a vision. He saw a taniwha."

"Like that guide, Nathan, said?"

"Yes."

Danny looked puzzled. "Seeing visions. Were they stoned? Because they've been stoned before and it hasn't stopped us from doing stuff."

"They weren't stoned."

"Then, I don't get it. Why didn't Eldridge and the others take the soldiers hostage like we planned?"

"I don't know, Danny."

"And what does that mean anyway? A vision of a taniwha? Why should a picture in someone's head stop us from protecting people's rights?"

Jason was sick of Danny's questions and his whining. He was like a kid insisting on having just the right plastic toy with his Happy Meal. How was Jason supposed to know what it all meant? He was still trying to make sense of what he *saw* and *smelled* out there in the forest.

He wiped his face with his hands, massaging his eye sockets with his fingertips. If he didn't know better, he'd say the cold and the mist had been playing tricks on his mind. Only, Te Kooti and the others had seen it too – they *must* have – because they'd turned tail and fled as if the hounds of hell were on their heels...

"Jason?" Danny'd had enough of trying to undo his laces. He levered the boot off with the toe of his other foot and it tumbled into the rust-coloured bracken that spilled out from under the deck. Startled by the thud, the tui bounced away into the canopy. Jason lost sight of it.

"There was no need for us to punish them, Danny," Jason said, his eyes on the skyline. "The taniwha was there to do the job for us."

CHAPTER 22

Te Urewera Forest, Day Four, Third Campsite

Leaning against the gnarled trunk of an ancient rimu, Taine shifted slightly, rolling his shoulders and wiggling his toes in an attempt to get his circulation moving again. The camp was quiet, except for the normal pre-dawn noises, muffled snores and the first twitters from the birds. A movement at the periphery of his vision had Taine on alert. He sniffed deeply, relieved there was no reek of Sphenodon drifting in on the soft mist. Nothing unusual. But he'd heard something. Someone moving about? One of the sentries? No, they were still at their posts. One of the others then? Taine waited, listening.

Jules.

She disappeared into Richard Foster's tent.

Taine's eyes widened. He knew Foster had designs on the biologist – the man could hardly keep his hands off her, putting his arm about her at every conceivable opportunity – but he hadn't been aware Jules felt the same way. How had he not seen that? A jab worried at his ribcage. Was he disappointed? Of course not. He hardly knew the woman.

I faced down a Sphenodon for her.

But even as he thought it, he knew she wouldn't have seen it that way. It was his job to serve and protect. She'd have expected him to act the same way no matter who the creature had charged.

Was he really that noble? Would he have done the same if the creature had attacked de Haas? Or Foster?

He clamped his lips tight. Jules and Foster. Well, why not? It wasn't unheard of. People sought reassurance when they were under stress. Maybe that was why he had feelings for Jules himself… Taine shook his head. So what? It's not like she felt the same way. She and Foster had history. They were both consenting adults. It was none of his fucking business what they did.

"Um… Taine, can I talk to you a second?"

He straightened. Lost in thought, he hadn't seen her leave the tent. Legs bare, she'd thrust her feet into her boots without bothering to tie the laces and her lower legs were covered in tiny droplets where she's pushed through the grass picking up the morning dew. He pulled his gaze from her exposed thighs. Her face flushed and her hair tousled, she was wearing a long t-shirt and a loose jumper, one creamy shoulder exposed to the cold.

"Taine?"

"Dr Asher. Sorry, I was miles away."

She brushed a tendril of hair off her face. "You have a lot to think about. Trying to keep us all safe."

Taine did his best to smile.

She pulled her jumper up her arm, slipping the wool up onto her shoulder. "It's just… Richard's gone. I've been to his tent…" Jules reddened, obviously aware of how that must have sounded. "The thing is, we had a bit of a set-to last night and we said some things… I regretted it straight away… I was awake half the night wanting to apologise. Anyway, this morning I went to his tent, only he's not there. I think de Haas has gone, too. They've taken their gear."

What?

Taine stepped around Jules and stalked to Richard's tent. Crouching, he pushed back the flap and peered inside.

"Foster?" It was empty, only the ground sheet remained. Taine backed out of the tent. "He's gone."

Of course, he's gone. She just told you that.

Shivering, Jules hugged her arms around her body. "I think they went off together."

Taine strode two steps to the right, and checked de Haas' tent. Miller's gear was in there, but there was no sign of the geologist. He dropped the tent flap and stepped back, nearly bowling Jules over in the process. "Damn it."

"I'm sorry."

"It's fine. I should look where I'm going."

"I don't mean for stepping on me."

Taine sighed deeply. "It isn't your fault," he said. "They obviously didn't want anyone else to know. What time did you have your argument with Foster?"

"It was more of a disagreement than an argument. Around ten, maybe."

Taine rubbed his chin. "Then they must have slipped away not long after that, while Miller was on his watch." Everything had been quiet when Taine and Coolie had taken up the second watch at 0200 hours, and Taine was sure the pair hadn't left the camp since. But for two civilians to slip away unnoticed with all their gear was surprising. It was possible, of course. Miller and Eriksen had been concentrating on the threat coming from the forest, they wouldn't have expected the civilians to stray outside their circle of protection. Not with a monster looking to pick them off one-by-one.

Still, Taine could murder de Haas. Convincing Foster they could make better time on their own. Richard Foster wasn't officially Taine's responsibility, not really, given that the biologist joined the task force at the last minute, and as a volunteer. But that didn't change anything. Foster was as much Taine's responsibility as anyone else on this mission.

"They'll have headed for the road," Taine told Jules, as she tucked her hands under her arms to keep them warm. "Don't worry, we'll catch them up. They might have a few hours' head-start, but it was dark and they didn't have Nathan to guide them." He called to Coolie. "Get the boys packed up. We're heading out in ten minutes," he said.

He turned back to Jules. She was shivering, chewing lips tinged with blue. "Jules, go and get changed. Warm up. And try to eat something if you can. You're going to need some fuel on board if we're going to catch them."

"Taine, I don't think they're heading for the road." She chewed at her lip some more.

Taine looked hard at her. Was it possible she'd gone even paler? "Why would you think that?"

"It's what Richard and I were arguing about last night." She paused.

"Dr Asher, I don't need to know about your personal life – whatever you and Dr Foster were arguing about is your concern—"

She blushed, the colour returning to her cheeks and lips. "Oh, it's nothing like that. No, it wasn't anything *personal*. It was just that Richard was going on and on about the Sphenodon being the only example of its kind in the world. He couldn't let it go. He's a scientist. For him, even finding a fossil of something like this would be a huge coup. It's an obscure group, so the leap in knowledge that could be obtained from a partial skeleton, from just a *phalange*, would be enough to sustain a career. But to discover a live specimen? And two hundred million years after the fact? A find like that, he'd be a science superstar—"

"Jules, where is he?" Taine cut in.

"I think he went to look for the Sphenodon. He wants to capture it for humanity."

Taine shook his head. "But they've both gone. Foster and de Haas. Yesterday, de Haas couldn't get out of this forest fast enough. Why would he decide to hang about now? He doesn't strike me as the sort to risk his own skin for the betterment of humanity."

Jules shrugged; a tiny movement, apologetic. "They're both scientists," she said, flatly.

Taine felt his cheek twitch. "And you think Foster has convinced de Haas to take a share in the glory?"

Nodding, Jules dropped her eyes.

"Damn it," Taine muttered. "Coolie!" he shouted. "Make that five minutes!"

Te Urewera Forest, Trail Back to the Second Campsite
De Haas slowed to hitch up his pack, the weight of the rope he was carrying making the straps dig into his shoulders. He took a moment to unravel an irritating twist in one of them, before looking up.

INTO THE MIST

Damn.

Already he was losing Foster, the biologist's shape coalescing into the grey of the trees ahead. Keeping his eyes on Foster's back, de Haas hurried to close the distance. They mustn't get separated.

Ben Fogarty got separated and look where that got him.

"Try to keep up," said Foster when de Haas joined him. "We're nearly there."

De Haas bit back a retort. This was Foster's show... for the moment.

Last night, when the biologist had come to him with the idea of capturing the Sphenodon, de Haas hadn't wanted a bar of it. Two men going after a monster? You could count him out. De Haas wanted out of this forest – and the sooner the better. But the more Foster had talked, the more the idea of catching the animal had grown on him. Foster said he had a plan – one based on guile and wit. Between the two of them, surely they had the brainpower to take down an entire herd of Sphenodon. The plan had made de Haas reconsider. His mineral exploration was already down the tubes – that damned Te Kooti had stolen the nugget, and salting the samples was always going to be a risk – but if he played his cards right, he could still salvage something from this mission. Perhaps more than just *salvage*. What Foster was proposing wouldn't be a *geological* discovery, but people were always finding new sources of ore. Not every day, but it happened. This beast – this Sphenodon – was something radically different; a creature from the late Jurassic according to Foster. A real-life Loch Ness monster, never before seen by humans. It was the kind of discovery guaranteed to get your name written in every new history book. Foster had whispered the words, Nobel Prize. Now *that* was a press clipping he'd love to send his father. Nobel Prize winner. How many rugby players could say they were one of those?

"This is it," Foster said, pulling up.

De Haas took a look around the clearing. Yes, this was the place. He recognised the track leading down to the stream, and over there the grass was trampled flat where a tent had been. At least they weren't lost. Without Nathan Kerei, de Haas hadn't been certain Foster would be able to find his way back.

"Okay," de Haas said, removing the pack from his shoulders and setting it on the ground. "Tell me more about this plan of yours."

"We need to search the stream," Foster said.

"What for?"

"Winters' body." De Haas' face must have shown his surprise because Foster went on. "Even with the two of us, there's no way we can capture it using brawn. We're going to have to use our *brains*."

"That goes without saying, Foster," de Haas said, impatient. "But you can't really be thinking about using Winters' body as bait?"

"Why not? He's dead – what's he going to care? Winters will be the bait, and we'll do it the way the Māori trapped birds, just on a bigger scale."

"Bigger being the operative word," de Haas mumbled, picking up his pack and slipping his arms through the straps. "I hope you know what you're doing." He followed Foster. He didn't bother to fasten the clips. The stream was only another fifty metres away. Foster was talking; something about crocodiles leaving their kills in the water to soften before they ate them, and perhaps the cousin did the same.

"All we need to do is find the corpse and remove it from the body bag. Hey presto, ready bait," he said.

De Haas' stomach roiled at the idea of handling the cadaver, but Foster's suggestion made sense. Winters had no use for it, and while the creature was busy devouring the corpse, it wouldn't be focused on them. Nevertheless, he patted his jacket pocket for the pistol he'd stolen last night from the one of the soldier's tents, taking comfort in its weight. The Sphenodon might be a scientific marvel, but it'd already consumed two men. Foster could wax lyrical about brains over brawn, but de Haas didn't intend to take any chances.

"Here it is," shouted Foster, pointing at the submerged body bag. He dropped his pack on the bank. Wading into the stream, he started lifting off the rocks that weighted the body down, and tossed them into the water.

And once they've captured the beast, he'll have Foster to contend with.

Feeling the pistol bump against his hip, de Haas dropped his own pack, glanced at the trees, and waded in after Foster, the freezing water swirling around his knees. He grabbed at the body bag with both hands, straining to lift one end clear of the water.

There'd be plenty of time to sort out the details later, when they'd captured the specimen.

The lady scientist needed a toilet stop so the sergeant called a time out, giving Hamish the chance he needed. He stepped off the trail and into the bush, doing a quick CTR before getting the foil packet out of his DPM smock. He'd been patient, waited all night, and now he wanted it. He deserved it too. He'd thought about telling Read, as they said you shouldn't do the first few doses on your own, but Read could be a bit of a goodie-two-shoes and the Army was even worse. The NZDF didn't even go for ciggies, for chrissakes. It was 'highly discouraged'. You weren't supposed to bring them on an op. They were like a beacon to anyone wearing infrared gear. He laughed silently.

Whatever.

Hamish placed the packet on a flat branch close to the trunk of a tree, where the precious dust would be protected from the wind, and opened the foil with care. Even in the low light, the tiny crystals glistened like sugar. He was going to have to snort it. He hadn't the time to smoke or inject it. That lady scientist mightn't take that long to pee. Snorting didn't appeal, though. Chris said it could hurt like shit. Like when you accidentally snorted beer through your nose. But snorting was quicker, both for getting the drug inside you and for the effect to hit you, so that was that. He took another quick look about, in case anyone was nearby. Then, taking his spoon from another pocket in his vest, he used the handle to create a sandcastle of meth: 4cm long and 1cm wide. He held up the spoon. A few crystals still clung to the handle. Not wanting to waste any – this shit cost a fortune – he licked it carefully before putting the utensil back in his vest. That done, he lowered his nose to the foil.

"Are you nearly done over there?" de Haas asked, impatient. It was late afternoon and Foster's trap still wasn't ready. De Haas' nerves were in shreds.

"Nearly," Foster said, his hair dropping over his face like a girl's. "I just need to finish a few more knots, test them for strength, and then we can set up. It's important we get these knots right, it's been a while since I was in the boy scouts." He paused for the hundredth time to scrub the hair out of his eyes.

"Speaking of boy scouts, where do you think McKenna and his jarheads are?" de Haas asked.

Foster picked up the rope and, nodding to him, shifted his weight backwards to test the knot. "They'll be back at the road."

De Haas leaned back, putting his weight on the other end of the net and acted as a counterbalance in a two-man tug of war. They'd got it off pat now, having tested every knot that made up the net.

"Not tracking us here? We're civilians. The army were sent in here to protect us." The knot held. Both men released the tension and straightened up.

With one hand holding his end, Foster examined a callus on his other palm. "Except I don't count," he said. "I joined as a volunteer."

"Well, me then," de Haas replied. "I'm the Task Force leader. If he leaves without me, there'll be questions to answer."

"They'll save the women and children first, just like in the navy. My guess is McKenna will see Jules to safety before coming after us. That should give us a day, maybe two at the outside, to catch our Sphenodon and write ourselves into history."

Writing themselves into history! De Haas couldn't wait. Still, he wished Foster would shut up and get on with it. It'd be dark soon and he didn't want to be exposed here with Winters' corpse stinking up the air, and the trap not set. Foster was convinced these were the monster's regular hunting grounds, since it had already killed here more than once. The Sphenodon could come back at any minute, which was what they intended, only preferably not *this* minute.

De Haas wasn't sure he'd have the energy to react if the creature attacked right now. Up half the night running back here, and busy concocting Foster's net-trap since then, his shoulders were burning, and his leg muscles cramping from cold and damp; and unless you counted a handful of scroggin, he'd hardly eaten anything in the past two days.

"How many more knots?"

"… three, four, five… another six."

Taking up the slack in the rope, de Haas glanced into the trees and wished again that Foster would hurry it up.

Not far out from the campsite, Coolie's skin prickled again. He slowed and listened. The muted scuffs and murmurs of the group in front carried back to him on the breeze. He frowned, straining to filter them out, and concentrated on the sounds from the forest. Nothing. The bush was quiet.

But something's not right.

Turning to face the way they'd come, Coolie brought his rifle up, using the sight to scan the trees for movement. He sniffed. Nothing. Just the damp odour of beech and leaf litter.

Where is it?

A faint whine reached him, drifting through the tree trunks. With a glance at Eriksen who'd disappeared around a bend in the track, Coolie stepped off into the bush and listened again. Above him, in the canopy, two branches creaked as they rubbed together. Coolie jumped back, his heart thumping. He shouldn't have risked stepping off the track. What if it'd been the Sphenodon? He had to be more careful. It was how they'd lost Winters.

He checked back along the narrow track before stepping out, his weapon at the ready. He hadn't actually laid eyes on the creature since the morning it had charged through the camp and trampled the radio, but still…

"I know you're there," he whispered, turning to follow Eriksen.

For about an hour now he'd had the same crawling feeling he'd had on the ridge when they'd been searching for cell reception. His imagination playing tricks on him? Like the pig-hunter had said, after a while the forest put ideas in your head. But Coolie trusted his instincts. They'd served him well in Afghanistan, getting them out of trouble on more than one occasion. Now, when they kicked in, he was inclined to trust them.

Something in his peripheral vision caught his attention. He swung his Steyr to face the blur; squinted into the murk. Nothing there. No movement. Just that infernal unease. It was here. And getting closer. He'd better push forward and let McKenna know.

Coolie jogged after Eriksen, his skin still prickling.

He scanned the trees. It was canny, that's for sure. You'd think a creature that big would make a lot of noise. It could teach the army a thing or two about stealth. The forest was calm. Tranquil. Coolie wasn't fooled.

On his left there was a small crunch. He swivelled.

Tricky.

That smell.

The Sphenodon loomed on his right.

How did you get there?

He didn't even get in a shot.

Voices up ahead. The separatists again, or the missing scientists? Jug's money was on the scientists, since they were getting close to the campsite where Winters had been killed. Nathan had tracked the pair for that first half hour after they left the camp last night. Once it was clear de Haas and Foster were retracing their steps, McKenna guessed they'd come here, to the last place they'd been. It was the last place Jug wanted to be, too. He'd rather be at home with Priya and the kids.

Picking up the pace, they followed the path down to the water, passing the spot where two days ago he and Lefty had discovered Winters. Jug glanced nervously into the shadows, hoping McKenna wasn't inadvertently serving *them* up for dinner, but when they emerged from the forest beside the stream bed, Foster and de Haas were there.

Immediately, the section spread out, Trigger and Eriksen crossing the stream to watch the trees, and Lefty and Read positioning themselves on either side of McKenna. Jug hung back with Nathan and Miller. Jug couldn't see where Coolie had got to, but then when did he ever see Coolie? He'd been around, probably creeping forward to cover the situation from some other angle. The little corporal was as canny as they came.

Jules was rushing over to where her colleague seemed to be assembling some kind of net. "Richard, what on earth were you thinking, leaving the camp like that? You could've got yourselves killed!"

Foster pushed past her, carrying one end of the net to a nearby tree and circling its trunk with the free end of the rope. "So you want us to walk away? That Sphenodon is the first of its kind ever seen by man. I can't let it be the last."

"But we talked about this last night. It's too dangerous. Please, we need to get out of the forest."

"Dr Asher is right," McKenna interjected. "That animal has caused too many deaths."

"It's not the animal's fault. It's a predator. It kills for food," Foster insisted, yanking on the rope to tighten the knot.

"And for sport," the sergeant said.

"You don't know that."

"No. Only what I've seen."

One hand still holding the rope, Foster rounded on McKenna now, stabbing his finger at the sergeant. "Which is exactly my point. How can we know *anything* about it unless we study it!"

"Your study will have to wait. Your safety is my responsibility."

Foster tossed his head, flicking his hair. "You can't make me. I'm not part of your precious task force."

You can't make me? Jug shook his head, incredulous. That was the sort of thing his daughter Navil said, except she was twelve.

"And I exonerate you from any responsibility," de Haas told McKenna. He handed Foster his end of the net. "We're grown men. We'll make our own decisions. We certainly don't need *your* permission." He turned his back on McKenna, as if to put an end to the discussion.

McKenna's expression hardened and Jug caught the involuntary twitch of his jaw. Jug couldn't blame him. It was a tough position to be in. Jug'd faced it himself when patients refused treatment – you end up trying to protect someone who didn't want to be protected.

If it were up to him he'd leave them, seeing as they were stupid enough to want to stay, but that was probably because he was a doctor first, and medical ethics dictated that patients be allowed to make decisions for themselves. Informed decisions, though. Maybe that was the problem here: Foster and de Haas underestimated what they were up against. Because, although the two scientists saw the beast stampede through the campsite, they hadn't seen what Jug and Lefty had. They hadn't seen it pick up a man as if he were a poppadum and crunch him between its jaws...

Jug shuddered. He'd seen death before, but even in the army it was usually from accidents or disease, or some kind of disorder. In those cases, at least there were new treatments coming on line all the time, and even if you couldn't do anything, there was always palliative care, allowing the patient to die with dignity.

He'd been trying not to think too hard about Winters. There wasn't much dignity in being eaten.

"Oi," said Lefty abruptly, making Jug look up. "What's with the body bag? What's it doing here on the bank—?"

Jug hadn't seen it there before, but now that he had, it didn't take much to put two and two together. Lefty must have done the same because even from here, Jug saw his eyes widen in disgust.

Before Foster could answer, de Haas whipped about, a pistol grasped in both hands.

"Hey!" Trigger shouted as de Haas pointed the weapon – an army issue Sig Sauer P226 pistol – like it were a hosepipe.

Instinctively, the soldiers dived and crouched, finding cover, while McKenna leaped sideways, pushing Jules behind a large boulder. Jug edged himself behind a tree trunk.

Prone on the bank, McKenna called out, "Put that gun away, de Haas. Save it for the Sphenodon."

"We're *not* going to kill it!" Foster shrieked from alongside de Haas, the muscles in his neck straining. "We're trying to *save* it."

"And get yourselves killed in the process," McKenna said.

"If you're so desperate to play the big man and protect someone, McKenna, why don't you and your men take Jules and get out of here? We don't need your help."

"Dr de Haas—"McKenna raised his head.

"Back off!"' shrieked de Haas. He fired at the ground in front of McKenna's face. The gun cracked and pebbles flew. McKenna covered his head with his hands, but Lefty was already on the move, rising from a crouch, coming at de Haas.

De Haas jerked the muzzle round to aim at the soldier.

"Christian," Foster said, putting his hand on the geologist's forearm, and Lefty took advantage of the movement to veer off, diving into a dip in the beach.

His fingers gripping de Haas' arm, Foster took a step backwards, his face contorting in terror. He pointed towards Jug.

What? He's pointing at me? No, not at me, behind me.

Jug's stomach lurched. He went cold. There was only one reason Foster would point in this direction. He turned his head, the smell of rot hitting him. The Sphenodon was only metres away! So quiet, Jug hadn't known it was there.

It's coming this way!

Jug didn't think. Blood thundering in his veins, he threw himself to one side. The monster lumbered past. Razored scales grazed his arm as it passed. Jug's feet churned, like a paddle steamer. Desperate, he scrambled though the ferns. If it had a mind to, the creature could reach out with those talons and eviscerate him. Thankfully, it didn't slow. Didn't look his way. It broke from the bush, heading for the others.

"Look out," Jug yelled, still scrambling. He plunged into a narrow depression, squeezing his body in, the earth solid around him. Trembling, he peeped out from beneath a log.

Beside the stream, de Haas stared as the monster advanced on the group at the stream. Even from here Jug could see him recoil. He foundered backward, his mouth open, and dropped the gun.

At the same time, McKenna rolled, and came up running. In seconds he covered the few steps to Jules and grasped her by the arm, dragging her to her feet to pull her to the cover of the bush.

"Go, go!" he yelled.

The creature swung its head to eyeball McKenna. Jug could swear it hesitated. Could it be intelligent enough to recognise the sergeant? Did it know they had some unfinished business? But it was distracted by Foster, who was sploshing along the rocky streambed.

"Foster! Get out of the way!" Trigger yelled, the rocket launcher jammed hard against his shoulder. "I can't get off a shot!"

"Firing," Read shouted. On one knee, the young soldier lifted his Steyr, sighted the Sphenodon and fired. He fired again. Smoke and noise filled the air. But like before, the bullets pinged off the animal's hide.

"Read, save it for the eyes!" shouted Trigger, who was clambering over the rocks with the rocket launcher, trying to get out in front of it so he could blow off its head. "McKenna, Lefty, get the hell out of there!" The beast looked first at Foster, and then at Jules. Jug imagined he saw it make its decision. It slowed and spun, its spiked tail sweeping outwards in counterbalance, nearly knocking Read off his feet. Its gaze fixed on the biologist, it started to run.

From his hidey hole, Jug watched the party scatter, everyone wanting to get the hell out.

CHAPTER 23

"**M**cKenna! Incoming!" cried Eriksen.

Taine looked up to see the beast bearing down on them, its burned eye fixed on Jules. He was hit with a sudden sense of *déjà vu*. The Sphenodon was after *her*. Again.

"Jules!" She looked up, her face pale with shock.

Adrenaline pumping, Taine steeled himself. It couldn't have her.

Not on your bloody life.

Tightening his grip on her hand, Taine half-pulled, half-dragged her, stumbling over the rocks and across the open ground towards the forest.

"Give them some cover!" Trigger yelled. "Miller, get the fuck over here. Help me load this thing."

Jules struggled on the uneven rocks, her stride too short to make the gaps between the boulders. They weren't going to make it. The creature would overtake them. Kill them.

Taine used his strength to tow Jules with him, almost lifting her, the momentum carrying her across the cracks.

His mind raced for a way to drive it off. His men were doing their best, but the Steyrs were no better than pellet guns. Maybe the noise would turn it. And like a cricket ball to the leg, those bullets had to hurt, even if they couldn't penetrate.

Taine chanced a backward look. The Sphenodon was closing fast. It lowered his head, maw open, and hissed. The tongue lashed forward. Strings of drool dripped from between razored teeth. At that instant, a long narrow tube rolled in front of the animal's front talons.

Smoke grenade. Whoever lobbed it had good aim. Coolie probably. If they could only take advantage of it. He had five seconds at most. Facing the trees, Taine scanned the area in front of them, trying desperately to memorise the rocks that lay ahead. "Jules, don't let go of my hand," he said.

The smoke grenade exploded. Thick white smoke billowed outwards, stinking of burned propellant. Jules hadn't been expecting it.

"Taine!" she gasped.

"Just follow me."

But damned if the breeze wasn't blowing in their faces and, just moments later, the Sphenodon barrelled out of the mist, as if it were stepping from a steamy shower. Double-edged sword was right. The Sphenodon hardly slowed.

The eyes are sensitive. Go for the eyes.

The smoke dissipating, Taine pushed Jules ahead of him.

"Run!"

"But—"

"Just go!"

He concentrated for a few seconds on slowing his heartbeat. Twisted his torso. Fired.

Like a choreographed fight scene, the Sphenodon swerved. The bullet flew over the creature's head, barely grazing the spines.

Fuck.

It was still coming.

Taine spun on his heel and sprinted after Jules.

The sound of the Charlie G exploding warmed him, like the second shot of whisky at a New Year's party.

"It's a hit!" Read yelled, barely audible over the animal's bellow.

Finally reaching the trees, Taine turned, expecting to see the creature fall. Instead, it twisted its torso about, and Taine spied the bloody gouge in its flank. The wound was significant, the flesh seared like overdone sirloin. But it wasn't fatal.

Taine sagged with disappointment. There was nothing Trigger could've done. The creature was facing the other way, so he couldn't aim for its eyes and mouth. And with the remains of the smoke grenade drifting at him, it was a gutsy call. But the big soldier hadn't given up. The weapon already reloaded, he fired again, the forest reverberating with the blast. Another chunk of meat was torn from the animal, this time from its shoulder. Wild with fury, the Sphenodon swung its massive head from side to side, looking for the source of its pain.

Its gaze settled on de Haas.

The geologist was closest to the animal. He hadn't moved far from where they'd found him beside the stream.

"'De Haas!" Taine shouted. "For god's sake, man. Run!"

And de Haas did run, but *back* towards the monster.

He was going to retrieve the gun from the stream!

The Sphenodon hurtled towards de Haas, its head dropped like an armoured front-end loader.

The grenade launcher primed, Trigger waivered, his face wracked with indecision. If he shot for the creature's eyes, he might hit de Haas.

De Haas plunged into the stream. Knee deep in the water, he rummaged amongst the rocks.

Leave the gun, you fool!

It was as if de Haas could read Taine's mind because, contrary as ever, he raised the pistol, water dripping down his arms and, standing like a cowboy in the middle of the stream, squeezed the trigger. Unused to the recoil, the blast forced him to take a step back. Not a bad shot for a civilian, but the bullet missed the animal's eyes. Instead, it grazed its skull and went wide.

The Sphenodon tossed its head, its vicious crest of spines slicing through the air. It swung to face de Haas. He shot again. A hit this time, but to the animal's chest armour. The bullet bounced away. The Sphenodon threw back its head and bellowed.

Oh shit.

Enraged and gravely wounded, the animal descended on the geologist, its head lowered. At last, de Haas decided to run. He scrambled away, splashing, his thighs churning through the water. It was too late. The Sphenodon charged, running the geologist through. The spiny crest on its snout pierced the skin under the man's ribcage near his kidneys, continuing right through to exit his abdomen.

De Haas could only stare in shock, gaping at the projection emerging from his belly. Jules screamed for him as the creature threw its head back, carrying him into the air.

When the two gun blasts sounded, Jules had reached the treeline. She whipped around.

Gasped.

No!

The Sphenodon had speared de Haas, running him through like a samurai.

It lifted its snout in the air, de Haas pinioned on the spine. Bellowing, it flung him from side to side. De Haas grasped the spine in his hands, a macabre version of a rider on a mechanical bull. His face was a rictus of agony. Blood trickled from the spike.

"Taine, my God, he isn't dead!" Jules cried as the Sphenodon tossed de Haas, sending him flying twenty, thirty metres through the air towards her. There was a cruel thunk as he smashed against a nearby tree trunk. His head lolled, his back surely broken. He flopped to the ground.

Jules started forward, but Taine, reaching her side, hauled her back – the animal wasn't finished yet. In a bound, it was there, standing over its prey, slicing the body apart with its talons. Lazily, the way a cat sharpened its claws on the carpet.

Jules put her hand to her mouth to hold back her scream, almost fainting when the creature dipped a talon into de Haas' gut and ripped free a piece of intestine, throwing the viscera on the ground before scooping it up in its jaws.

Her breath came in short gasps.

No, no, no.

Read rushed in, yelling.

Taine leaped up, waving his rifle. "Read, no!" he shouted. The creature paused, intestine dangling from its jaw. Read jabbed at it with his rifle.

"Read, what the fuck? Get out of there!" Trigger yelped.

The Sphenodon hissed. Read jabbed at it again. He danced in and out, stabbing and feinting.

Oh my god. He's going to get himself killed.

The creature stepped over de Haas. It darted towards Read. Hooting, Read turned on his heel and ran. The Sphenodon gave chase. The rocket launcher on his shoulder, Trigger charged after it. Eriksen and Lefty followed suit.

With the animal gone, Jules burst from the thicket and ran to de Haas. He lay in the scrub, hardly more than a shredded bag of rags. Gently, she turned him over. He was unrecognisable. His face was pulped, a gore of blood and bone. A pink bubble formed where his mouth should have been. And yet his lungs were still working, their laboured sucking more than Jules could bear.

He's not dead. How can he not be dead?

Taine pulled her away. Jules clutched at him, grabbing his arm in both hands. A muscle in his jaw twitched. He raised his other hand, cocked his pistol, and shot de Haas in the head.

Jules closed her eyes. As the boom faded, Eriksen's voice carried through the trees.

"Go, go, go! It's coming back!"

It hasn't finished its meal.

Taine grabbed her by the hand, and they ran.

Hamish laughed wildly, dashing down the gully, slipping and skidding in the greasy clay. He scrambled over a tree trunk and slid down a bank into a ditch, dropping his gun. He got up, and was bending to retrieve his gun when someone called his name.

"Miller! Over here!"

"Who's that?"

"Up here. It's me, Jug."

Hamish swivelled. Jug was peering down at him from behind a clump of flax at the top of the gully. "Hey there Jug!" Hamish giggled. "What are you doing hiding up there?"

"Shhh!" Jug whispered, checking all around him. "The Sphenodon!"

"Yeah," Hamish said, scrambling back up the slope to Jug. "The Sphenodon. Did you see it kill de Haas?" He shook his head gravely. "That was bloody nasty. But it's okay because I'm going to get it – me and not Read, okay? – and when I do, they're going to give me a medal."

Jugs eyes narrowed. He took a step out of the flax. "Miller, are you okay?"

"Sure! I'm great." Hamish put his hand to his face, talking from behind it like he was sharing his secret. "I'm going to kill the monster before Read. Afterwards, they're going to give me a medal."

"What's this about Read?"

"Yeah, I don't mind telling you, Jug, because you're a friend, but Read, he's just a goodie good, isn't he? A goodie-goodie-good. Makes you sick. Everyone's darling. I used to tell him things, but now I don't. Except when they give me the medal. I'll tell him when they give me the medal."

"What medal is that, then?" said Jug, taking another step out of the clump of flax.

"The fucking medal from the fucking government, that's what!" He giggled again. "The word government is funny, don't you think? Govern-ment. Hear that? Govern-ment." He collapsed into laughter.

"Shhh, Hamish, not so loud." Reaching out a hand, Jug placed it firmly on Hamish's wrist. "You know, we should really hide," he said conspiratorially, but Hamish knew what he was up to. He was trying to do that doctor-thing and take his pulse. Fucking sneak.

Hamish snatched his hand away. "Don't touch me, you wanker. I didn't give you permission to do experiments on me. And don't tell me what to do either."

"Hamish, what have you taken? Was it a pill? Did you smoke something?"

"Me? No. I'm fine. I'm great. But I have to go and look for

that Sphenodon. Otherwise, they're going to give the medal to Read. I can't wait to see the look on my parents' faces when I get that medal."

"Hamish, it's too risky. I really think we should hide," Jug said carefully.

Hamish sniggered. *Jug's such a scaredy cat.* Hamish wasn't afraid of the Sphenodon. There was no need to be afraid if you were the one attacking. That's why they were in this mess. McKenna'd been *reacting*. He was a decent guy and all that, but he wasn't proactive, was he? Reacting when he should have been attacking. Everyone knew the best form of defence was attack. Even the Sphenodon knew it – attacking them all the time.

Jug's voice came to Hamish, telling him they'd better keep quiet and hide, but he just didn't get it, did he? If you were going to win a battle and get yourself a medal, then you couldn't be hiding out in a hidey-hole. And since no one else understood that, he'd have to do it. But that was okay, because he'd never felt so alive. He was totally pumped.

"Jug," he said, pushing Jug back into the bush. "You stay here. I'm going to find the Sphenodon. I'll come back for you when I've killed it."

Turning, Hamish skidded down the gully, gripping his gun as he slid, so he didn't lose it a second time.

Jug shouted from up the top.

Hamish swivelled.

What? The Sphenodon? Up there with Jug? He scrambled back up the bank, feet slipping in the clay, his eyes blurring with sweat, and stood panting at the top. The flax moved, the grey-green spears fluttering. That Sphenodon was a canny bastard. It was in there with Jug. Hamish was sure of it. He could see the swish of the tail, the crest of spines visible over the top of the flax. He lifted the Steyr, painting the target with the IRAD on the side of the rifle.

"No!" Jug said, and Hamish glimpsed his face etched with worry.

"Don't worry, Jug. I'm going to save you," he whispered.

Read or Trigger, they wouldn't dare take this shot. They'd be worried about hitting Jug. But Hamish backed himself. In situations like these, you had to have confidence. If you faltered, you failed. He checked the sight. Breathed deeply.

"No!" Jug yelled.

Hamish would have liked a clearer shot, but there was no time. The monster was going to kill Jug.

He fired.

Jug dived out of the flax, a burst of pain exploding at his side. He cried out, his arms wind-milling, and tumbled down the gully. Coming down heavily, his leg twisted beneath him.

Jug shrieked.

The pain was raw, threatening to overwhelm him. He fought to draw breath, gripped at the earth, his knuckles taut. Forced himself to breathe deeply. Again. His head spun. Another breath. Jug patted his side. His hand came away wet. The bullet had grazed his side just under his ribs. Miller had shot him! Fired on him. Jug patted again, finding the edges of the wound. It hurt to breathe, but it wasn't deep, thank God. Miller had been too high to aim straight and Jug, forewarned, had leapt a split second before he'd fired. That split second may have saved his life.

For now.

A wave of pain made him draw in a shallow breath. Jug waited for it to pass, then looked down the length of his body, seeing the gleam of white bone against his ebony skin. His lower leg was twisted at an odd angle. His tibia, fractured. Jug broke into a cold sweat. Shivered. Not that. Not out here. He wouldn't be able to walk, let alone run.

He tried to sit up to examine his leg, but he didn't even get his elbow under him before the pain beat him back. His medical bag! It was at the top of the gully. As he took in the ramifications, his body started to shake uncontrollably. Shock.

Then he heard that tell-tale hiss as the ground beneath him trembled.

Jug fainted.

They gathered back by the stream. It was logical. It was what parents always told their children: 'Stay where you are, don't wander off, or you'll end up even more lost.'

Taine watched as Richard Foster crept out of the trees to stand beside Jules. Taine hoped the idiot realised what he'd done. He'd only gone and got de Haas killed with his stupid scheme to save the Sphenodon. Taine hadn't liked the man, but it didn't mean he deserved to die. And not like that.

Turning away, Taine spied de Haas' geologist's pick lodged in the stream. He scooped it up and shook it off, fastening it on his pack.

"So, are we all here?" he asked.

He scanned their faces: Read, Miller, Eriksen, Lefty… Jug and Coolie weren't back yet.

Taine shivered. "Anyone seen Jug or Coolie?"

"Last I saw of Coolie he was on the trail just before we found the scientists," said Eriksen. Richard dropped his head, his hair flopping forward to hide his face.

"When exactly?"

"He was just behind me at the campsite."

"Anyone see Coolie at the stream?" Taine demanded. No one replied. Catching Taine's eye, Trigger shook his head.

No. Not Coolie too. Taine bunched his fists. "What about Jug? Anyone see what happened to him?"

"He was at the stream. I saw him jump out of the way when the Sphenodon came charging through the trees," Lefty said, pointing towards the treeline. "He ducked behind that log."

"Well, he's not there now, is he?" Eriksen whispered.

There was a hush. Jules' forehead creased, her breath catching. "Poor Jug," she murmured sadly.

"Coolie's a good soldier. He knows how to look after himself. If he's out there, he'll find us," Trigger said encouragingly. "Could be he's just being cautious."

Taine acknowledged the comment with a curt nod, although they both knew Coolie's chances were crap. Together they'd faced some ruthless enemies, but nothing like this. Silent and stealthy, the Sphenodon was like a sniper, biding its time, waiting for them to be exposed, and then picking them off.

"Jug could be fine, too. Doctors are smart. He's probably holed up somewhere safe. Maybe even with Coolie," Read suggested.

"Yeah, could be," said Trigger, putting his hand on Read's shoulder. Miller kicked at a stone.

Taine wanted to stalk over and punch Richard Foster into next week. That selfish piece of work had just got three men killed. Three! Including two of the finest soldiers he'd had the privilege of serving with. There was no time for grieving. For Jug or for Coolie. No time for Taine to mourn the loss of his friend. Standing smack in the middle of the creature's hunting grounds, they were on the back foot, and the Sphenodon knew it. Taine had to get these people the hell out of here.

Swallowing hard, he faced the group. "Okay, this looks like all of us for the moment," he said. "We're not getting out of the forest tonight, so we're going to need a bolt hole to spend the night. Somewhere safe, or at least easy to defend. Nathan? Any ideas?"

The guide rubbed his chin. "There are caves."

"Nearby?"

Nathan nodded.

"Can you find us one? One big enough for all of us?"

A pause.

"Nathan, it'll be dark in a couple of hours, maybe less. We need a trench to hunker down in. Can you help us?"

"Yes."

"Good. Read, I don't want to see any more heroics, and that goes for all of you. Trigger, if you get a sight on that monster's eye, shoot the goddamned thing."

Richard Foster opened his mouth to protest, but Taine cut him off. "And Trigger?"

"Yes, Boss?"

"If Dr Foster gets in the way this time, you have my permission to shoot him."

Foster paled.

"Everyone stay close. Let's move."

Chapter 24

Jules slipped sideways on the soft ground, but Taine grasped her upper arm and hauled her back to her feet. The tread of her boots was clogged with slippery clay and almost instantly she tripped again, this time on a darkened log.

The log moaned.

Jules jumped, startled. "Wait! I heard something," she said, pulling out of Taine's grasp. Crouching, she shoved a large fern frond out of the way. A man's gold watch glinted in the dim light.

Jules' hope surged. "It's Jug! Taine, I've found Jug."

"What? Let me see."

Quickly tucking the fern leaf behind its neighbour, Jules stepped aside to let him through.

"Jug, can you hear me, mate?" Taine put his gun down and leaned in to palpate Jug's neck.

Jules sucked in a breath. "Is he alive?"

He nodded grimly.

"Thank goodness—"

"He's going to wish he wasn't, though," Taine muttered. He stood, and it was only now, seeing Jug lying flat out, that she spied the tattered state of his clothes, the angry slice of bone jutting from his leg, and a wound the size of a saucer in his side. She covered her mouth with her hand.

"Read, Eriksen, Miller, set up a perimeter. Nathan, Lefty, we're going to need a stretcher. Use whatever you can find. Branches, shirts, whatever. Foster, see if you can help them." He crouched beside Jug, then obviously thought the better of it, standing and turning again. "Miller, before you go…" he said.

"What?" The young soldier seemed dazed.

"Give me your bandage, will you?"

"What?"

"Your bandage! The one in your pocket."

Jules felt a jab of sympathy for him. Barely out of school uniform and faced with all this. Taine clearly understood his hesitation, because he tore open the Velcro of his own pocket and removed the dressing so Miller could see, his actions slow and deliberate. He ripped the wrapping apart with his teeth and packed the gauze gently around the crag of bone protruding from Jug's leg, holding it in place with one hand. Flustered, Miller fumbled with his pocket, finally managing to hand Taine a second dressing.

"Open it," Taine said patiently. "And cut me down that branch too, will you? We're going to need to immobilise his leg."

Miller fought with the wrapper.

"Here, why don't you give me the bandage?" Jules said gently, putting a hand out to him. "I can do that. You get the branch." Her fingertips brushed his as she took the dressing. Miller jumped.

Jules looked to Taine.

"That branch," he said, not moving his hands from the wound. He nodded at a flattish branch without too many burrs.

"This one, Hamish," Jules said, stepping over and placing a hand on the branch. With shaky hands, Miller pulled out a knife and began to hack at it, but Taine changed his mind.

"No, that one won't work. Maybe that one over to your right? Yes, that one looks more solid. And when you're done, pass me your spare socks. I'll need to pad the splint. Jug's going to be in enough pain as it is."

While Miller cut the splint, Jules pulled one of her own t-shirts out of her pack to cover the wound at Jug's side. Oozing and blackened, there didn't seem to be much blood.

"This looks like a burn," she said to Taine.

Taine nodded. "His gun must have gone off in the fall. He's lucky it's just a graze. It's a miracle he didn't kill himself."

Moments later, standing alongside them, his fingers gripping the splint, Miller looked as grey as Jug.

"You feeling okay, Hamish?" Jules asked.

"Just worried about Jug."

"He'll live. It's not as bad as it looks," Taine said. "Is that the splint?"

"Hang on," Jules said, taking the branch from Miller. She broke off the protruding twigs before handing it to Taine, who laid it lengthwise alongside Jug's injured leg. Then, taking care not to bump him, Taine lifted Jug's good leg close to the injured one, and slipped the bandage under the gap in the doctor's knees.

"Your spare socks, Miller?"

"Oh yeah. Sorry."

Hamish rummaged in his pack, eventually producing a pair, which Taine used to pack around the splint. Then he tied the bandage off against the splint.

"A couple more – below the break, and at his ankles – should keep it still. Jules, can you see if you can locate Jug's pack anywhere? Don't go too far, just see if it's somewhere nearby."

"Right." Jules dropped to her hands and knees to search for Jug's pack. She scrambled around in the undergrowth, lifting ferns and branches and sweeping her hands underneath in case the pack had rolled when Jug fell.

"How's that stretcher coming?" Taine said, glancing down the track.

"Nearly done, Boss," Lefty called back.

"Jules? Anything?" Jules could hear the hope in his voice. Perhaps he'd hoped she'd find Coolie lying in the ferns, too.

"No, not here. He must have dropped it earlier. I can't see his rifle, either."

"The rifle we can do without, but I would've liked to have had his pack. Right now, he's slipping in and out of consciousness, but when he wakes up properly he's going to know all about it. I was hoping to give him something for the pain."

"I have some Paracetamol," Jules said. She got to her feet. Straight away, she felt stupid. The poor man had a bone sticking out of his leg. Fat lot of good Paracetamol would do.

But Taine disagreed. "Anything that could take the edge off

his pain is good. I've immobilised it as best I can, but it's going to be a rough trip. We'll need to keep him quiet…"

He didn't need to tell her why. Slipping a hand into her pants' pockets, Jules pulled out a silver strip of capsules.

"I'll crush a couple, see if I can get him to take them with some water when he comes to," she said.

Taine's smile was grim. "That'd be great."

Lefty and Nathan brought the stretcher over and lay it alongside the medic.

"Miller, come and lend a hand. We're going to need the four of us on either side of him. Grip him by his clothes if you can, and try to keep your movements smooth. Jules, if you could support his head. On three. One, two, three."

Together, they lifted the medic onto the stretcher.

Lefty's hands burned. A deep ache had set in across his shoulders and his forearms were pumped, the veins raised. Singh wasn't a big bloke either, although the guy's leg was fat enough now. The swelling had blown it up something ugly. Lefty shifted the weight of the stretcher in his palms. It was a small movement, but it made Singh groan. The sudden jolts of the last half hour must have been killing him.

Poor bastard.

At last, McKenna called a break, leaving Trigger, Read and Miller on guard, while he and Nathan scouted out a cave. Lefty and Eriksen put the stretcher down where they were. Lefty flexed his fingers, relaxing his cramped palms. Eriksen paused to check on the medic, although there wasn't much they could do for him. They sat down beside the stretcher. Lefty took his water bottle from his pack, chugging down a few mouthfuls before offering it to Eriksen.

"Thanks." Eriksen drank deeply then screwed the lid back on the bottle. "You holding up?" he said quietly.

"Yeah."

"Shitty day."

"Yeah."

"Scared?"

Lefty paused. "A bit. Who wouldn't be? You have to clock one up for the animal kingdom though, don't you? That Sphenodon is more cunning than a weasel, going around our little herd, carving off the weak and picking us off one by one. Sooner or later, you've gotta think it's going to get around to you."

"I'm trying not to think about it."

"Yeah, probably the best policy," Lefty said. He reached out and snapped a small twig off a nearby mānukā, nervously stripping the bark off the smooth wood inside. "Look, about Sheryl, I'm sorry I went off my head the other day."

Eriksen said, "It's not mine."

Lefty suppressed a wave of anger. Did he really want to start a fight now, while he was in the middle of apologising? There might not be time for apologising after. The way this fucking trip was panning out, there'd be a good chance neither of them would make it out alive.

He did his best to keep his voice even. "Yeah, you already said. But Sheryl thinks it is."

"It's not."

"So that's it? She says it is and you say it isn't and that's the end of it? Come on Adrian, there's a kid's life at stake here."

"So? I've already got two kids. Sheryl knew I wasn't looking to have any more. My divorce from Carla only came through two months ago."

Lefty shook his head. "How many kids you've got doesn't change anything. If you didn't want another one, you should've worn a rubber."

"You think I don't know that?" Eriksen took another drink.

"Look, I know my sister. She likes her fun, but she's not a liar."

Singh moaned softly from the stretcher. Lefty and Eriksen looked in his direction, but after a second the medic fell quiet again.

Lefty continued to mutilate the stick, peeling back the layers of wood until a tiny pile of bark scrapings formed between his legs. "There're some things you should know about Sheryl."

"I don't want to hear—"

"Come on, Adrian. Just hear me out okay? I might not get another chance."

Eriksen sniffed then nodded for Lefty to go on.

"Sheryl's old man wasn't decent like mine. Shot through when she was only five. Then, years later, he went to court, rewrote history and got visitation. Those weekends, I used to hear Sheryl crying when she got home. She'd get into bed and hide her face under the covers, but I knew. Hank – that's her dad – he's the sort who gets off on running women down. Used to tell Sheryl she was useless at everything. They'd go to McDonalds and he'd tell her she was getting fat. She'd write him a story and he'd say it was dumb. Then, later on, Hank hooked up with someone else, had some other kids, and it got worse. Those kids were princesses compared to Sheryl, who was too fat, too dumb, too ugly, too useless – whatever."

"You trying to make me feel sorry for her?"

"No!" Lefty snapped. He paused a second, inhaling deep to calm himself. "I want you to understand why my sister is the way she is. Sure, she's flirtatious – yeah okay, I know what they call her behind my back – but I reckon all she's ever wanted is someone to tell her she's all right, you know? Make her feel special." Lefty sighed. Talking about his sister had made him feel as worn and calloused as his palms.

Eriksen didn't reply, just sat there, turning the water bottle in his hands. Read signalled to say they were on the move again and they got to their feet.

Eriksen passed Lefty back his bottle. "Tell Sheryl I'll do the test. If the baby's mine, I'll see her right financially," he said.

"That's great. Thanks man."

"But that's it, okay? I don't want to marry her."

Lefty's mouth twitched. "Well, that's good because you're not my first choice for brother-in-law."

Taine pushed his night vision glasses to the top of his head and wiped his forehead with his palm. His head was pounding, and he massaged his temple with his fingers.

Foster stepped past him, pushing deeper into the cave. Miller did the same.

"We all in?"

"All in, Boss," Trigger replied, the last of the group to squeeze through the narrow gap.

They were lucky to find it. Nathan had nearly missed the cave. A recent rock fall had blocked part of the entrance, mud and stones making it even narrower than the guide remembered. It had been barely wide enough for Lefty and Eriksen to squeeze the stretcher through, their knuckles scraping against the rock as they stepped over the tumble of debris to descend into the cool of the cave.

Too narrow for a certain Sphenodon, which makes it perfect for us.

"Jules, you can take those off now," Taine said, gesturing to her night vision glasses. She'd been wearing Jug's pair. Too big for her, they made her look like a little insect. Taine was almost sorry when she pushed them up on the top of her head.

Trigger and Miller used the lights on their picatinny rails to illuminate the cave. In spite of its less than impressive entrance, the inside was grand. A vaulted cavern, the ground sloped upwards on one side and tapered into a ledge. On the low side, a stream flowed from one end of the cave to another, entering and exiting at each end through holes in the wall.

Lefty and Eriksen sat down where they were. Lefty threw his head back, and puffed out hard, his shoulders drooping. Eriksen dropped a hand on his back.

"It's like a cathedral in here," Read said, walking deeper into the cavern.

"Say some bloody prayers then," someone muttered, Taine wasn't sure who. Trigger maybe. Truth be told, a few prayers wouldn't hurt. Taine sent one up to the gods for Coolie as he stepped across the cave to talk to Nathan.

Seated on the sloping rock with his knees up, the guide had dropped his head into his hands. He breathed in and out, each intake slow and deliberate.

"Nathan, you okay?"

"Yeah, yeah, I'm good. Just not too keen on caves. Bit claustrophobic. I prefer to see the stars."

"Maybe not tonight, though?"

"No, maybe not tonight."

They were quiet for a moment, Taine watching while Jules bent over Jug, wrapping more clothing around his shoulders and murmuring softly, as if she were tucking a child into bed.

"Anything I can do to help?"

Straightening, Nathan flared his nostrils and sniffed in. He clapped his hands on his knees. "No, that's okay. I'll be fine," he said. "Just as soon as I get myself a beer from the bar."

Taine grinned. "Getting something inside you might help," he agreed. "We're all a bit low on reserves. I'm not sure about beer, but the staff here might be able to brew us up a mug of tea. Do you know if the stream water's safe to drink?"

"I've only been here once before, and I didn't hang around, but as far as I know the water's safe – only, be careful, because away from the banks, it could be deep. And we need to keep an eye out on the weather. A flash flood could trap us in here."

Taine glanced up at the entrance; a light grey stripe overhead. "It never rains, it pours, huh?" he quipped.

"Something like that," Nathan said wryly.

Belmont, Wellington City

In his plaid dressing gown, James Arnold sat on the sofa in the dark, nursing a cold cup of tea and looking out over Wellington Harbour. There were one or two boats on the water, over Eastbourne way, and to his right, lights in the capital's CBD winked on and off. The Hutt motorway was lit up like a glow-stick.

INTO THE MIST

A wet nose and a nudge.

Placing his cup on the side table, James lifted the animal, plopping it gently on his lap. "Here we are again, Puss," James whispered. "Two of us who can't sleep."

The old girl turned a few times, her paws poking imprints on his thighs, until eventually she found a position she was satisfied with and settled down. She purred loudly, the vibrations rumbling against James' stomach.

There'd been no further news of McKenna and his men, or of Kevin's section sent out earlier. There'd been a problem with the radio. Some damage. The corporal had mentioned it the last time he'd called in. And since then, there'd been no word, so the comms must have given up the ghost. Of course, there was no mobile phone coverage in there. GPS wasn't much chop either. State-of-the-art technology and it couldn't see past a few trees.

They'd be fine, James told himself. They were big boys, and McKenna knew what he was about. Odds were, he'd walk them out of the forest in a few days and everyone would take a collective sigh and wonder what the fuss was about.

Except, something very strange is going on in that forest.

The cat shifted her weight in his lap, kneading her paws on his thigh before settling again.

If there was no news from McKenna in the next 48 hours James would have to call it in, higher up the line. And then there was his sister-in-law. That was a call he wasn't looking forward to. At the moment, she thought her grandson was peacekeeping on a Pacific island, giving out school books, installing public taps and whitewashing fences. That was Noeline for you. What exactly did she think they issued the guns for? No point in worrying her just yet. McKenna could turn up something. Still, it might be wise for him to drive back to Waiouru and wait for news. He might as well wait there as anywhere. Gently, James lifted the cat off his lap and onto the sofa.

He'd get dressed now. Hell, he was practically up already.

Taine and Nathan slipped out of the cave and returned with armfuls of firewood. With the fire going, the group prepared the first hot meal they'd had in two days. They said an army marched on its belly; Taine was pretty sure it applied to morale as well. Only Miller wasn't eating – not hungry he said – but they'd all seen what happened to de Haas, and then coming across Jug like that... well, people reacted differently to trauma, and the soldier had been pretty upset. Taine made a note to keep an eye on him. At least Read seemed to be holding up okay.

"It's not exactly Mum's cooking, but I never knew camp food could taste so good," Read said, between mouthfuls. "I was starving."

"You have to be starving to eat my mum's cooking," Lefty said. "The woman can burn water."

Grinning, Taine offered Jug a second mug of tea. "How are you doing?" he asked.

Jug winced. "Not so good."

Taine turned to Jules. "Jules?"

She patted Jug gently on the arm. "I haven't got any painkillers left," she said apologetically.

Jug paled. "It's okay. I'll be fine. I'll sleep in a bit. The pain will ease off."

Hearing that, Nathan got up and walked across to the pile of firewood. He searched through the logs and branches and pulled out a branch of mānuka. Stripping the bark off the branches, he put some in a billy with water, and boiled it over the coals of the fire. When it was well steeped, he poured some of the mixture into a cup, and the rest into an empty water container.

He handed the cup to Jules. "Hold this for a second, will you?" he said. He gestured to Miller to help him prop Jug up. The gunshot wound must've hurt like hell because Jug flinched before they even touched him, looking up with alarm at Miller when the soldier approached him on his wounded side.

"Take it easy, guys," Taine said.

They shifted him gently, Nathan using his own pack to support the medic's back. That done, he took the mug from

Jules, and handed it to Jug. "Old Māori recipe," he stated. "Tastes awful, but it'll help with the pain."

"Thanks," Jug said, grimacing. Even holding the cup looked painful. He took a sip of Nathan's home brew. "Gawd that *is* awful," he said.

"Well, let's hope it's enough to dampen the pain," Taine said, standing. He made his way to the stream to rinse his plate. Nathan was right, this stream was deep. Taine walked the length of the cave and put his hand on the cave wall, stooping to check out the tunnel where the stream exited the cave. There was a gap of about a foot between the tunnel ceiling and the stream gurgling and bubbling its way into the darkness. The area was probably riddled with streams like these, miles of them crisscrossing under the ground.

"Boss, Read's found something." Eriksen interrupted his exploring. Taine almost hit his head on the roof of the tunnel.

"What is it?"

"Over here."

Taine followed Eriksen to where the others had congregated not far from the cave's entrance. Read shone his torch at the wall, illuminating two ovoid shapes poking from the rock. Eggs. From the looks of it, they were uncovered recently, possibly in the landslip that had caused the blockage at the cave entrance.

The sight of them filled Taine with dread. "Sphenodon eggs?" he asked.

Foster laughed derisively.

Jules flicked him a stern look. "No, I think these are more likely to be fossilised moa eggs," she replied.

"Well, that's a bloody relief," Lefty says. "One Sphenodon is enough."

Foster snorted.

Jules cocked her head to one side as she considered the fossils.

"Jules?"

"Nothing really. I was just thinking. Moa only laid one or two eggs, like these ones here, but tuatara lay lots of eggs, sometimes as many as ten. From an evolutionary stand-point it makes sense. Plenty of animals enjoy an egg for breakfast, so laying more eggs means a greater probability of one of your offspring making it to maturity."

"Could there be more?" Taine asked.

She shook her head. "No. Richard and I discussed it. We think it's unlikely."

Read lowered his torch and the party moved back towards the fire. They sat on the rocks scattered about it. Taking a seat near Jug, Taine took out his carving and began to whittle. The general shape complete, he began to decorate the piece with sweeping whorls and bold fluid lines. He carved without thinking, almost by instinct, taking pleasure in the solid feel of the wood, its resin smell and its warmth.

Lefty took up the conversation where it left off. "Well, what if the Sphenodon's female? Could it lay eggs?"

"I can't say if it's female or not," Jules replied. "Most tuatara reproduce sexually, and for that there would need to be two. I think this one's a juvenile."

"That monster's a *baby?*" Eriksen said. "It could get bigger?" He shook his head and murmured "Fuck me" under his breath.

"It's got good skills for a baby," said Lefty.

Taine had to agree. "How can you tell it's a juvenile?" he said, as he chiselled a curve in the wood.

"A few things; like the fact that it hunts during the day. And earlier... when I was close to it..." She gave a little shiver. "...I noticed a parietal eye, or third eye, in the centre of its forehead. When the tuatara reaches maturity that third eye gets encrusted with a horny plate, like a scab, but our creature's eye is still visible."

Taine remembered that eye. It was the first thing he'd noticed when the creature had appeared out of the mist.

Leaned up against his pack, Read said, "When I was nine my mother got us a kitten from the SPCA. Sampson we called it."

"What's that got to do with the price of fish?" Eriksen said.

"Yeah, is there a point to this story, Read?" said Trigger.

"Every day Sampson used to drag in a bird or a mouse and drop it on the mat by the kitchen door. My mother wasn't that impressed with the mice, but she thought it was cute, the kitten wanting to give us a present. The bird would always be missing a wing or, if it was a mouse, the head would be gone. Once, he brought in a rabbit. It was almost as big as he was. Sampson had bitten its leg off. Left a trail of blood on the back step. One day, Sampson took off. My brother reckoned he saw the cat sitting on the neighbour's fence licking his paws once, but that was the last time any of us saw him. He never came back home. He was already the best hunter in the neighbourhood, he didn't need us feeding him Whiskas."

"So, what's your point? That if we stop feeding it, it'll move on somewhere else?" Trigger said.

"No, that's not what he means," Taine replied. "Read's saying the Sphenodon is behaving like his kitten. Every time we come up against it, it's learning more about us. It's learning to hunt us…"

"Dr Asher?" Nathan asked, his voice quiet.

Jules looked up wearily. "Yes?"

"That third eye? It's not an ordinary eye, right?"

"No. We just call it that because of its location. And because of the way it looks."

"So, if it's not really an eye, what's it for?"

"We don't actually know. Some scientists think it's for testing the temperature of the air, to sense fluctuations which would indicate a change in season."

There was a sudden stillness, as if all the oxygen had been sucked out of the cave.

Eriksen gave a low whistle.

"Shit," said Lefty.

"What is it?" asked Jules.

Taine fingers tightened on his penknife. He glanced at the top of her head, where Jug's Mini N/SEAS goggles rested. "Our Sampson has his own night vision glasses."

Beside Jules, on his stretcher, Jug shifted slightly. The poor man had finally nodded off, Nathan's home-made analgesic doing the trick. Jules was exhausted too, but today's nightmare kept repeating in her head. Looked like she wasn't the only one. Miller, sitting upright, his back supported by his pack, was staring at his hands in his lap and mumbling to himself.

Over by the fire, Taine was also awake, whittling.

Sighing, Jules got up and, wrapping her sleeping bag around her, went to join him.

"You should be sleeping," he said as she approached.

"So should you."

"I'll wake Trigger in a bit."

They sat listening to the fire crackle, Taine passing the time with his carving and Jules watching the coals glow.

"What's that you're making?"

Taine turned the little carving in his hands. "You know, I'm not sure I'm making it. It seems to be making itself. It's a pūrerehua. A Māori wind instrument. You swing it around your head, and it conjures up the sound of the wind. Some people call it a bullroarer. Here, I'll show you."

He went to the pile of firewood and searched through it, pulling out a long strand of flax. Tearing off a thin strip, he attached the fibres to one end of the lozenge-shaped instrument, then moving into a clear space, he spun the instrument around his head like a hammer thrower in warm up.

It was the oddest sound, white noise, like the drone of a plane. The men shifted in their sleep.

Taine slowed the instrument. When the bullroarer had stopped oscillating, he wound the flax cord around it and slipped it into his pocket. "I guess it's not everybody's cup of tea," he said, taking his seat again.

She gave him a small smile, her voice dropping to a whisper. "Taine, what happens next? Are we going to be able to get Jug out?"

He turned to her, his eyes reflecting the amber glow of the fire. "I'm going to do everything I can to keep us all safe."

She smiled at him again. "I know that. I saw what you did for Jug." She glanced at the medic, sleeping quietly for the moment.

Taine grunted. "What I did for Jug was some basic first aid. It's part of our training."

"Whereas Sphenodon 101 is not?"

His smile was short. "Something like that. There's no textbook for dealing with this kind of enemy."

Jules paused. "There could be quite a lot of information actually."

"You mean science?"

"No, I'm talking about oral histories of lizard-like creatures living in New Zealand."

"Legends?"

Jules shrugged. "Maybe they're not just legends. If you asked me a week ago if a giant tuatara was skulking about in the Ureweras I would've said you were dreaming."

Taine chuckled softly. "Okay, I'll give you that. Any particular oral history?"

"Captain Cook wrote a paper about a Māori who'd befriended him – a man who warned him that the land was inhabited by enormous lizards that captured and ate men. He drew Cook a picture."

"I thought you said the Sphenodon isn't a lizard."

"But Cook wouldn't have known that. If an indigenous man draws a thing he calls a taniwha, Cook's going to call it a lizard because that's what he sees. It's Cook's interpretation. So from the earliest contact between European and Māori, we have this reference to a giant lizard from a respected scholar."

Taine frowned, taking in what Jules has said. "How does that help us? What if the Māori made it up to scare the Europeans off? Just say you were that chief and, out of the blue, a ship turns up and parks itself offshore alongside your village. The ship is bigger than anything you've ever seen. Taller than a rimu, it's like a mountain floating on the horizon and it can carry an entire village of pale-skinned people on its deck. The chief knows he hasn't got a hope against an enemy like that, so he sends in a messenger, someone to befriend the enemy and warn him about the terrifying monsters that roam the land devouring men. I'd say that's a good way to get rid of the invaders without having to throw a single spear."

"Maybe. Except in Cook's journals, the messenger also told him how to kill the taniwha. Why would he do that if he meant to scare the pākehā off—"

Taine placed his hand on her arm, stopping her from talking. "Can you hear hissing?"

"The stream?" she whispered.

"I don't think so."

He slipped his rifle on over his head. "Jules, wake everyone up."

As she hurried to wake the others, the Sphenodon's eye loomed in the fissure. Jules swallowed hard as its gaze followed her across the cave.

CHAPTER 25

Taine ran to the cave entrance. The Sphenodon glared through the gap. It spied him and hissed. Using its powerful forelegs, it dragged a large boulder away from the entrance and extended a horny talon into the cave, swiping at Taine.

Trigger came at a run, the Charlie G grenade launcher already hoisted onto his shoulder. Taine showed him the flat of his hand.

"No, we can't risk it. It's too much firepower."

"What are you talking about?" Trigger said. "It hardly bruised the bastard last time."

"It'll blast the edges of the cave entrance away, letting him in sooner."

"Oh shit," Trigger said, his face falling. "What about the rifles?" he suggested. "We're close enough, we could take out its eyes, like you said."

"Too close. The rounds could ricochet off the walls and kill one of us."

"Fuck! First we're not close enough, now we're fucking too close?" Trigger mumbled.

"What about fire?" Read said. "It worked that first time." Before Taine could respond, Read ran back to the fire and returned with a glowing log. Holding it in both hands, he stabbed it at the entrance.

"Hey Sampson," he taunted, jabbing the fire into the gap. "Remember this?"

Sampson moved away, but in seconds he was back, raking a taloned foreleg into the space again, scrabbling at the rocks either side of the entrance, and brushing aside a large boulder on the inside of the cave. Read jumped out of the way as Sampson leaned in as far as he could, trying to hook him with a talon. The edges of the fissure crumbled under its weight, stones and debris tumbling into the cavern, the two ovoid eggs included.

Still, Read waved the fire in front of its face and made the animal hesitate. It wasn't much, but it might hold it until they could think of something else. Taine darted deeper into the cave and scooped up the rest of the firewood, bringing the bundle back and tossing it down in a heap as close to the entrance as he dared.

Sampson was throwing himself at the gap, which was now significantly wider.

"It's working. He's going to get through," Read observed, flatly.

"Give me the torch," Taine said.

Read handed it over and Taine thrust it into the pile of wood. The burning embers smouldered a second before catching, causing the tiny twigs in the pile to glow red and blacken before the thicker branches did the same.

"Think it will hold him?" Trigger asked.

Taine shook his head. "Not for long."

"But how are we—?" Read started.

"Back of the cave, now," Taine ordered.

All three of them turned and ran.

Taine headed for the stream, pulling his rifle off while he ran. Detaching the light from the picatinny rail of his Steyr, he held it in his palm, diving into the icy stream and coming back up, water streaming off his face.

Shit, that's cold!

Treading water, his hand pressed on the rock ceiling, he entered the tunnel, allowing the current to carry him.

Nathan poked his head into the tunnel. "McKenna," Nathan shouted over the chatter of the stream. "What do you think you're doing? This tunnel could lead anywhere!"

Taine looked back; Jules and Trigger had joined the guide at the tunnel entrance.

"So long as it's anywhere but here," he replied, wryly. "I'll only be a minute," he quipped, and seeing the panic on Jules' face, gave her a quick wink.

Turning, Taine continued until he ran out of head space, then he took a deep breath to fill his lungs and dived, kicking out hard. He swam downwards, counting in his head: *One Whakatane, Two Whakatane, Three Whakatane…*, a hand brushing the wall to orient himself. The underground canyon was convoluted, but smooth, the walls' rough edges worn away by centuries of water flowing over them. Abruptly, the tunnel narrowed. Taine forced himself to stay calm. If it got too narrow, he wouldn't be able to turn around. But if he couldn't find an egress in a hurry, they'd all be stuck. This was the only way. Except it wasn't. Taine had come to a fork in the tunnel, the stream splitting two ways. *Which way? Left or Right?* Right, he decided, and he hoped his intuition was good. The decision made, he kicked forward, blowing out slowly, expelling the carbon dioxide from his lungs in a gradual stream of tiny bubbles. *Thirty-two Whakatane…*

Time's up. He had to go back now. He couldn't afford any more precious seconds; swimming upstream was going to take him longer. But what was that up ahead? A light? He turned off the torch. *Thirty-eight Whakatane…* It could be light. Faint and still a few metres off. He turned the torch on again. Should he push forward or go back? His lungs screamed at him to go back, but the stream's current encouraged him to go on. He thought of Jules and the others, waiting back at the other end of the tunnel.

If you're wrong, it'll be the last time.

Kicking his feet hard, Taine pushed forward.

Jules stood in the freezing water, vaguely aware that Read was dashing about the cavern searching for another way out. It didn't matter. Even if he found one, they couldn't go without Taine. The water swirling at her waist, she stared into the tunnel.

"Come on, man!" Trigger whispered beside her.

"Trigger, it's been longer than a minute." Jules was surprised at her own voice. Surely she couldn't sound that calm.

"I know," Trigger said. "But it's McKenna. We'll give him a bit longer."

Read came back.

"Anything?" Nathan asked him.

"No."

Jules' shoulders sagged. Even Read had lost his enthusiasm. She stared into the tunnel, as if staring would bring him back, watching the water bubble as it disappeared into nothingness. She held her breath. Let it out. Held it again. It'd been too long. No one could survive being under water for that long.

"It's McKenna," Trigger said again, as if daring her to say otherwise.

Taine exploded from the water, sucking in huge lungsful of air. Already in the stream, Trigger took two strides forward and yanked him upwards, helping him to find his feet.

"Jesus, man, you gave us a scare."

"Trigger, there's another cave, a beach," Taine gasped, his chest heaving. He inhaled deeply again, pushing back his shoulders to fill his lungs. "Forty-two seconds with the current! It's a push, but we can make it."

From the front of the cave came the rumble of Sampson bringing down another rock. The dust rose and the crash of falling debris reverberated around the cavern, persistent and chilling, like a requiem mass. They paused to listen a moment. Taine waded out of the stream. "Take only what you can't do without," he called to the group. "Keep it light. Anything bulky, leave behind. We can't risk blocking the channel."

Richard waded into the water, making for the tunnel entrance. He put his beanie on, pulled it down over his hair, took a deep breath and approached the shaft.

"Foster!" Richard looked up. "There's a fork," Taine said. "Take the right-hand entrance. And be careful because the current will pull you to the left. I don't know where that goes."

Richard nodded briefly before disappearing. He didn't look back. Taking care of himself. They said people showed their true colours in a crisis. It occurred to Jules the only colours Richard had ever waved were his own.

"Nathan, will you be okay?" Taine asked.

The guide's arms were wrapped about his body. He glanced towards the front of the cave. "I'll manage," he said. He waded in, Miller following him.

"Read!" shouted Taine.

"Yep, coming, Boss!"

Jules turned to see who was left.

Jug.

The medic was clutching the sides of the stretcher, his knuckles stretched taut. He dropped his chin on his chest. "Leave me," he whispered. "If you give me a gun, I'll do my best to…"

Crouching, Jules put a hand on his shoulder. "Jug, we're not leaving you," she said firmly.

Jug looked up at McKenna, who was dripping water on the cave floor. "You've got no choice," Jug said. "Trying to haul me through there is going to put everyone at risk."

"You're coming," Taine said. "Lefty, Eriksen, let's get him off the stretcher. You boys okay to guide him through?"

"We got him this far, didn't we?" Lefty said.

"Good man. Eriksen?"

'Yeah, sure.'

Jules felt Jug tremble under her hand, from relief or fear, she couldn't tell.

"I'll help the boys with Jug," Trigger said.

Taine shook his head. "It's a kind offer, mate, but you can't. There's a spot where the tunnel narrows. You're going to need to make like a stick insect."

Trigger nodded sombrely and Jules wondered if the size of the tunnel had been on his mind. "The Charlie G?" he said.

"I'll bring it," Taine replied.

Trigger ducked his head and, wading into the water, he entered the tunnel.

"Read!" Taine called again.

"On my way!"

Taine turned to Jules. "Give Trigger a head start and then you can go through. You're going to need to take a deep breath," he said. "It's a long swim to the other side."

"Nuh-uh," she said, folding her arms across her chest. "I think I'll go last. Bring the stretcher."

"Jules, you can't. You won't make it through. The tunnel's too narrow."

"And I'm the smallest. If it won't go through and blocks the way, then I'm the only one small enough to slip past it. I'm doing this, Taine. Jug's going to need it on the other side."

"We'll make a new one."

She threw a pointed look towards the front of the cave. "We might not have time."

Lefty and Eriksen were carrying Jug to the stream. Jules ran to support his head and shoulders. They lowered him into the water, Jug sucking in his breath when the cold hit him.

"Pretty bracing huh?" Lefty said, his own body almost fully immersed now.

"Well, at least it's clean," Eriksen said.

Jules looked at him, puzzled.

"You know, less chance of Jug getting an infection." He hadn't finished speaking when Sampson brought down something huge at the front of the cave, the crash causing the ground to quiver. A shower of tiny rocks and stones fell from the cave roof.

Jules giggled. "Yep, less chance of infection," she agreed. Even Jug smiled.

"Okay, Jug, let's do this, man," Eriksen said.

"I'll help as much as I can. If it gets too much, you should just let me go."

"Shut up, Jug," Lefty said. The pair guided him feet first into the tunnel. "Save it for breathing."

"Read, you're up!" Taine yelled, as he helped Jules carry the stretcher to the water, stepping nearer, his face close to hers. "Read and I'll go through first. Now remember to breathe out because of the—"

"CO_2 saturation. Yes, I know."

Taine picked up the Charlie G. "And if the stretcher won't go through, then ditch it."

A rifle blast echoed through the chamber.

Taine swivelled.

Read came careering across the cavern. "It's through!" he shrieked. He clambered over the tapered slope, Sampson hard on his heels, its maw and those razored teeth in full view. Taine lifted the launcher, checked the sight, and fired. But standing in the stream, the rocks beneath him weren't stable. His shot went astray, only hitting Sampson on the shoulder. Nevertheless, the explosion rocked the cavern, giving off fumes and dust. Bellowing, Sampson fell back.

"Move it!" Taine shouted.

"I took out its third eye when it came through the entrance," Read yelled cheerfully, as if he and Taine were discussing the cricket scores while out for a weekend run. "Scaled the wall, and poked it from above with a burning log. When Sampson jumped back, I jumped down. I figured it would even the odds a bit."

Jules watched Sampson's reaction and shivered. Read may have damaged its night vision, but Sampson's hearing was just fine. The animal took a step in Read's direction, lowering its jaw to the ground. Jules had seen that hoovering motion before. She adjusted the night vision glasses on her face.

"Hey there, Sampson!" she cried, stepping out of the stream before Taine could stop her. She darted to the left a short way up the bank. "Over here. It's me, Jules. Nice of you to drop in. What say you and I have a wee chat?"

A wee chat? No, Jules... Taine wanted to yell.

Taine surged forward, the abandoned stretcher butting him in the stomach, but alerted by the splash, Sampson cocked its massive head. *Trying to determine where I am?* Taine cursed silently. No ear holes and still the damn thing could hear.

"Taine, I am trying to have a conversation with Sampson here, so I'd appreciate it if you didn't move," Jules told him, almost singing the words. "Now where was I? Oh yes, our little chat. You may be one of a kind, but that doesn't give you the right to terrorise my friends." The animal crouched, creeping forward on its belly, squeezing between two large rocks. "Yes, that's right," she said. "Follow the sound of my voice while Private Read gets into that little tunnel over there."

Read did as he was told, flinging himself over the ledge towards Taine, and running headlong into the stream. The animal looked up at the sound of him splashing, but Jules kept up her crooning, pulling its focus back to her. The monster batted a foreleg, its talon raking the air in front of her, like a playful kitten pawing at a scrap of newspaper. If he wasn't so terrified for her, Taine would have been impressed. Jules had it completely mesmerised.

But how long will it be willing to play?

"Taine, if Read is safe, I'm going to step back now," Jules said, her voice wobbling.

Taine stood flatfooted in the water, unsure what to do. With no rounds to hand, the launcher was useless. He could only watch helplessly as Jules turned and ran, crossing the ground between them at a sprint, her face a grimace of concentration. Sampson pounced. Taine stopped breathing. *Just short.* He exhaled as Jules plunged into the water.

She tripped, putting her hands out to stop herself, falling to her knees in the water.

Get up. Get up!

The stretcher was bumping about at the entrance of the cave. Flinging the Charlie G aside, Taine grabbed the stretcher, lifting it out of the water. He swung it towards Jules.

"Grab on!"

She clasped the crooked rails, and he hauled her in. A fisherman with a net. It took his everything – his body weight, his determination, and every last ounce of his strength – to skim her through the water ahead of the Sphenodon's jaws. They dove into the tunnel, Sampson throwing himself at the entrance. His teeth snapped behind them. Taine released the stretcher, grabbed Jules up, and pulled her to him. "It's okay. It's okay," he said as she buried her head in his shoulder.

Sampson's scorched eye appeared at the tunnel entrance. After a second, the eye moved away.

Suddenly, Read bobbed up next to them, breathing hard.

"Read?"

"It's Trigger. Must have been coming back to help. He's stuck."

Shit!

Taine thrust Jules at the private. "Give me a minute then bring Jules through. And Read, no bloody heroics, you hear me?" He took a breath and dived.

Halfway along the tunnel, Taine found Trigger, wedged tight. He was conscious, but it wouldn't be long before he passed out. He gave Taine a sad smile, and the thumbs down signal. Taine couldn't let Trigger die here, stuck in a hole like Winnie the fucking Pooh.

Taine dived for a closer look; Trigger's lats wouldn't pass.

If there was ever a better advertisement for not working out… Picking up Trigger's arm, Taine yanked it. Trigger's body didn't budge. In the water Taine had no purchase…

He needed to hurry. Jules and Read would come through soon. If Taine couldn't get Trigger out of the channel, they'd all be stuck in this godforsaken stream…

Taine removed his Steyr from across his back, and wedged it across the channel, jamming it in tight between the rock walls. Read and Jules might struggle to get past it. But there was nothing else he could do. Trigger had gone limp. He had to be running out of air. Might already be dead…

Holding off his panic, Taine placed his boots on Trigger's shoulders, and his hands on the gun. Then he straightened his body out, pushing off and driving through his skeleton, forcing Trigger through the gap.

There was a gurgle and Trigger popped free. Taine turned and dived after him, grabbing him just as the current surged, but Trigger slipped out of his grasp, missing the right hand turn. They both slid into the left hand tunnel. Taine hadn't scouted this tunnel. It could go on for hours. There was no way of knowing. Taine closed his eyes and gave himself over to the current.

Jules gasped, sucking in air. Nathan hauled her from the freezing water and dragged her onto a tiny beach. She sat with her head between her knees, panting heavily.

"Read?" she asked, when she got her breathing under control.

"He's here," Nathan said.

"What about the stretcher?" Nathan shook his head. "Damn it," Jules said. "It must have got stuck. Sorry Jug," she said. "I guess we'll have to make you a new one."

Jules hugged her arms to herself to ward against the chill. They were in another cavern, much like the last one, only better lit. Metres above them, an opening in the rock let in the moonlight.

"Shame we had to leave the fire behind," she said wistfully.

No one answered. She looked about. Nathan, Eriksen, Richard... they were all staring at her. Jules' heart lurched.

Something's wrong.

"What is it?" she demanded, searching their faces.

Lying alongside her on the beach, Read turned to her. "It's McKenna. He didn't come through yet. Trigger's gone, too."

Jules leaped up.

That's not right.

She waded knee-deep into the stream. The tunnel entrance on this side was under the water. "But they were ahead of us! Taine went to help Trigger. They were *ahead*."

Nathan ran a hand through his hair. "They haven't come through, Jules," he said softly.

"But they must have!" she insisted. "The channel was clear. Read and I passed through it."

"There was the other tunnel, the left-hand one," Lefty said. He lobbed a pebble into the stream where it landed with a tiny plop and sank. "I reckon they got swept down there."

No. That tunnel was an unknown. They had no idea where it went or how far. Taine wouldn't have taken it. Not unless he was disoriented. Or unconscious. Or perhaps Trigger had gone that way, and Taine had dived after him? It was just the sort of thing he would do.

Jules pushed deeper into the stream, her body trembling.

The water eddied, and up popped the stretcher.

Taine shot out of the tunnel and was thrown in a heap in the middle of a small stream.

"Ouf!" Stones jabbed into his back.

Not dead. I'm not dead.

And he wasn't under the ground anymore either, but outside, in the forest. Coughing violently, he rolled over, sucking in air as he crawled out of the stream and up onto the bank.

"Trigger?" Still on his hands and knees, Taine scanned the shadows. "Where are you?"

Taine staggered to his feet, stumbling noisily on the loose pebbles. "Trigger," he called, louder this time. Unless there were more tunnels, and more tributaries, he should have washed up here too. He couldn't see. He patted himself, his heart lifting. His night vision goggles! He pulled them up, adjusting them on his face, and immediately spied Trigger further along the bank.

He ran to him and gave him a shake. "Trigger!"

No response.

Taine palpated his neck. He still had a pulse! It was weak, but it was there. Quickly, Taine heaved the big man onto his side, supporting Trigger's back with his knees. Trigger sputtered, spewing water, but didn't inhale. Taine pushed him even further, so he was almost on his stomach, and slapped him hard on the back. More water spurted from Trigger's mouth and nose.

"Come on, dammit. Breathe."

But Trigger wasn't breathing. Yet. Taine was going to have to do mouth-to-mouth. Stepping over him, Taine crouched to shove him onto his back again. Then, tilting Trigger's head back, he hooked a finger into the man's mouth to clear the airway. Lifting his tongue did the trick. Trigger blinked. Opened his eyes. And gulped in a mouthful of air. Taine hadn't heard anything as blissful as the rasping sound of that big man inhaling. Flopping onto his side, Trigger vomited some more.

Taine clapped him on the shoulder, wearily. "Welcome back, man."

Swearing, Trigger wiped his mouth with the back of his hand and sat up. He looked around. "Where are we?"

"Outside somewhere," Taine said, although that much was obvious.

"The others get through?"

Taine raised an eyebrow. "You mean, once I kicked your fat arse out of the way? I think so. Jules and Read were just behind me."

Trigger nodded. "Yeah, sorry about that. There was a delay after the boys came through with Jug, and I got worried. Thought I'd come back to help. I'd made it one way, so I figured the other direction wouldn't be any different." He shrugged. "Anyway, thanks for the nudge."

"No worries."

The stream chattered and sighed, running over the pebbles. Not far away, a morepork called.

"What now?" Trigger asked.

"Find the others, I guess."

Trigger nodded. "Where do you think they are?"

"Not far."

"How do you figure that?"

INTO THE MIST

Taine picked himself up off the rocks and stretched his battered body. "Well, for one thing, we're not dead, so we can't have been in that second tunnel for more than a few seconds. How far could the stream have carried us in that time? You okay to move?"

Trigger grumbled. "Just a minute ago I was dead and now you want me to move."

Grinning, Taine extended a hand to pull him up. "You're breathing, aren't you?"

CHAPTER 26

Te Urewera Forest, Day Four, Second Cavern

Her clothes still wet, Jules shivered in the cool of the cave. Nathan leaned over and gave her hand a gentle pat. "You okay, love?"

"Cold."

Nathan nodded. "Maybe you should get up, move around a bit?" he suggested. "Warm yourself up."

Jules sighed. Nathan was right. She wasn't doing anyone any favours sitting here allowing herself to succumb to hypothermia. She stood and waved her arms about a bit. Stamped her feet a few times. Jogged on the spot. Feeling some of the numbness leave her limbs, she took a walk across the little beach. When she was far enough away from the others, she dropped her head into her hands and lets the tears flow. So many deaths. Winters, Ben, de Haas, Coolie, Trigger...

And Taine.

She scrubbed at her face. This was silly. She hardly knew him, only met him a few days ago.

Whump!

A clump of mānukā brush landed beside her. Startled, Jules looked up.

"Hey, down there," Taine said, grinning, his face poking through the hole. "We thought you guys might like to warm up."

Taine and Trigger rigged up a vine, and belayed into the cave to join them. After a bout of back slapping and hand-shaking, the soldiers set to doing their boy-scout thing and, before long, they had a fire roaring. What little gear they had had come through the tunnel, a lot of it wet through. Everyone huddled close to the fire to dry off, Jug included.

Trigger told them all the story of how he'd almost died in the tunnel, and how he'd almost died again when he and the sergeant had washed up in the streambed outside, and how he'd almost died *a third time* when he'd woken and found McKenna leaned over him, all puckered up and about to give him a bloody kiss! Sitting on the other side of the fire, Taine winked and Jules smiled back, suddenly feeling warmer.

Eventually though, the bonhomie exhausted, Lefty asked, "So, now what?"

"We need to go after it," Hamish said quietly. Everyone looked at him. "Well, it makes sense, doesn't it? We're in a siege situation here. We're stuck in the castle, while Sampson catapults us with everything he's got. Some of us need to attack the enemy face-on, so the rest of us can escape out the back with Jug." His eyes darted to the medic, who was asleep on the sand.

"Go after it?" Taine asked carefully.

"Capture it, kill it, whatever."

"We should capture it," Richard said.

Trigger got up and walked away from the fire. He stood by the stream watching the current.

Taine wiped his face with his hands to cover his anger. Bloody Foster! The same stupid idea that got two men killed and a third one currently on the sand half-conscious from the pain, and Foster brings it up again.

Still, they needed ideas, and while Foster was a jerk, the guy was smart. Taine let his hands fall away from his face. He gave Foster a hard look. "Okay, I'm not saying I like the idea of capturing it—"

Trigger turned, his eyes stony in spite of the firelight.

Taine continued. "...but *anything* that can occupy the Sphenodon long enough to get the party to safety is worth considering."

"I vote we kill it," Trigger croaked.

"Kill it, capture it. I'm open to suggestions," Taine said.

"Christian and I..." Richard said, his face reddening, "...planned to drop a net on it, the way the Māori used to snare birds."

"Look how well that turned out," Eriksen said.

Richard sniffed. "We were trying to *save* it."

"The old Māori hunting method is an interesting one, though," said Taine, closing down the bickering. "Because earlier, Ju… Dr Asher and I thought there might be some clues in the Māori legends about taniwha."

Read piped up. "I know a story about a chief and a taniwha."

"Yeah, and I know a story about a flying fish," Miller said.

"How's a story supposed to help?" said Trigger, returning to the fireside.

"It's helpful if real Sphenodons inspired the legends in the first place," Jules said.

Nathan nodded. "It's possible."

Eriksen butted in. "I know one. It's from where my dad was brought up. They had a taniwha there called Ohinemuri. This taniwha fell in love with a chief's daughter. While the girl's father was at war with his neighbours, Ohinemuri snatched her up. Kept her in his cave-lair. But her old man had the last word, snatched her back."

"Hmm, that one might not actually be about a taniwha," Nathan said. "Sometimes a powerful Māori chief would be called a taniwha. It was symbolic."

Eriksen shrugged. "In Waihi, they said Ohinemuri was a taniwha."

Lefty piped up, "Of course, they did. The daughter of their chief was stolen from under their noses."

"Tell us your story, Read," Taine said.

"Well, there was this chief called Tara who lived on the plains at Heretaunga, near Hastings," Read said. "Tara's people were being killed by a taniwha – the taniwha had a name too, but I forget what it was – anyhow, Tara couldn't let it continue, so he made a giant eel pot—"

"A hīnaki," said Nathan.

"… a… hīnaki,' Read said, "which he baited with two hundred live dogs and set in the middle of a lake. When the taniwha entered the trap, Tara dragged it ashore and killed it."

"Dragged it ashore, huh. How did he do that?" Lefty asked. "Sampson's got to weigh the same as a logging truck."

Read shook his head. "I don't know."

"My kuia used to tell me a story like Read's," Nathan said. "But in her story instead of using dogs for bait, the people used eels. And they killed it using spears, stabbing it in the belly. When they opened up its stomach, they found hundreds of people inside."

Everyone went quiet.

"Killed it with spears, huh?" Eriksen said after a moment. "Well, they can't be any worse than a Steyr. Piece of piss."

"You guys are off your heads. They're just *stories*," Trigger said.

Taine pulled Trigger aside. "I think our taniwha is attracted to Jules."

"What?"

"He's *interested* in her."

Trigger laughed, his sides shaking. "Now I've heard everything."

"No listen..."

But Trigger was still laughing. "You gotta get a handle on your jealousy..."

"Jealousy? I'm not jealous."

"Really?" Trigger clasped his hands to his chest.

Taine's face grew hot. "That's ridiculous. It's my job to look after her."

Raising bushy eyebrows, Trigger puckered his lips and made kissy noises.

"I'm not... I don't...it's not..." Taine stammered. Who was he trying to kid? Jules only had to look at him and Taine could hardly breathe. He sighed.

"Okay, so I like her. Are you done?"

Trigger wiped his eyes with the back of his hand. "Yeah."

"I'm serious about the taniwha liking Jules, though. You remember when we were talking, Eriksen told a story about a taniwha who stole a woman? To take her back to his lair and mate with her?"

Trigger shook his head. "They're *stories*, Taine. You heard Nathan; it's a symbol. If a story says a taniwha took a woman as a spoil of war, it meant the chief."

"But what if they weren't just stories?"

"I'm not getting you."

"What if Sampson can detect the difference between men and women? I don't know, pick up a woman's scent or something."

Trigger shrugged.

"Listen, he has a thing about Jules. I saw it. He could have killed her in the cave before, but he didn't. He was *interested* in her."

"Maybe he decided she needed fattening up first," Trigger said grimly.

Taine frowned. "The briefing Arnold gave me mentioned a woman hiker. When the first section found her she'd only been dead for a couple of days. Somehow she'd managed to stay alive after being separated from her group."

"That doesn't mean Sampson took her. She could've been hiding."

"But what if he did take her? I need to go back to where we first saw Sampson. I have to leave the cave. I've got to check something."

"Okay," Trigger said, all traces of laughter now gone.

"I'm not asking you to come."

"Coming anyway, so save your breath."

Te Urewera Forest, Second Campsite
"Louise ran from this point here," Taine said, when he and Trigger arrived back at the site of Winters' death. "Jug and Lefty reckoned they could hear her running away in this direction." He opened his arms like a preacher, pointing both hands at the trees.

"We already searched that sector. We didn't find anything," Trigger replied.

"Humour me."

"It'll take hours."

"We'll give it one hour. If we don't find anything, we'll give up, head back."

In the end, they didn't need that long. On the tree trunk near a steep ravine, they found a clay hand print. Barely a smudge in the bark, at eye level, it was visible enough.

Trigger cursed. "How the fuck did we miss that?"

Taine could've kicked himself. This was his fault. He'd assumed Louise Hemphill had been injured and had told the others to search underfoot.

"At least we know she was here," Trigger said. "If Sampson got her and carried her off like you said, maybe we can track him, find out where he took her."

Taine shook his head. "It was raining, plus we trampled all over this area looking for her. Any tracks will be ruined by now."

"I should've put up crime scene tape. Stopped the boys making a mess of the evidence."

"It was only a theory."

"You've got to feel sorry for her though," said Trigger morosely. "Face-to-face with that stinking, drooling beast. What if she was conscious when it carried her off? I can't think of anything worse."

Taine could think of something worse: being the soldier who failed to keep her safe.

"We should be getting back to the others."

But Trigger's words echoed in Taine's ears. *I can't think of anything worse.*

Abruptly, Taine turned on his heel, stepped close to the cliff. Hooking his arm around the tree trunk, he leaned out over the edge.

"Trigger, we need to get to the bottom of this ravine. What if Louise Hemphill couldn't think of anything worse either? What if she made a choice and jumped?"

Trigger raised his eyebrows, but he followed Taine along the cliff top. They had to go quite a way before they found a spot with enough roots and rocks to use as handholds. They scrambled to the foot of the cliff.

"You sure this is it?" Trigger asked when they arrived in the ravine directly beneath the handprint tree.

Taine nodded. "I used that landslip on the other side as a landmark. See those boulders near the top? They're about to tumble into the ravine."

"Well, it was a waste of time, anyway," Trigger said. "There's nothing here."

"Not right here, but let's look around a bit," said Taine. "It's possible—" He stooped to pick up an object amongst the stones, turning it over and examining in his hands.

The cracked sole of a tramping boot.

They found Louise Hemphill just metres away, her body crammed into a narrow crack in the wall, as if she'd hoped to fuse with the landscape.

She'd still been alive after she jumped.

Trigger and Taine hauled the body out. Wedged in tight, it tumbled out in a rush, coming to rest in an awkward heap.

Trigger took a step back. "Jesus."

The woman's face was blue with bruising, one eye so swollen it was merely a slit. She had a deep cut in one hand, several of her nails were missing, and the perverse angle of one of her legs pointed to a break just below the knee. Her hair, ordinarily smooth and tidy in its ponytail, had fallen out of its elastic band, the strands a tangled mass. Her clothes were torn in a million places, as if she'd come off second best in a hit and run with a road sweeper.

Taine's jaw clenched. "Sampson found her. He's been *playing* with her."

Shielding his eyes, Trigger looked up at top of the cliff. "She could've got these injuries from the fall. That's a thirty metre drop. And she was terrified, remember. Maybe, after falling, she squeezed herself in this gap to hide."

Taine needed to know for sure. Crouching close, he peeled back the sleeve of Louise's merino top. Her arm was black with contusions.

"People bruise for a short time after death," Taine said. "But not this much." He lowered what remained of the tattered garment then rolled up the leg of her trousers on the uninjured side, respectfully, as if she were alive and about to show him nothing more innocuous than an unfortunate bee-sting.

Over Taine's shoulder, the big soldier gasped.

Running diagonally across Louise's leg was a deep line of ragged bite marks caused by a double row of wedged teeth.

They returned Louise's body to the cleft in the wall until it could be retrieved, then ran back along the bottom of the gully to where they could climb out of the ravine.

"We could use this information," Taine told Trigger when they'd almost reached the top.

Trigger put out his hand. "How?"

Taine grasped it firmly and Trigger hauled him over the lip. "'For Sampson, women are like a lure. What if we were to take advantage of that to trap and kill him? It's what the Māori did."

"Those are just stories."

"Stories exist for a reason."

"Yeah, for reading to kids at bedtime!"

"Sometimes they're about passing on information. It's how we knew about Louise."

Trigger grunted. "It was a lucky guess."

"Based on a *story*."

"You can't, man. You just can't. Dangling her on a line for that monster? Jules isn't a dog or an eel. It's even worse than Foster's idea of using Winters' corpse."

"I'd use the dog instead," Taine said, sardonically, "but Sampson ate it. So far, that thing is winning every round."

"This isn't a joke, Taine. I thought you liked Jules."

"I do like her!"

"Then, don't do it!"

"But don't you see? I don't think he'll kill her. I think he'll keep her alive, like he did with Louise."

Trigger grabbed Taine's smock in his fist, pulling Taine around to face him. "Tell. Me. You're. Not. Serious."

Taine broke free from Trigger's grasp, pushing him away. "I don't want to place her in harm's way. The *last* thing I want is for Jules to be hurt, but it's the only way. I'm convinced Sampson will want to toy with her first, like a kitten with a pom-pom. And while he's playing, we'll kill him."

"You don't think I want to kill that thing for what it did to Coolie? I'd like to stuff the bastard with C4 and bake it in the oven, but what you're suggesting is just too dangerous."

"Well, you tell me what to do then, Trigger. How are we going to keep these people alive? I don't see you coming up with any great ideas."

"We stay in the cave. Make a signal fire. Eventually, Arnold will have to send another section."

Didn't Trigger suggest this once before?

"With the end result: in a week more soldiers will be dead. Arnold won't risk it anyway, not when two other sections have already failed."

Trigger's eyes were flinty. "James Arnold won't abandon us."

Taine sighed. "The major will do what he can, but this is an off-record mission. We need to face facts. Arnold might be forced to sacrifice us, for plausible deniability."

"Taine, you can't do this."

"What if Jules agrees to do it?"

Trigger clamped his lips shut.

Taine didn't like it either, but Sampson wasn't leaving them a whole lot of options.

"That thing is playing with us," Taine said aloud. "It's like Read's kitten. Sooner or later, it's gonna bite off our heads."

Te Urewera Forest, Second Cavern

Taine said he had something to ask her. They walked to the beach and sat on the sand. Jules sifted the grains through her fingers while he explained.

"You want me to be the bait in a trap?" she said.

"You can say no, Jules. I'm not forcing you. I know Foster thinks we should try and save it, but if Sampson isn't stopped—"

She placed two fingers across his lips, stopping him from saying any more. "I know."

Picking up a stick, she poked at the ground with it. "Supposing I said yes, how do you plan to do it?"

"We'll use Foster's net. There's a cliff where we found Louise…"

Jules sucked in her breath. *A cliff…*

She can't. No, she can't.

But an image of Louise came to her, the way she was when they'd put the tent together that first night. Laughing and joking. *Alive.* Not anymore. Taine and Trigger thought Sampson toyed with her, perhaps for hours. If Jules didn't do this, the Sphenodon would go on to torture someone else. Someone just like Louise. Jules swallowed. She didn't have a choice.

"Taine, you remember how Richard arrived at the last minute to join this expedition?"

He nodded.

"I know he told everyone he came because he discovered he had some leave owing, but that's not the real reason. It's because I hadn't been out in the field for ages."

"Your file said two years."

"You knew?"

"Just that much."

"Oh." Jules bit her lip. Of course, he would know. "It didn't say why?"

"No. Do you want to tell me?"

She tugged her hands through her hair, smoothing it to her nape, collecting her thoughts. "It used to be I couldn't wait to get in the field. I loved getting my hands dirty, you know? We got to do some cool things, counting tusked wētā populations, possum control… that sort of thing." She paused, Taine silent, listening. "The thing is, I hadn't been in the forest because I was scared."

"Something happened?" he finally asked.

Now it was Jules turn to nod. "I was on Te Puka Hereka island," she said, "studying the mōhua-yellowhead population. The whole time we were there, it'd been awful weather; constant rain, drizzle. Typical Fiordland. We were about to wrap things up, so several of us braved the rain to do a final check of the birds' nest holes for new clutches…" Jules eyes welled with tears. She scrubbed at them with the heels of her palms.

"Sarah, my friend, was in front of me. She disappeared. Just like that. One moment she was there and the next…

"There was a subsidence." She swallowed. "Sarah fell in. Instead of grabbing for her, I snatched at the air for a handhold, something, *anything* to stop myself from falling too. I caught hold of a lancewood. They have serrated leaves, so my hands were shredded." She looked at her palms, almost expecting the cuts to still be there. "But it was just a sapling and eventually the roots gave way." She gave a grim chuckle. "I was holding on to it when I fell. I waited to hit the bottom, but I never did. Instead, I stopped and found myself perched on a ledge…" Jules trailed off.

"Luckily, only the two of us were caught out, and I was better off than poor Sarah. I stayed on that tiny shelf for two days. When they pulled me to the surface, I was fine; some minor dehydration, a few lacerations and a twisted wrist. Nothing like Sarah. The only thing I really damaged was my confidence."

Taine's face was stony. "Jules, you don't have to do it. We'll find another way."

Jules leaned across the gap and took his hand, almost crumbling when he curled his fingers around hers. "It's okay, I'll do it."

"Jules…" he started.

"No, I have to. *We* have to. Sampson can't be allowed to carry on. He's adapting to his environment, Taine. The moa isn't here anymore, so he's looking for new food sources. It isn't too hard to work out that he's developing a taste for people."

Releasing her hand, Taine stood and stepped away, his eyes boring into hers. "And the cliff?"

"Perhaps it's not the cliff that frightens me so much as the consequences. Since the accident Sarah's never been the same. Every day is a torture for her. I'm a coward really. I don't have her strength. Faced with that, I'd rather die."

"Jules, I won't let you die. I promise."

Looking down, she discovered she's been twisting her hands in her lap. She clasped them together now, forcing them to be still. "But that's just the point, Taine. If I fall, or if Sampson gets me, I think I'd prefer that you did."

CHAPTER 27

Te Urewera Forest, Day Five

Taine called everyone together.

"We'll go with Miller's suggestion. A diversion's the only way to get Jug out. Eriksen, I'd like you to head up the escape team. Up to you how you get the stretcher out of the cave—" He tilted his chin towards the hole in the roof. "The lift or the water slide – take your pick. Once you're out, Nathan will see you out of the forest. I suggest you head south, away from Sampson's main hunting grounds. Maybe try to connect with the Waikaremoana Track – there's more likely to be help there. Get DoC to close the park, at least until you hear from us. Tell them whatever you need. Separatists, whatever."

"And if we don't hear anything?"

"Then assume we're not coming and Sampson is lording over the forest. Major Arnold will debrief you. You need to tell him everything. He'll take it from there. Lefty and Miller, you'll go with Eriksen to carry the stretcher."

"Read—"

"Put me on the diversion team, sir."

Taine didn't have to ask Trigger. He waved his rifle for yes. Taine was relieved. Trigger might not approve of the plan, but he'd always had Taine's back.

Foster piped up. "You forgot to mention Jules and me."

Taine couldn't help himself. "You might like to be on my team, Dr Foster, in case we're able to capture it. I thought we could retrieve the net that you and Dr de Haas were making—"

At the mention of de Haas, Foster blanched, perhaps because the last time anyone saw the geologist his entrails had been strewn across the forest floor. "Um… I think I'd prefer to be sure Jules gets out safely."

"I'm staying, Richard," Jules said.

Foster gaped at her. "After telling *me* it was too dangerous?"

"Yes," she said flatly. Squaring her shoulders she looked away, ending the discussion.

"Dr Foster?" Taine prompted.

Richard waved his hand dismissively. "Take the net if you want it. I'll go back with Eriksen." He stalked back to the fire.

"So how do we make sure Sampson follows you, and not us?" Lefty asked when Foster had gone.

It was a good question, and one Taine didn't have the answer to.

"If Sampson were smaller, I might have an idea," Nathan said. "Our people used to use a wind instrument, a pūrerehua, to bring lizards out of hiding. They're attracted by its sound, like a moth's wings."

Trigger rolled his eyes. "More legends."

Nathan rubbed a hand across his burgeoning beard. "It's not a legend; just something Māori people have always known. A bit like using mānukā to help with pain," he said, lifting his eyes to Jug.

Taine frowned. A bullroarer? He'd played his bullroarer for Jules, in the other cave, before the Sphenodon had tracked them there. What if it hadn't tracked them? What if Taine had summoned it?

Taine took his carving out of his pocket, unwound its flax cord, and turned it over in his hand.

Richard pulled her aside, yanking hard on her elbow.

"Ow, Richard, you're hurting—"

"You can't do this," he said.

"I have to."

"Ten years. Ten!" he spat. "Doesn't our friendship mean *anything* to you?"

"That's not fair. You know it does. I—"

"Spare me the bullshit. I ask you to help me capture it – just to help – and you say, 'oh, no, it's too dangerous!'" He flapped a hand near his face, like a Victorian lady having the vapours. "But Sergeant *McKenna* asks," his voice dripped with sarcasm, "a man you've only known for *four* days, and that's okay? Jesus, Jules, can't you see what he's doing? He's using you as bait. Bait!"

Jules looked at Richard, his face contorted in anger. He was right. Was she really so shallow that she could be taken in by a handsome face and a decent set of abs? She was bait. She could die. Why had she agreed to do it?

Turning her head, Jules glanced at Taine, who was connecting the flax cord of his bullroarer to a nylon rope. Deep in thought, his jaw twitched.

Because he makes me feel safe, that's why.

Abruptly, she was wrenched about, Richard twisting hard on her wrist, dragging her arm across her body so her face was close to his. "Jules. Come back with me. We're a pair, you and I. I can't lose you."

"Richard, no. I'm sorry..."

He tightened his grip on her wrist. His breath was hot in her face. A fleck of his spittle landed on her cheek.

"Let me go."

"You're *sorry?* You owe me, Jules. All these years; I've been propping you up. You're an average scientist bordering on mediocre. You wouldn't even have this job if it weren't for me. And don't think it'll be there waiting for you when you come back – excuse me, that is *if* you come back—"

She slapped him, the smack of her palm on his cheek reverberating in the cavern.

He stared at her a moment, his fringe flopping in his eyes, then pushed her away. "Fuck you, then," he hissed.

Eriksen stood and took a step in their direction. "Jules, you okay?"

"I'm fine."

Richard turned on his heel and stalked off.

Rubbing at her wrist Jules watched him go. She really was sorry. All these years… Richard had never had her heart, and now he never would.

Te Urewera Forest, Near the Second Campsite
Taine checked his watch; time to get started. Eriksen would be impatient to get his group underway. Taine paused to look at Jules, further along at the edge of the narrow ravine. She had to be terrified, standing on a clifftop served up as kitty meal for the giant Sphenodon. Perhaps sensing his gaze, she looked over and, smiling, gave him a little wave.

Nothing was going to happen to her.

Turning away, Taine took the bullroarer from his pocket, and unravelled the flaxen string.

This is shit. It's never going to work.

Sitting in the beech tree on the edge of the cliff, Foster's net laid out on the ground below him, its free end in his hand, Trigger felt like Wile E Coyote with the latest ACME invention. They might as well have been facing Goliath with a fucking slingshot. Give him mortar fire and snipers any day. At least with guns, it was a clean death.

Was that it then? Was he afraid to die? He shifted his bum, trying to find a more comfortable spot on the branch. He never used to think so. But then, maybe he'd never been so close to dying before either. No, it wasn't the dying, or even *how* he died that bothered him. You signed up for a career as a soldier; you knew it was a possibility. If a sniper took you out, you'd be dead before you hit the ground. One second you were okay, and the next, dead. Quick, silent, painless. But this Sphenodon was a different kind of enemy. With Sampson, you saw your death coming and it wasn't pretty. Shredded muscle, cracked bones, guts spattered everywhere. Trigger wasn't afraid to die, he just didn't want to witness it.

From where she was standing on the edge of the ravine, Jules gave Taine a wave. Trigger snorted quietly. Imagine Taine thinking he hadn't noticed. Not hard to see those two had a thing for each other. They could be good together. Trigger hoped they got a chance. He hoped Taine wouldn't let her slip through his fingers. Maybe facing down this monster would make his sergeant realise just how little time there was in life. Taine was a good soldier, and Trigger trusted him, but it wasn't like he'd never made a mistake before.

A few metres away, in another beech, Read signalled that they were ready.

Trigger closed his eyes a moment. "Beep beep," he muttered under his breath.

Rotorua township

The morepork was at his window again. Tonight the cry was tremulous. Poignant. Maybe Temera only thought that because he was frightened. Maybe the cry was as it'd always been. In any case, he wished he could blot out the sound.

No point resisting.

He got up, leaving his old body slumbering, and stepped into the spirit world, where once again he was a young boy chasing barefoot through the bush.

Tonight the morepork was leading him deep into the forest. At first the trail was wide and he flew along, breaking newly-spun cobwebs heavy with dew, but soon the undergrowth thickened and he was forced to pick his route carefully, brushing past ferns and climbing through the twisted black netting of the pirita-supplejack vines. Deeper into the forest, dense stretches of mānuka slowed him down, their woody grey stems scratching at his face and hands.

"This is getting old, my friend," he grumbled under his

breath. But the owl simply urged him on until finally, after what seemed hours, they came to a ravine where a heap of boulders teetered on the verge.

"Here?"

The morepork hooted.

"I don't see what…" But then, on the other side, Temera saw the woman, standing on her own at the edge of the chasm. He knew her! She was there that day when Temera and Wayne had tried to intercept the group as they'd entered the forest. Temera recalled she'd got down from the vehicle and stood at the side of the road. So, she was with the army. With the warrior.

McKenna.

What are they trying to do? Sacrifice her?

Because the taniwha was coming. Temera couldn't see or hear it, but already his heart was pounding with the knowledge.

The warrior, not far from her on the edge of the narrow ravine, was twirling a rope around his head. There was something attached.

A pūrerehua!

That's why the beast was coming. McKenna was *summoning* it. Hypnotising the monster with its music, like a snake charmer bedazzling a serpent.

Temera lifted his hand to the pūrerehua at his neck. Was that why he'd felt compelled to make his own wind instrument? No, there must have been more to it than that. He focused hard on the object in McKenna's hand, stilling time so its image reached him. Shuddering with effort, he pulled the picture into his core, to a place where he could examine it. He wouldn't be able to hold it for long. Just a few seconds at best. He forced himself to put the woman out of his mind, to concentrate on the pūrerehua. Turning it in his core, he studied it hard. Yes, the patterned surface of the instrument was the same as his own. Temera was sure of it. He recognised the large swirls and tight coils etched into the wood grain. Even the resin tang of the wood was familiar. The shape. The tiny dog's-tooth notches. The size.

Releasing the image, Temera sat down abruptly. The ground

was sodden. He was gonna have a wet arse. He wondered if back in his bed, he might have had an accident. He shook his head at that, angry with himself. A woman's life was in danger and all he could think about was whether or not he'd pissed in his bed?

Think!

McKenna was using a pūrerehua, a twin of his own. What did it mean? In the near distance, a tremor rippled through the ground. And on the wind came a faint hiss. Temera closed his eyes…

Te Urewera Forest, Near the Second Campsite
Taine's bullroarer droned on.

Trigger glanced back into the forest and caught the movement of something big coming through the trees. It was working. Sampson was on his way. Trigger kept his eyes on the creature's passage. Seeing it snake its way closer unnerved him. They'd never seen Sampson approach this way. Up until now the animal had always been stealthy, cunning. Maybe even more invisible than Coolie. But today the Sphenodon was making no secret of its arrival. Why? Was Taine really calling it? Trigger doubted it. More likely, it knew they had nothing to touch it; that their weapons were useless against it, and that all they had in their arsenal was a flimsy net, a girl, and an ancient whistle.

It was here.

Trigger glanced at Read and gave him the thumbs up.

Just because the odds are stacked against us, doesn't mean we have to roll over and give up.

Listening to the hum of McKenna's pūrerehua, Temera took his own carving from around his neck and unrolled the string. When he was sure it was free from tangles, he lifted his arm and twirled it above his head, feeling a surge of excitement as it gathered pace, the cord whizzing though the air, making it sing. The voice of Temera's own wairua resonated in his chest, in his head, and in his heart. Not sound, but the note was as pure as a spoon tapped on the side of a crystal glass.

"McKenna," he called.

The soldier didn't look Temera's way. He made no sign to show he'd heard.

There must have been something Temera missed. Was it the cadence? The size of the circles? Frustrated, Temera let the cord drop to the ground.

A torpedo would have been easier.

The morepork hooted, and Temera chuckled. "Yes, you're right, my friend," Temera told the owl. "My old mātua would agree with you: I'm too impatient, expecting everything to work on the first go."

He picked up his pūrerehua again, this time focusing hard on matching McKenna's rhythm in spite of his shorter, nine-year-old arms. He gave himself over to the music, losing himself in its timbre and its resonance, finally realising that to speak to a living person from within the spirit realm, their two pūrerehua had to first harmonise in a duet of souls.

"McKenna!"

"Who's that?"

"A friend."

"Coolie?"

Temera felt the voice quaver, as though McKenna's pūrerehua had slowed, the cord quivering.

"No, not Coolie."

"Who are you? Why don't you show yourself?"

"Because I'm not actually here. I'm in your head, carried to you through the music. But you could see me, or a form of me, if you concentrate hard and—"

"I can't see anything…"

Temera sighed. They were not so different, he and McKenna. "It doesn't matter. There's no time to—"

"Wait! I see you. But… you're a boy!"

"Yes, as you see me now, I'm nine years old."

"I don't understand," McKenna said, the hum becoming indistinct.

"I can explain," Temera said quickly, afraid to lose the link between them. "But it's complicated and we don't have time. I need you to do something…"

"I can't," McKenna said, the hum muffled.

"But I'm trying to help you," Temera wailed. "With the *taniwha*."

The chord hummed, the song strong again. "What do you want?"

"Have you seen *Star Wars?*"

"Everyone's seen *Star Wars*."

"You're going to have to swing down into the ravine. When I say. And don't aim for the clifftop, you need to go lower, below the net…"

"This is crazy."

"You need to do it now."

Chapter 28

Trigger held his breath as Sampson strolled onto the battleground. It waited a distance from the cliff, where the trees were thinner. Unhurried, it lifted its head and sniffed the air. Did it know they were waiting for him? Could it smell their fear?

Amazing it can smell anything over the stench of its own rot and filth.

On the edge of the ravine, Taine continued to play his instrument, its buzz like a mosquito behind Trigger's eyes. Sweat trickled down his temples.

Sampson had spied Jules. He started to run in her direction. *Jesus.*

Even the beech tree trembled. Taine had better fucking know what he was doing. Jules' face paled. She took a step back.

"Not yet, not yet," Trigger whispered. "It's too soon!"

The bullroarer whirred.

Sampson approached Jules, approached the cliff. He was coming in fast. He wasn't going to stop! But Trigger was wrong. The monster thundered to a halt not much more than a car length from Jules. Her chest rose and fell, but she didn't move. Paralysed with fear? Trigger hoped not. She had to jump clear. Sampson stretched out a taloned foreleg, raking it lazily through the air. He hissed. Trigger's heart pounded.

Fuck.

Like a kitten? What was Taine talking about? Sampson was nothing like a fucking kitten. You called that playful? Jesus. And they'd put Jules in its path, with no way of saving herself. She was a fucking sacrifice!

The Sphenodon bellowed, the sound almost gleeful. It tossed its massive head, its deadly spines glinting. It stepped closer. Lowered its head and opened its mouth…

Soon, soon…

Trigger was about to show Read the chop, when Jules let out an involuntary squeak.

The animal hesitated.

Trigger threw up his palm instead. Not yet…

Sampson bunched his muscles.

"Now!"

Together Read and Trigger yanked the net skywards, just as Sampson lunged for Jules. The net swung up and around, its two rope-stays like the handles of a child's drawstring bag, the animal's forward movement pulling it tight and closed. Secured to the two solid beech trunks, the ropes snapped backwards.

The bullroarer in hand, Taine hurled the line upwards and across, aiming for a tree near Read. It caught in a fork between two branches. Taine twisted the cord around his arm, ignoring the bite of the fibre. He launched himself off the cliff, and prayed the Force was with him.

Jules was meant to jump sideways – sideways and away from the cliff. But she had to leave it to the very last second so Read and Trigger could bring up the net. She waited, trembling as Sampson approached. But then he lunged, coming at her with those teeth, the reek of its breath, and *oh my god, those teeth…* She was too terrified to move. She squeaked. Sampson slowed for a split second, startled by the pitch of her voice, then lunged, reaching with a curled talon.

The talon that had yanked de Haas' intestines out of his body.

No… not again…

Jules stepped back, and stumbled.

She grasped for a handhold.

Swinging into the ravine, Taine *saw* her fall. She tumbled downwards, grappling for a handhold, the rocks and debris raining from the cliff face. Taine steeled his grip on the line, angling his body to face her and, coming in sideways, collected her in his free arm. Together, they slammed into the cliff face in a shower of debris, Taine's arm nearly yanked out of its socket.

Shit!

They were swinging backwards. But Jules reached out and snatched at a root. Seized it. Her fist clenched around the root, the knuckles white, she pulled them back to the cliff.

Taine glanced about for a foothold. A metre or two below them was a tiny ledge, a shelf of rock about the size of a coffee table.

"When I tell you, I want you to let go, okay? I'm going to let out the line."

Her eyes widened, her heart pounding against his chest. "No! It's too far."

"I'll slide us down the rope. It's just a couple of metres." Taine's arm was beginning to shake from the strain, their combined weight causing his shoulder to burn. "Jules please, trust me," he said, his chest tightening when she bit her lip.

"Okay."

"You count. We'll go on three."

By the count of five, Taine's feet found the ledge. Jamming the line into a crack in the rock, he drew her to him. They took a moment to catch their breath.

"This wasn't in the plan," she said.

Up on the clifftop, the rope snapped back. An accidental loop closed about Trigger's wrist. It tightened, the weight of Sampson, thousands of tons of angry thrashing Sphenodon bore down on his wrist, crushing the bones. Trigger roared. White blue, the skin changed colour. His hand was in a noose. Being amputated. His head swam.

In the branches of the beech, Read twisted at Trigger's shout. Everything was going to hell in a handcart. Jules and McKenna were gone, the sergeant leaping after Jules, almost before Read saw her trip. They'd be dead, or if they weren't, Read could only pray they'd found a hand hold somewhere. The net didn't look as if it would hold – the rope tether on Trigger's side stretched to the limit. If Jules and McKenna were alive down there, they'd be crushed. Read had to secure that rope!

But it was already too late. The rope pinged free – Trigger was caught in the rope, the loose end dragging him towards the cliff. It yanked him from the tree he'd been sitting in, pulling him down the length of the trunk, slaloming him between the branches. His shoulder hit one, bouncing cruelly. His clothes were torn to shreds, and no doubt his skin with it.

He's going to go over.

Grabbing a nearby supplejack vine, Read swung into the air Tarzan-style, releasing the vine mid-arc to throw himself at Trigger. Landing beside him, he clutched at the big man's smock.

"Got you."

Only he hadn't yet. Read dug his boots in, slipping over the rock-strewn clay, straining to slow their advance. The cliff rushed at them. Gravel ground under his boots. Tumbled away. His ankle flip-flopped, snapping to one side. Pain shot up his leg.

Biting back a curse, Read tightened his grip on Trigger, his fingers clawing at the man's jacket as the remaining rope creaked, and dug in some more. He wasn't going to lose another man. The net listed way to one side.

They were going to go over the edge of a cliff with an angry thrashing Sphenodon!

Determined, Read dug his heels in, giving it everything, leaning backwards, his ankle screaming, and the backs of his legs burning.

No!

Still, they slid. He could do nothing more. His heart thundering, Read held his breath and watched the cliff approach.

They slowed to a stop, the net snare held only by a single tether.

No time to celebrate, Read scrambled to his feet, unwinding the rope from Trigger's mangled hand. Just in time. The remaining tether squealed and snapped, both ends free now to race away over the cliff. Read threw himself at the edge, sliding in on his stomach to peer down into the ravine.

"Look out below!" he shouted, but already it was too late, the net, Sampson inside it, was crashing down the ravine to the ground.

A hand appeared, extended out as if its owner was checking for rain.

Taine?

On a ledge below Read, McKenna grasped at the passing rope, letting it slip through his palms as it passed, until he was holding the end.

Sampson crashed to the ground.

Temera picked his way to the bottom of the ravine and ran panting along the gully floor. Nearing the taniwha, he could see the old wounds on its flanks, the eyes that were blackened and raw.

"Hello, little seer. I suppose you've come to gloat?" the taniwha sneered.

"I've come to watch you leave the forest."

"Is that so? I'm not quite beaten yet." The taniwha thrashed wildly in a demonstration of his power. The net strained to contain it. It might break yet. Terrified, Temera stepped back. He wasn't really there, but with the pūrerehua at his neck, he felt closer to the living world than normal.

"McKenna will kill you."

"He hasn't so far."

"He'll kill you," Temera said again.

"Ah, but that won't stop me visiting *you*, will it?" it said, and laughed cruelly.

Temera shuddered.

"Is it dead?" Jules asked hopefully. Taine felt her breath at his neck. He glanced at the crumpled mess at the bottom of the ravine.

Maybe we've done it?

But Sampson's tail twitched. Wrapped in the net, the fall had only stunned the monster. It wouldn't be long before it came to. Used those talons to cut its way free.

Taine didn't want to leave Jules on this ledge. If it were anyone else. *Anywhere* else.

"Jules…"

"I'll be perfectly safe. I'll lock the doors," she said, forcing a smile. "Just try not to be late home, okay?"'

Taine grinned. Looping the rope over a jagged rock in the cliff face, he pulled it tight. Tested it. He was about to rappel down the cliff when he stopped.

Fuck it.

His hand at her nape, he pulled her to him and kissed her, feeling her body melt into his. She put her arms around his neck, and kissed him back.

Sampson bellowed beneath them.

He forced himself to pull away. "Jules…"

"I'll be right here," she whispered, her eyes dark. "Go."

He leaped off the ledge, rappelling down the side of the ravine, and jumping the last metre onto Sampson's belly. The animal's head was already half out of the ropes, the nylon fibres severed by the crest of spines.

Taine raised his pistol, preparing to fire at the creature's eye.

"Not the pistol," the boy's voice came to him, far away but also close.

How are they talking? There was no music. Taine's bullroarer was hanging in a tree thirty metres above him. The answer came to him almost before he'd asked the question – *our souls have met before*.

"But I can finish this now," Taine replied.

"No! You'll only kill the lizard, and not the taniwha," said the boy cryptically.

"What do you want me to do? Strangle it with my bare hands?"

"I don't know. Give me a second to think. It'll be something traditional."

"The lead pipe in the conservatory?" Taine said bitterly.

"You're not helping!"

Taine raised his pistol. "We're wasting time. It'll be free soon."

"No! We have to get it right. The nightmares, they'll keep coming."

Taine lowered the gun. "They'll keep coming?"

"A spear!" the boy cried. "Use a spear and strike at the belly, the soft part. It's what our ancestors did. It has to be a spear!"

Taine didn't have a spear. But there were branches here, torn from the trees in recent slips. He could use one of them. *Make* a spear. He leaped off the Sphenodon and scooped up a branch. Four strikes of the penknife, and he had a crude spear. It looked pathetic.

"Quickly," the boy urged.

The creature was almost free of the net. It bucked and thrashed, tossing its head, spines slicing through the ropes, increasing its range of movement with every pass.

Drawing a deep breath, Taine pulled back his arm. He rushed in, pointing the spear at the Sphenodon's belly. It pierced the hide, the spear sliding into the creature's flesh. Taine felt a tiny surge of hope. It worked! A simple spear achieving what guns could not. The Māori warriors of old *had* known what they were doing! He drove the shaft deeper, using all his weight. But it didn't stop Sampson. He screwed his torso from one side to the other, bellowing, hissing. Clutching at the spear, Taine was flung from side to side. The tail won free, Taine jumping clear and onto the rocks just in time.

Shit!

The spear poked from the animal's belly. Enraged, Sampson lashed out, its tail scattering nearby rocks as it worked at finishing the ropes with its talons, slashing and clawing. Taine's hope faded. All he'd done was given it a teeny pinprick. A bee-sting. He'd annoyed it, nothing more. He should have used the pistol while he'd had the opportunity.

"Shallow-hearted," the boy's voice said, and Taine prickled. Let him stand in Taine's shoes and say that! But then he realised it wasn't what the boy meant; the beast's *heart* was in its underbelly!

"Again. Hurry!"

The net full of holes, Sampson kicked out, bursting the knots. He got to his feet. Taine darted under the net, and under the beast's legs. He yanked on the spear. Stuck fast, Taine hung off it, his feet dragging on the ground, straining to wrench it out of Sampson's hide. The Sphenodon reeled about. Tossed its head. The last of the net fell away.

It was free.

CHAPTER 29

Temera closed his eyes, the taniwha's laughter ringing in his ears. It hadn't always been like this. Even taniwha, when young, started out shy. Hiding in the shadows of Temera's dreams, it had hissed quietly. Perhaps the first few deaths had been accidents, a question of the creature killing to survive. It was a living thing, after all. But after each encounter with Temera's people, the beast had grown more confident, even arrogant, its wairua becoming puffed up with pride and importance.

Now it wasn't enough for it just to live in the forest and keep to itself. It wished to place itself above everyone, even Tāne, the god of the forest. If the taniwha was to be banished forever, he would have help McKenna. It wasn't enough to slay it; the taniwha's wairua had to also make the journey to the underworld. But Temera was only a man, and doing battle with a taniwha was not the same as predicting where a geyser might pop up. He stood in the canyon, watching McKenna struggle to free the wooden spear, and wished his mātua were here, to guide him.

Free the wooden spear...

Temera opened his eyes. Wood! Mātua Rata may not be here, but there was someone who might help him. Temera took his pūrerehua from around his neck and twirled it above his head, building the cadence, widening the circle, the air dancing over the sweeps and swirls and dog's-tooth notches of its korero-carvings until the instrument sung. He allowed it to hum for a moment, just long enough for his own wairua to gain confidence, and then he called on him, Tāne, god of the forest, who separated the earth and the sky and let light into the world.

Temera called on Tāne, who fashioned the first man, and told him of the taniwha who would destroy them. Tāne of the forest, spirit of the mist. His body trembling, Temera, the boy-seer, walked in the spirit world and summoned the god.

The mist rolled in, cloaking the forest in darkness. The birds fell silent, but Tāne's children, the trees, creaked and groaned. Cold seeped into the canyon. Temera's arm ached, but he dared not stop the music because someone was coming.

The pūrerehua resonated with strength. Not Temera's power. Temera was just the morepork, the humble messenger that darted between the worlds, but he felt the being's presence. And its rage. Then the mist thickened until Temera could see only shadows. The warrior and the taniwha lost in its drifts...

No!

The Sphenodon tore itself free of the net. Clutching at the rock wall, Jules stared in horror. Just seconds ago she'd seen Taine duck under Sampson's body, still clinging to the spear. Where was he now?

Jules could hardly breathe. She had to do something. What? Quivering, she bent her knees, her legs shaking, fingernails raking at the rock wall.

At last, she lowered her body enough to put her hands on the ledge floor.

Oh god.

Trembling, she pushed her legs backwards until she was lying on her stomach, her feet dangling off the ledge. A pebble toppled over the edge. It bounced off the side of the ravine, clinking to the ground. Jules shuddered.

Don't think about it. Taine's down there. He needs my help.

Nauseated, she leaned as far out over the ledge as she dared, so Sampson could see her face. "Hey Sampson!" she called. "I think it's time we had another one of our wee chats, you and I. What do you say?"

But the creature didn't respond, too intent on locating Taine, twisting and snaking to dislodge him. How long could Taine hold on? Jules needed to get its attention. She twisted her torso sideways, feeling with her fingertips until she found a loose rock. She closed her hand around it. Aimed. Hurled it. Hitting a boulder, it skittered away uselessly.

Damn.

Jules put her hand back and felt for another. Heavier this time. She grasped it. Concentrated hard on Sampson's head. Then she threw, the effort wrenching her shoulder.

Yes! The rock struck above the creature's eye, where the flesh was black and raw. It wasn't a strong blow. Not enough to do any damage, but Sampson stopped its thrashing and looked up.

At last, the spear slid free!

Taine dropped to the ground with it, Jules' voice in his ear. She was singing, her words soft and lilting, like a prayer. The creature paused.

This was his chance to kill it!

Where? Taine wouldn't get a third chance. But now the animal had stopped, he spotted the place where the heart throbbed beneath the soft belly of the animal. For a split second, watching it rise and fall, Taine was almost sorry. The last of its kind. But then he thought of Louise and Anaru and Coolie, and a sudden brutal surge of rage exploded inside him. He thrust the spear upwards, sliding it between the creature's ribs, into the pulse, feeling the power of the weapon in his hands. Blood gushed from the wound, soaking him. He plunged the spear deep into the animal's core. Taine drove the spear on, sinking the wooden shaft into Sampson's heart. He felt the organ falter. The vibrations slowed.

Sampson staggered sideways. Lurched. Bellowed. Taine watched it fall.

The ground trembled.

The monster glared at him from singed eye-sockets. It opened its mouth, baring murderous teeth, and hissed, its talons making a final lunge for him. Taine darted out of their way.

Is it dead?

Taine held his breath.

Seconds passed.

Finally, he pulled out the spear, stepping back to avoid the gush of blood. Sampson didn't move. Taine drove the spear in again for good measure. Then he turned, looking up to where Read and Jules waited, one above the other on the cliff face.

Rotorua township

"Temera!"

"What?" All at once the forest was quiet.

Temera opened his eyes, blinking as the flood of light hit him. With just his pyjama pants on, Wayne was leaning over the bed, his hands on Temera's shoulders.

"You've had another one of your dreams, Uncle."

"Ah." He was back in the present. No longer in his dreams. He didn't remember coming back through the forest. The morepork had abandoned him there. Temera had been sure he would die in his dreams, his wairua following so many others and slipping into the ocean far away at the tip of the country… and yet here he was, in his bed in his nephew's house.

Pania appeared at the door now, tying her dressing gown about her waist. Her hair was tousled and her eyes looked tired. "What's going on?"

"Just another of Uncle's nightmares," Wayne said.

"Wayne—"

"Pania," Wayne said softly, and Temera caught his look, his eyes begging her to leave off. "Not now, love. He's a bit disoriented."

Pania chewed her bottom lip. Temera could tell she didn't want to put off the conversation, but she thought the better of it. "I'll make us all some tea, shall I?" she said cheerfully. "Bring it through."

Wayne smiled at that. "That would be great, love." He

cuffed Temera on the shoulder teasingly. "Since we're all up and awake. A cup of tea'll be just the ticket."

She left the room.

Temera put his hands behind him and shuffled himself backwards until he was sitting. The sheets were damp with his perspiration. Temera slipped a hand under the covers and checked out his nether regions. His pyjamas were damp, but not sopping. He hadn't wet himself, although he was frightened enough.

But had they succeeded? Temera closed his eyes, straining to grasp at the last tattered threads of his nightmare. He could see the morning mist, thick and grey, rolling through the valley on its ghostly raids through the trees. There was a flash of the taniwha, its haunches rippling, spines erect. It hurtled through the air, lunging at the bait McKenna had set for it. The woman's face, her terror. Temera screwed up his eyes, a dull ache throbbing at his temples. He wrapped his arms about himself and concentrated. There had been bellowing, screaming. Temera had felt it fall… had it died? Had McKenna killed it? Was the forest free? Or was the taniwha still out there, hunting him?

The last dregs of the nightmare faded…

Temera threw off the covers, swung his legs over the side of the bed, and immediately felt his bones ache. But this was not the time for him to be whinging about his age.

"We have to go," he said.

"Go?" Wayne said, puzzled. "Go where? It's not even 5:00am. Nothing will be open now."

"Not to the shops. To the forest. The Ureweras."

Wayne shook his head. "I'm sorry. I can't take you out there today. I've got to go to work."

Temera put his hand on his nephew's knee. "It's the last time, Wayne. I promise. Folk need our help. They could be hurt."

When Pania entered the room, their tea on a tray, Temera was sitting on the bed, fully dressed and struggling to reach the laces of boots.

"What's going on? Why are you getting dressed? It's the middle of the night."

"We have to go into the forest," Temera replied.

She frowned. "You're going out now?"

"We have to."

Her lips tight, Pania put the tea tray down on the dresser, and went to the room next door.

Temera grabbed his Swanndri from the closet, yanking it off its hanger, and put his ear to the wall.

"Wayne? What's going on?" Pania said, her voice barely muffled. There was a whump as Wayne's pyjamas hit the washing basket.

"Uncle Rawiri's had another one of his premonitions."

"Again? Wayne, you can't just go careering off every time your uncle wakes up from a bad dream."

"Just this last time."

"You know you shouldn't be encouraging this. Taking an old man out in the cold to go traipsing around in the forest in the middle of the night. We're supposed to be taking *care* of him, getting him help."

"Baby, he's really distraught."

"All the more reason," Pania said. Temera imagined her folding her arms.

Wayne sighed. "Pania, my uncle is a matakite. He *sees* things. I've told you about the geyser that came up in our yard when I was a kid. If he hadn't warned my parents to keep me indoors, I wouldn't even be here now. We wouldn't be having this conversation. I owe him my life."

"Yes, yes, I know. You've told me the story. And I know you love your uncle. *I* love your uncle. But Wayne, you've *been* up there already. Sitting out there on the road since the summer, warning people off going into the forest. Indulging him like this isn't working. Whatever is going on in that head of his, he's becoming obsessed with it. He needs help."

His nephew must have turned away then, because Temera didn't hear his reply.

After a while, Pania went on, her voice rising. "Even if there *is* someone hurt out there, the forest is huge. How will you find them? On a *premonition?*"

"Let me humour him one last time, please," Wayne said.

They stopped talking. Quickly, Temera stepped away from the wall, putting on his Swanndri, battling to get his arms into the sleeves, and he stepped into the hall. Wayne was already there, his arms around Pania.

Agreeing with her, or kissing his girlfriend goodbye?

"You ready?" Temera said, hardly daring to breathe. What if Wayne said no? How would Temera get there? He'd have to steal Wayne's truck.

But, grabbing the keys off the hall table, Wayne nodded at Temera.

They were going! So Pania said yes. Wayne was going to drive him. Awash with relief, Temera hurried down the hall to the back door after his nephew, giving Pania a grateful pat on the back when he passed.

"Wait!" Pania said.

Wayne stopped in mid-step, his hand poised on the doorknob. Temera's heart thudded.

"If someone is hurt up there, then you're going to need the first aid box. It's under the sink in the bathroom. Uncle, you grab some blankets from the cupboard in the spare room. I'll put this tea in a thermos and see if I can rustle up some food."

Temera swallowed. She really was a good kid, that Pania.

CHAPTER 30

Te Urewera Forest, heading south

Nathan lifted his hand.

"Is it the Sphenodon?" Richard Foster whispered, his face pale.

Nathan shook his head. He raised two fingers at Eriksen, indicating the bush to their left. Eriksen slipped off the trail on the opposite side.

"I don't see what you're—" Foster started.

"Shh," Nathan said, interrupting him.

The bush parted and Eriksen herded two men – boys really, neither of them much older than Nathan's grandson, Brandon – into the clearing. Nathan recognised the pair from Te Kooti's group.

"Mr Kerei," one said, stepping forward. He threw a nervous glance back at Eriksen's gun. "My name's Jason, and this here is Danny." He scuffed his boot in the dirt. "We were wondering if you would mind if we travelled with you?"

"Why?" Nathan said.

"Yeah," said Eriksen. "I thought you lot didn't like the army."

"That's Te Kooti. Not us. We've got nothing against the army, have we, Danny?" Jason nudged his friend.

Danny shrugged. "Nah, we're good," he replied.

"What about a Tūhoe traitor like me, then?" Nathan said with quiet anger.

"Danny and I are Tūhoe too," said Jason. "Family. We don't want any trouble with family."

Eriksen lifted his chin. "What about your mate, Te Kooti? If I let you join us, I don't want him picking a fight with us further down the trail."

"Oh, you won't see him," Jason said quickly. "He's taken the boys east, somewhere up near Opōtoki. Decided he wanted to be closer to town. Nearer the pub." He grinned weakly.

Nathan folded his arms across his chest. "Why didn't you go with him?"

Jason picked at his fingers. He swallowed. "Got a bit sick of the bush," he said. "Thought I might go back to uni."

Nathan raised an eyebrow.

His shoulders on fire, Taine staggered, his legs buckling under the weight on his back. He grabbed at a branch to stop himself from going down, hardly feeling the pain in his hand as he lurched forward. At the last second, he found his balance and righted himself.

Too close.

Breathing hard, Taine looked to the newbie – hardly a newbie now – following with Jules. Read threw him a look, but Taine shook his head at the unspoken request – Trigger was *his* responsibility.

"You okay?" Jules asked, coming up alongside Taine, her eyes filled with concern.

"Just catching my breath," he said. He gave her what he hoped was a cheery smile.

"We could help, if you'd let us…"

"I'm fine, Jules."

"You look exhausted."

In fact, Taine had never been so tired. For hours now, he'd carried Trigger through the bush without a spell. There was nothing else for it. Read was willing enough, but with a sprained ankle he was limping as it was. Mercifully for Trigger, he'd lost consciousness hours ago, his groans slowing to nothing. Now all Taine could hear was his quiet breathing. From time to time, Trigger gave an involuntary jerk. Taine marvelled at the human body's response to pain, shutting down, focussing on only essential functions. Taine, too, dreamed of oblivion; his legs felt like he'd been on the hack squat machine non-stop for a week. Enough of feeling sorry for himself! He needed to keep going. Trigger's life could depend on it.

Using his arms to push himself off the tree, Taine forced himself to advance. His legs slowly found their rhythm again and he plodded forward, breathing through his nose, his lips clamped shut.

They were going on instinct now, heading vaguely north-east, hoping to reach the road. A niggle worried at his mind. They hadn't been moving fast, but they should have made it by now. Taine prayed they hadn't missed it. Easy enough to pass right by if there was no traffic to alert them. Given the nature of their mission, Arnold wouldn't have made a public song and dance about it, but Taine hoped he had the army patrolling the roads, looking for them. With a bit of luck there'd be a Unimog just around the bend.

"Light, up ahead," Read said. "I reckon the trees might be thinning."

Taine barely had enough energy to lift his eyes. Could they have found the road? Or just another clearing? They'd been disappointed before. Gently, Taine hoisted his friend higher on his back. He took one step, and then another, counting them out in his head. Every step another half metre closer to the edge of the trees.

Suddenly, Read was shouting, and the weight on his shoulders lessened. Trigger was falling off his back.

"No!" he shouted, adrenaline surging. He stumbled sideways.

Read barrelled in. "Careful there," he said. "The big guy's injured."

"Jesus," a man's voice came at a whisper. "Quickly, help me get him in the back of the truck," he said. "We need to get him to hospital."

The weight lessened. *It's help.* Someone on the road, helping them. Read. Trigger. Taine slumped in relief. Suddenly, Jules was there, her hands on his cheeks, steadying him. "Taine, you did it. It's over," she said. "You got us out."

Even streaked with tears, she was beautiful. Holding her gaze, Taine kissed the inside of her palm.

The man's voice again. Insistent. "The blankets in the truck – Miss, can you lay one out, while we carry him over there?" Jules hurried away.

Shattered and dazed, Taine closed his eyes.

It's over.

The Sphenodon was dead, buried. It seemed so long ago… The climb to the opposite side of the ravine, to the boulders teetering near the top. Using de Haas' pick as a crowbar to create a landslide. Rocks tumbling to the valley floor, burying Sampson's remains, and Louise's body, wedged in its crevice. Taine felt a pang of sadness for Louise's family. It'd be hard on them, not knowing – but the truth was crueller. When the rocks had settled, he'd taken the longer route back to the cliff edge, where he and Read had hoisted Jules up from the ledge…

Someone laid a hand on his shoulder. Taine turned, exhausted. The old man. The one from the blockade. Temera.

Creases formed at the edges of his eyes, and the old man reached into his Swanndri. On a string at his neck was a bullroarer, the twin of his own.

Taine looked at Temera. But he… Taine squinted a little. He'd seen the old man before, and not just on the road.

"You were there," he whispered. "The boy."

Smiling, Temera nodded.

Taine ignored his outstretched hand. Instead, close to collapse, he reached out and clasped the old man to him.

Te Urewera Forest, Heading South

Jug could hardly believe it. They'd reached the Waikaremoana tourist trail! Wide and well-maintained, it was like a state highway after what they'd been through. They might just make it. Calling a break, Eriksen kept an eye on Te Kooti's boys, while Nathan and Foster slipped into the trees for a leak. Lefty and Miller put the stretcher down.

"Hamish? Would you mind passing me a drink, please?" Jug pointed to the bottle of cold mānuka tea. Crouching, Miller handed the bottle to Jug, his eyes rimmed red from lack of sleep and heaven knew what else.

"Thank you," Jug said.

"No worries."

"You sure about that?" Jug said, keeping his voice low.

"I'm sorry?"

"I've been thinking about when I had my accident. You were there in the forest with me. We were hiding together."

"Yes..." Miller said carefully, "... and then you fell and shot yourself."

"I fell and shot myself." Jug twisted the top on the water bottle. He took a sip. "The thing is, that's not how I remember it."

Surprise flashed across the boy's face, but he quickly got himself under control, laughing nervously. "I think you've been drinking too much of Nathan's happy-tea, you know that?"

He was about to stand, but Jug laid his hand on his arm. "That's not what you've been taking though is it, son? You've been taking something much, much stronger. You forget that I'm a doctor, Hamish. I'm trained to recognise the signs. Besides, it's easy enough to verify with a simple hair follicle test..." Jug trailed off deliberately.

Miller's eyes hardened. He shrugged off Jug's hand. "I don't know what the fuck you're talking about," he hissed under his breath.

Jug looked at him. "Yes, you do. You know exactly what I'm talking about. So here's the deal. If we make it out of this forest, then I'll continue to have amnesia. I'll continue to say 'silly me, my gun must've gone off when I stumbled', and I'll go on saying that for as long as you stay clean. But if I hear anything, anything at all, that suggests you're using again, if I see something that makes me suspect, if I even hear a *rumour* that you are taking drugs again, then you're going to find that my amnesia is suddenly cured."

Miller opened his mouth to protest, but Lefty returned, allowing Jug the last word. Jug hoped it was enough.

"On three," Lefty said. "One, two, three, lift."

Jug lay back and closed his eyes.

James braced himself as the Unimog bounced over the pothole. "What about that track?" he said. "Just ahead on the right."

At the wheel, Dawson said, "We've already checked that one, Major."

"It was hours ago," James said, his fingers gripping the dash.

The radio crackled. Dawson pulled up, stopping the vehicle in the middle of the road. "Dawson."

James stared into the trees.

"Yes, I'll tell the Major. Out." Dawson put the vehicle into gear, turning the steering wheel hard right. "They've located them, sir. A couple of civilians picked up four people east of Maungapōhatu. There's a casualty—"

"McKenna?"

Looking over her shoulder, Dawson reversed the vehicle. "They didn't say."

"We need to get to Rotorua Hospital."

"Already on it, sir," she said.

The Unimog swayed when they took the bend. A man wearing long-johns and carrying a gun ran onto the road in front of them.

"Look out!" James shouted.

Dawson had seen him. She braked, the Unimog lurching to a stop.

The man halted, panting. Wild-eyed, he stared at James.

Seconds passed.

When he didn't shoot, James reached for the door handle,

INTO THE MIST

but the man bolted, disappearing into the mist on the other side of the road.

CHAPTER 31

Wellington, Three Weeks Later

Ken picked up his phone. "Regulatory Policy, Chesterman speaking."

"What the fuck is going on?"

Australian accent. Female.

Ken smiled. He'd wondered when the bitch would call. Getting up from his chair, Ken closed his office door, then, faced away from his Conservation Department staff to Roseneath on the other side of the harbour. "I'm sorry, who is this?"

"You know exactly who this is. Where the hell is that Task Force?"

"What task force?"

"Don't play silly buggers with me, Kenneth," the woman snarled. "I can still make that phone call."

He needed to play this carefully. Andrew was gone, but he'd asked Sandra for a divorce and it would be inconvenient if the information about their liaison came out now. He kept his voice even. "The recent mineral exploration team to Te Urewera forest? Would that be the one you mean?"

No answer.

Ken smirked. He returned to his desk. "I have the report right here on my desk. What is it you'd like to know?"

"Where the fuck are they?"

"The Task Force has been disbanded; Dr de Haas and Mr Fogarty agreed that the site didn't warrant exploiting. Both consultants have returned to their native countries."

"Fogarty wouldn't have said that." The tone was glacial.

"Really?" Ken feigned surprise. "His name is right here alongside Dr de Haas'. I can read the report to you if you like." Taking a seat, Ken swivelled his chair so he was facing the window again. Then he turned to the summary, and cleared his throat theatrically. "Sampling took place over a ten day period from the prescribed area... the co-ordinates are here. Would you like me to read them?"

"Don't fuck with me, Kenneth."

Ken smiled. "Let's skip to the report's key recommendation. Here it is. In our expert opinions the relatively small quantities of ore represented in the samples do not warrant the cost of extraction. There's more. I could email it to you if you like—"

"Don't be funny, Kenneth. Just read it."

"Regarding the discovery of the gold nugget that prompted the establishment of the Task Force, it's our view that the nugget is not from the region at all, and was most likely taken from the Martha mine area to the north during its boom period in the last century. While it is purely conjecture on our part, we believe the nugget may have been transported—"

"One nugget, but..." Her voice was suddenly less sure, she broke off. "It doesn't make any sense. Fogarty I can understand... but de Haas has dropped off the grid, too. The South African government has no record of him entering the country."

Kenneth couldn't resist. "There's something else here in the report which might be of interest to you..."

"What?"

"It's a statement from Jules Asher, recommending that the area be retained as a mainland island conservation park. It seems Dr Asher uncovered some unique fauna in the area." Ken chuckled. "The Urewera region is quite the nature reserve. Home to the rare whio duck. A little grey duck that needs protecting. So, you see, even if the geological findings *had* been positive, the Conservation Minister is duty-bound—"

There was a click. Ken smiled. The bunny boiler'd hung up.

Rotorua township, Six Weeks Later
Temera was pulled from his slumber by the cheeky warble of a tui at his bedroom window.

INTO THE MIST

It was Sunday morning and, once again, the morepork had forgotten to call. He checked his alarm. 7:00am. Another full night of delicious kip. For weeks, Temera had laid awake, fearing sleep. But since his experience with McKenna, the morepork had remained silent. Was the horror over? Had the encounter cured Temera of his night terrors?

Outside, the tui chirped his wake-up call. Temera heard Wayne's muffled groan through the wall. "Shuddup..."

Temera chuckled out loud.

Still laughing, he wriggled down into the warmth of the duvet to listen to the bird's cheery song.

Thanks for reading *Into the Mist*.

We hope you enjoyed it, and if so, please consider leaving a review on Amazon and/or Goodreads. As a small press, even though we do have a marketing budget for each book, we also rely heavily on word-of-mouth for marketing, and reviews help most of all when it comes to Amazon deciding to promote our books.

We specialise in military horror, creature-horror, and military sci-fi.

COHESION PRESS